SIDEWINDERS:
MASSACRE AT WHISKEY FLATS

William W. Johnstone
with J. A. Johnstone

PINNACLE BOOKS
Kensington Publishing Corp.
www.kensingtonbooks.com

PINNACLE BOOKS are published by

Kensington Publishing Corp.
850 Third Avenue
New York, NY 10022

PUBLISHER'S NOTE
Following the death of William W. Johnstone, the Johnstone family is working with a carefully selected writer to organize and complete Mr. Johnstone's outlines and many unfinished manuscripts to create additional novels in all of his series like The Last Gunfighter, Mountain Man, and Eagles, among others. This novel was inspired by Mr. Johnstone's superb storytelling.

All Kensington titles, imprints, and distributed lines are available at special quantity discounts for bulk purchases for sales promotions, premiums, fund-raising, educational, or institutional use. Special book excerpts or customized printings can also be created to fit specific needs. For details, write or phone the office of the Kensington special sales manager: Kensington Publishing Corp., 850 Third Avenue, New York, NY 10022, attn: Special Sales Department; Phone: 1-800-221-2647.

ISBN-13: 978-0-7860-1922-9
ISBN-10: 0-7860-1922-0

First Printing: November 2008

10 9 8 7 6 5 4 3 2 1

Printed in the United States of America

*He who would avoid trouble
should learn to recognize it
when it walks up and introduces itself.*
      —Ling Yuan, ancient Chinese
         warrior-philosopher

Howdy. I'm Scratch, he's Bo.
      —Scratch Morton

CHAPTER 1

"Sounds like a ruckus brewin' out there."

Bo Creel tried to ignore his trail partner's comment, as well as the elbow that Scratch Morton prodded insistently into his side. The two Texans had spent a long, hot, dusty day in the saddle, and all Bo wanted to concentrate on at the moment was the cold beer in front of him on the bar. Condensation ran down the sides of the mug to form a puddle on the hardwood. It was a moment of delicious anticipation.

But then someone in the street outside, where a commotion had erupted in the past few minutes, shouted, "Somebody find a bucket of tar and some feathers!"

Bo sighed. He was an easygoing hombre, but some things stuck in his craw.

Tarring and feathering some luckless bastard was one of them.

"Think we ought to go see what's goin' on?" Scratch prodded.

"Might as well," Bo said. "You won't be satisfied until we do."

He turned toward the batwinged entrance of the Buffalo Bar, casting a look of regret over his shoulder at that mug of cold beer as he did.

The Texans walked side by side, a pair of tough frontiersmen who had wandered the West from the Rio Grande to the Milk River, from the Mississippi to the Pacific Coast, for nigh on to forty years now. They had first met as youngsters, back when their homeland was still part of Mexico and General Santa Anna's army had sent the Texican settlers fleeing in the great exodus known as the Runaway Scrape, in those dark days after the fall of the Alamo.

Bo's father and Scratch's pa had both been members of Sam Houston's ragtag army, and the newfound friends had run away to join up, too, arriving just in time to swap lead with the Mexicans during the Battle of San Jacinto, the clash that had won freedom for Texas and Texans. Scratch had saved Bo's life that day, the first time among many that each of them had risked his hide for the other, and they had been best friends ever since. Through tragedy and triumph, they had ridden together, and even though they never went looking for trouble, the acrid scent of powder smoke always seemed to follow them.

They were both tall, muscular men, but that was where the resemblance ended. Scratch's hair had turned silver at an early age, but he was still handsome, with a ready grin that the ladies found quite appealing. He was something of a dandy, too, sporting a cream-colored Stetson and a fringed buckskin jacket over whipcord trousers tucked into high-topped boots. An elaborately tooled leather gunbelt was strapped around his waist, and in its holsters rode twin, long-barreled Remington revolvers with ivory grips on their handles.

Where Scratch had a touch of flamboyance about him, Bo was more restrained and sober, in a dusty black suit with a long coat that made him look a little like a reverend. He wore a white shirt and a string tie, and his flat-crowned black hat rested on thick brown hair with gray threaded through it. Bo carried only one gun, a Colt .45 with well-worn walnut grips.

The faces of both men had been weathered by the long years of wandering . . . tanned by countless desert suns and seamed by the frigid winds of the high country, living maps of the frontier and all its harsh beauty. Their deep-set eyes, framed by perpetual squints, had witnessed just about everything there was to witness.

In other words, they had been to see the elephant, and more than once at that.

So as they pushed past the curious customers in the Buffalo Bar who had congregated at the entrance and front windows of the saloon, slapped aside the batwings, and stepped out onto the boardwalk, Bo and Scratch didn't see anything they hadn't seen before. An angry mob of more than a dozen men clustered in the street, shoving their hapless victim back and forth as they jeered and taunted him about what they were fixing to do to him.

In the fading light of day, Bo and Scratch saw that the man was young, no more than twenty-five or so. He wore a dark suit and a black hat. His duds were fancier and more expensive than Bo's similar outfit. As one of the members of the mob gave him a hard shove, his hat fell off, revealing a shock of blond hair. He looked scared, Bo thought . . . as well he might be.

"Here comes Ralston," one of the men bellowed. He was the biggest man in the crowd, with powerful, slab-muscled shoulders and a prominent gut. "Did you get it?" he called to the four or five men who approached the scene in the middle of the street.

One of them waved something in the air and replied, "Here's a couple o' my wife's feather pillows, and Duncan's got a bucket o' tar! That'll fix that four-flusher up mighty fine!"

"What'd your wife say about you takin' them pillows, Ralston," a man called with a jeering tone in his voice, "or did you sneak 'em out without her knowin'?"

"Damn it," Ralston said. "I'll have you know I wear the pants in my family!"

"Leave it alone," snapped the big-gutted man. "We got more important things to deal with, like teaching this no-good swindler a lesson he'll never forget!"

The mob's victim spoke up, trying to sound reasonable. But the quaver in his voice betrayed his fear as he said, "Now, Mr. Harding, there's no need for this to get out of hand. I'm sure if you'll just let me explain, you'll see that this is all just a big misunderstanding—"

"Misunderstanding, hell!" the man called Harding bellowed. "You tried to gyp everybody around here out of what they got comin' to them! You'll be sorry you ever set foot in these parts, mister!"

It looked to Bo like the gent was already sorry, as well as scared for his life. Most of the time, men who were tarred and feathered survived the painful, humiliating experience, but sometimes they died of the burns inflicted by the hot tar. It was one step short of a lynching, but potentially just as fatal.

Quite a few of the townspeople had gathered on the boardwalks to watch the grim scene being played out in the street. Bo looked over at one of them, a balding man with a prominent Adam's apple who wore a store-keeper's apron. The man had a frown of disapproval on his face.

"Who's the fella with the big belly?" Bo asked the townsman.

"You mean the one running the show, like he runs everything else around here?"

Bo nodded.

"That's Tom Harding," the storekeeper went on. "Owns the biggest ranch in these parts, as well as having his fingers in half a dozen businesses here in town."

"Big skookum he-wolf, is he?" Scratch asked.

"He thinks he is anyway." The man sighed. "And I reckon he is. He's got some tough hombres working for him, so most folks just go along with whatever he wants. Simpler that way."

"And less dangerous," Bo commented.

The merchant shrugged. "We're just common folks, mister, not gunhands."

"What about the law? Don't you have a marshal?"

"That's him with the pillows," the man replied dis-gustedly. "Marshal Ed Ralston. He hasn't seen the outside of Harding's hip pocket since Harding got him appointed to the job."

Bo and Scratch glanced at each other in the fading light. If they took a hand in this game, they would be going up against not only a wealthy, powerful rancher who fancied himself the lord of his own little kingdom, but also the official forces of law and order, corrupt though they might be.

But it wouldn't be the first time they had gotten crosswise with the law. In their travels they had always been more concerned with doing what was *right,* rather than what was necessarily legal.

"What do you think, Bo?" Scratch asked.

Bo's face was grim as he replied, "I think it's time we put a stop to this."

The storekeeper stared at them in amazement. "Are you fellas loco?" he asked. "Going up against Tom Harding is a good way to get yourselves killed! Not only that, but that hombre they're going to tar and feather really is a crook. He tried to swindle the whole town!"

"Then he ought to be dealt with legally," Bo said. He took a step down from the boardwalk into the street and started toward the mob.

He didn't have to look around to make sure that Scratch was with him. He knew that his trail partner would be there.

A couple of Harding's men had grabbed hold of the swindler's arms. He writhed in their grasp and tried desperately to pull free, his instincts forcing him to struggle even though it was obvious he couldn't escape from the ring of angry men that encircled him. He let out a yell as another man approached him carrying a bucket from which tendrils of steam rose. The bucket contained hot tar, ready to be dumped on the luckless victim.

"Hold it!" Harding yelled.

At this apparent last-minute reprieve, the swindler sagged in the grip of the men holding him. "I've learned my lesson, Mr. Harding," he babbled. "I surely have."

"Strip him first," Harding ordered harshly, "then put the tar on him."

The swindler's face twisted in horror. He cried out and started to struggle again as hands reached for him to tear his clothes off.

That was when Bo said in a loud, clear, powerful voice that carried to everyone on the street, "That's enough!"

CHAPTER 2

Everyone froze for a second, from Tom Harding to the man who struggled in the grip of Harding's cronies. Then the rancher turned to glare at Bo and Scratch, who stood about ten feet away, apparently as casual as if they'd been out just enjoying the evening air.

"What the hell did you say, mister?" Harding demanded furiously.

"I said that's enough," Bo repeated coolly and calmly. "Let that man go."

Harding took a step toward the Texans, his prominent belly preceding him. "I think you're mixed up, hombre," he said. "*I* give the orders around here."

"The way I understand it, you're not the law." Bo pointed at Ralston, who still stood there looking a little ludicrous as he clutched a pair of feather pillows. "He is. If this man has committed a crime, he ought to be arrested and held in jail for trial."

Harding sneered. "The circuit judge isn't due through here for three weeks yet. We're just saving him some work. We can take care of things like this ourselves. Isn't that right, Marshal?"

Ralston swallowed hard and bobbed his head in a nod. "That's right," he said. "You fellas are strangers here. You better just go on your way."

"I'm afraid we can't do that," Bo said. "We'll ride out . . . but we're taking that man with us."

Harding stared at him in disbelief for a second before he roared, "Do you know who I am, you old son of a bitch?"

"Reckon I do," Scratch drawled. "You're a big bag o' hot air just achin' to be popped."

Harding gawked, then his face contorted in fury. "Jenkins!" he called. "Thomas! Show these old geezers what happens when somebody butts into my business!"

Two hard-faced, gun-hung hombres stepped forward from the mob. "You want us to kill them, Boss?" one of them asked.

Harding hesitated. Even a man as powerful in the community as he was couldn't order cold-blooded murder in front of this many witnesses. He growled, "Of course not. Just bust 'em up so they hurt for the next week."

"Our pleasure, Mr. Harding," the other man said with a cold grin. "Nothin' I like better'n beatin' on some sanctimonious old fart. Learned that from my pa, I did."

The two men advanced on Bo and Scratch while the rest of the mob looked on in rapt attention. The townspeople on the boardwalks watched nervously, too. The storekeeper Bo had spoken to earlier ventured, "This ain't right, Harding."

"Shut up, Gus," Harding snapped. "Don't forget, the bank I own a half interest in still has a lien on your store."

The merchant grimaced, half in anger and half in fear, but didn't say anything else.

The two hardcases were almost within reach of Bo and Scratch now. One of them sneered and said, "Say your prayers, old-timers." Then he lunged at Bo and swung a fist at the Texan's head in a swift, brutal blow.

But Bo suddenly wasn't there anymore, and the punch whipped harmlessly through the empty air where he'd been. Bo had weaved forward and to the right with seemingly effortless ease, and as his opponent stumbled forward, thrown off balance by the missed blow, Bo hooked a hard left into the man's gut. His fist sank almost wrist-deep. The hardcase gasped in pain as his breath puffed out of him and he doubled over. That put him in perfect position for the roundhouse right that Bo brought around and crashed into his jaw.

At the same time, the other man tried to grapple with Scratch, only to find himself sailing through the air as Scratch grabbed his arm, twisted around in a sharp pivot, and flung the man over his hip. The hardcase had time to yelp once in surprise before he came crashing down on his back in the street.

"An old Injun taught me that move nigh on to thirty years ago," Scratch said with a grin into the stunned silence. "Injuns love to rassle."

The man Bo had belted in the jaw had collapsed, too, but he was stunned only for a couple of seconds.

Then he started to surge back to his feet, clawing at his gun as he shouted, "I'll kill you for that, you old buzzard!"

Bo's hand seemed to flicker faster than the eye could follow as he brushed aside the long black coat and palmed the Colt from its simple black holster. The hardcase's gun hadn't finished clearing leather when he found himself staring down the muzzle of Bo's .45.

"Better let it go, son," Bo advised softly. "I'd purely hate to have to kill you, because then your amigos would probably try to kill me and there'd be guns going off all up and down this street and innocent folks might get hurt. But you'd never know about that, because you'd already be dead."

"Son of a bitch!" somebody on the boardwalk said in the hush that followed Bo's draw and his quiet words. "That old-timer must be as fast with a gun as Matt Bodine!"

Bo didn't smile, but amusement appeared in his eyes for a second. As a matter of fact, he had met the famous Matt Bodine, along with Bodine's blood brother Sam Two Wolves, and he knew he wasn't as slick on the draw as either of those two young hell-raisers. Bodine was in a class almost by himself, matched in gun-speed and prowess only by a few others such as Smoke Jensen, Ben Thompson, and Louis Longmont.

But truth to tell, Bo and Scratch were fast enough to hold their own in most corpse-and-cartridge sessions, as they had been forced to prove on countless occasions.

The gunman who worked for Tom Harding stared

at Bo's Colt in disbelief that he had been outdrawn. A muscle in the man's jaw twitched as he warred against the impulse to complete his draw. He had to know that if he did that, he would die, plain and simple.

After a second, his fingers opened and allowed his revolver to slide back down into its holster.

"Take it easy, old-timer," he said hoarsely. "That gun's liable to go off."

"Not unless I want it to," Bo said.

Scratch unlimbered his Remingtons just in case. A fighting light gleamed in his eyes. Just like Bo, he was ready to go down with guns a-blazin' if it came to that. He grinned directly at Tom Harding, and the message was obvious. If any shooting started, Scratch aimed to ventilate the cattle baron first and foremost.

"What the hell!" someone in the mob suddenly exclaimed. "That crook's gone!"

Harding swung around, rage darkening his face. "What?" he bellowed. "Gone, you say?"

It was true. The young, fair-haired swindler was nowhere to be seen. He had slipped away while the brief ruckus and the near-gunfight had everyone distracted.

Harding roared curses at the men who were supposed to be holding the swindler, but that did no good. Like a rat, the varmint had slipped away in the gathering darkness. No telling where he was now, but in all likelihood he was putting as much distance as he could between himself and this settlement.

"Looks like we don't have any reason to fight anymore," Bo observed. "If you'd locked that gent up like you should have to start with, Harding, he'd still be here. Now he's long gone."

"Thanks to you two," Harding snarled. "I ought to—"

"But you won't," Scratch broke in as he shifted the barrels of his Remingtons significantly.

"I've got a dozen men here! If I give the word, you'll both be shot to pieces!"

"Yes, but it'll be the last word you'll give," Bo said.

Harding looked like he was struggling to swallow something that tasted mighty bad. But after a moment he turned and choked out to his men, "Get back to the ranch—now!"

Bo could tell that those lean, hard-faced gunwolves didn't want to go, but they slowly turned away and headed for their horses, which were tied at hitch rails along the street. Marshal Ralston and the other townies who had been part of the mob started to disperse as well. Harding was the last to go, and before he did, he told Bo and Scratch, "You'd better get out of this town. You'll be sorry if you don't."

"Mister, we're already sorry we stopped here," Scratch said. "It's a plumb unfriendly place."

"You don't know how unfriendly," Harding said. He stalked off, jerking the reins of a chestnut free and swinging up into the saddle. It was a big horse. It had to be in order to carry a man of Harding's bulk. He rode away without looking back.

Bo and Scratch didn't holster their guns until the street was empty again. Then, as they slid their irons back into leather, Scratch asked, "Are we lightin' a shuck like Harding said?"

"Not until I get that beer," Bo said. "Or another one rather. I expect the first one's warm by now."

The storekeeper they had spoken to earlier was still on the boardwalk, and as the Texans approached, he said, "I'll buy you that beer, fellas. It's been a long time since anybody around here stood up to Tom Harding. Quite a show."

"You sure you want to risk being seen associating with us?" Bo asked. "Sounded like Harding's got a hold over you."

"His bank's got a lien on my store, but I'm no fool. He can't call the note in early. I made sure of that before I signed it." The man motioned for them to follow him into the Buffalo Bar. "Come on."

The merchant, whose name was Gus Hobart, bought beers for all three of them and joined the Texans at a table in the corner. After he had downed a healthy swallow of the drink, he licked his lips and went on. "I admire your gumption, fellas, but it might be better if you moseyed on. Having to back down like that is going to stick in Harding's craw. There's no telling what he might do."

"We ain't made a habit o' runnin' from trouble," Scratch said.

"On the other hand," Bo said, "sometimes there's some truth to that old saying about discretion being the better part of valor." He took a long drink of the cold beer and sighed in satisfaction. "I'm curious, though. What did that young fella do to nearly get himself tarred and feathered?"

Hobart snorted. "That's the worst of it. You boys were risking your hides for somebody who didn't deserve it. He came damn close to making off with a fortune that rightfully belongs to folks around here. You see, the railroad's talking about building a spur line up here from the main route down south."

"Ah," Bo said. "The railroad." He understood perfectly well that although the coming of the iron horse had done a lot to help with the civilizing of the West, it was also responsible for a great deal of violence and chicanery in recent years.

"Yeah," Hobart nodded. "We'd been hearing rumors about that spur for a while, and then that young fella showed up. Called himself Charles Wortham, but that was probably a lie like everything else. He claimed to be working for the railroad and said he was here to arrange for the donation of land for the right-of-way. Folks had figured that the railroad would buy the land, but the way Wortham explained it, the only way they'd build the spur was if they could acquire the right-of-way free of charge. A trade-off, he called it. Folks around here would provide the land, and the railroad would provide the prosperity. So what we had to do was transfer the deeds to the property over to him, and then he would transfer it to the railroad in one big piece. So he said."

Bo and Scratch were both shaking their heads already. Scratch said, "Nobody believed that line o' bull, did they?"

"I'm afraid they did," Hobart replied with a sigh. "We were that desperate for the railroad to come in."

"Wortham would have *sold* that land to the railroad and made a killing," Bo said. "Then he'd disappear before anybody found out that he'd acquired it by underhanded means."

"Yeah, but he hadn't counted on Tom Harding having a friend in Santa Fe," Hobart said. "Harding got this fella to look into the matter, and he found out that Wortham didn't work for the railroad at all. As soon as Harding got the letter telling him that, he went after Wortham. Grabbed him in his hotel room, got the deeds out of Wortham's carpetbag, and dragged him out in the street." Hobart shrugged. "I reckon you know the rest."

Scratch gave a disgusted snort. "Sounds like we really did risk our necks for a skunk who didn't deserve it."

"He didn't deserve to be tarred and feathered either," Bo said. "That could have killed him. A couple of years in prison would've been more appropriate."

Hobart said, "Maybe so. I got to admit, I felt a mite queasy myself at the idea of doing that to him. Nobody from around here, though, would've stood up to Tom Harding to stop it."

Bo started to tell him that until the townspeople stood up to Harding, the cattle baron would continue running roughshod over them, but he decided to save his breath. Hobart had to be aware of that, and so did everybody else in the settlement. What they did about it was up to them, and no business of his and Scratch's.

"Any towns south of here?" he asked after taking another swig of the beer. "It's been a while since we've been through these parts, but to the best of my recollection, there's not much until you hit Santa Fe."

Hobart shook his head. "No, that's not true. There

are several settlements between here and there. Closest one is several days' ride, though."

"You're not thinkin' of movin' on, are you?" Scratch asked with a frown. "We were gonna stay here a few days and stock up on supplies, amongst other things."

That had been the plan, all right. Despite looking like a parson, Bo was a highly skilled poker player, and when the Texans' stake ran low, he could usually fatten it up in a few days just by sitting in on a few games. That was what he would have done here, if fate hadn't intervened.

"We still have enough provisions to last us for a while," he said. Nor were they flat broke yet, although he didn't mention that. "It might be best if we moved on." At Scratch's grimace, he added, "Best for the town, that is. If Harding knows we're still here, he's liable to be like a bear with a hurt paw. He'll lash out at anything that comes near him."

"Yeah, you're right," Scratch admitted. "I was sure lookin' forward to sleepin' in a real bed with a roof over my head again, though."

Bo grinned. "We'll find us a nice comfortable spot to camp tonight."

Scratch just snorted.

They finished their beers, and Bo said, "We're much obliged to you, Mr. Hobart."

The storekeeper nodded. "I just wish we could be more hospitable to you fellas. You understand, though."

"Sure," Bo said. He and Scratch stood up, nodded their farewells, and started toward the batwings. The other men in the saloon nervously watched them leave.

As they stepped out onto the boardwalk, Scratch growled, "It's like we got a dark cloud hangin' over our heads, and those gents are afraid it's gonna rain all over 'em."

"You can't blame them for feeling that way," Bo said. "We're strangers, just passing through, but they have to live here and try to get along with Harding—"

He didn't have time to say anything else before muzzle flame spurted from the darkness of a nearby alley mouth and the roar of guns filled the night.

CHAPTER 3

Bo and Scratch reacted instinctively as bullets sang past their heads. They split up, Bo hugging the front wall of the saloon to the right, Scratch going to the left toward the street. The silver-haired Texan put one hand on the railing along the edge of the boardwalk and vaulted over it, rolling lithely as he landed in the street. He came up on one knee with both hands filled with the butts of his Remingtons.

Meanwhile, Bo crouched behind a bench that sat on the boardwalk. As the bushwhackers' guns continued to blare from the alley, slugs chewed splinters from the arms of the bench. One of the wooden slivers stung Bo's cheek as he lined up his Colt and squeezed the trigger. He had aimed just above one of the muzzle flashes, and as the revolver bucked against his palm, he saw another gout of flame from a gun barrel, only this one was aimed skyward as the man who pulled the trigger was driven over backward by the smashing impact of the bullet from Bo's gun.

Scratch opened fire, too. Instead of the single

precise shot that had come from Bo's gun, Scratch set both smokepoles to roaring in a thunderous volley of death. Left, right, left, right, he squeezed off the shots, each Remington blasting in turn as the barrel of the other gun kicked upward from the recoil. Lead poured into the alley mouth. The second bushwhacker, even though he managed to get off another couple of rounds, never had a chance.

After triggering half a dozen shots in less than five seconds, Scratch held his fire. On the boardwalk, Bo straightened from his crouch and walked toward the alley, advancing slowly and cautiously with the Colt thrust out in front of him, ready to fire again if need be.

No more shots came from the alley mouth. When Bo reached the end of the boardwalk, he fished a lucifer out of his coat pocket with his left hand and snapped it into life with his thumbnail. The harsh flare of light from the match revealed two men lying motionless on the dirt, their rough range clothes splotched with spreading bloodstains. Bo recognized both men.

So did Scratch, who had holstered one gun and was using that hand to slap dust off his clothes as he came closer. He grunted and said, "The same two varmints who tried to hand us a beatin' earlier."

"Yeah," Bo agreed. "Jenkins and Thomas, I think Harding called them."

"You reckon he sent them back to kill us?"

Bo shrugged. "Could be. Or they might've come after us on their own, since we showed them up. You can bet Harding would say he didn't know anything about them being here, if the law ever called him on it." Bo's mouth twisted. "But of course that won't ever happen, since the only law around here is Harding's tame star packer."

Scratch leaned forward to take a closer look. "Both dead, ain't they?"

"Oh, yeah. Shot through and through." In fact, spreading blood was forming dark pools around both men.

Bo shook the match out and dropped it as boot heels rang on the boardwalk, hurrying closer. He and Scratch swung around in case they were about to be attacked again, but instead of more bushwhackers, all they saw were curious townsmen, drawn by the flurry of shots. The marshal, Ralston, was in the lead, carrying a lantern.

"What in blazes happened here?" he demanded. He held the lantern higher so that its yellow glow washed over the corpses. "My God! You've murdered two of Mr. Harding's men!"

Gus Hobart, who was in the curious crowd that had emerged from the Buffalo Bar, said sharply, "Don't even think about trying that, Ralston! Those Texans had barely stepped outside when the shooting started, and the first shots came from the alley over here. They were just defending themselves, and there are a dozen men here who will swear to it!"

Ralston regarded the storekeeper narrowly. "You better watch what you're sayin', Hobart. You're liable to wind up neck-deep in trouble."

Hobart thrust out his jaw and said, "You know I'll go along with most anything Tom Harding wants. I'm no fool. But I'll be damned if I'll go along with these two men being railroaded for murder when all they were doing was defending themselves from Harding's hired killers!"

Ralston jerked his head around, nervous as a rabbit as he looked at the townspeople surrounding him. "You're sure that's the way it was?" he asked.

"Damn sure," Hobart responded. He didn't look like a meek little storekeeper at this moment. Growing a mite of backbone seemed to have straightened him and even made him taller.

Ralston pulled at his chin. "Well, then, I, uh, I reckon I can't hold you two," he said to Bo and Scratch. He squared his shoulders in an attempt to regain a little dignity. "But you're troublemakers, both of you, and I'm damn sure within my rights to tell you to get out of my town! Vamoose and don't come back!"

Bo saw Scratch stiffening, and knew that the marshal's words had put a burr under his partner's saddle. Scratch was stubborn enough to argue with Ralston just on general principles. Instead, Bo put a restraining hand on Scratch's arm and said, "As a matter of fact, Marshal, we were just about to ride out."

"We're still leavin'?" Scratch growled from the corner of his mouth.

"That's right, we are," Bo said, his voice as firm as the hand on Scratch's arm.

After a second, Scratch gave an explosive, disgusted grunt and said, "Fine. I'm sick o' this place anyway. It's as unfriendly a burg as I've seen in all my borned days."

As the Texans started toward their horses, Gus Hobart called after them, "You fellas take care. Keep an eye on your back trail, if you know what I mean."

Bo knew exactly what the storekeeper meant. Harding might not let this lie, even after the deaths of two of his men. That might make him even more determined to exact vengeance on the two drifters who had dared to defy him.

But there was no point in borrowing trouble. Plenty of it came to a man naturally.

Bo rode a rangy dun with a dark stripe down its back, an ugly, nasty-tempered brute that didn't look like much . . . but it was a horse that could and would run all day if you asked it to. Scratch's mount, in keeping with his dandified nature, was a big, handsome bay, the sort of animal that impressed the ladies. But Scratch's horse, unlike some that were pretty, had just as much sand and grit as Bo's more unprepossessing mount.

The Texans untied the reins of both animals now from the hitch rail where they had left them upon arriving in the settlement. They had intended to just have a quick drink and then tend to the horses' needs, stabling them and seeing to it that they were unsaddled, rubbed down, and properly grained and watered, before finding lodging for the night themselves.

Things hadn't worked out that way, though, and as Bo and Scratch swung up into their saddles, Scratch said, "I sure hate to take these big fellas back out on the trail tonight. They deserve better."

"Folks don't always get what they deserve, for good or bad," Bo said, "and I reckon that applies to horses, too."

They rode out, heading south. The main street of the town became a narrow road, little more than a path. A wagon could negotiate it, but the driver would have to be careful. The horses had no trouble following it, though.

Around them rose the thickly timbered hills of northern New Mexico Territory. The tang of pine and juniper and sage perfumed the air. Mountains loomed in the distance to both east and west, dark and mysterious in the night. What seemed like at least a million stars glittered in the heavens overhead, casting a silvery illumination over the landscape. A sliver of moon floated in the sky as well. It was a beautiful scene, although the sharp contrast between light and dark gave it a weird, otherworldly aspect as well.

"You think Harding's gonna come after us?" Scratch asked when they had put a couple of miles between them and the settlement.

"No telling," Bo said. "He struck me as just arrogant enough, and just mean enough, to do pretty much anything."

"Yeah, I know what you mean. I never did like that sort. Thinks he's better'n ever'body else and likes to be the big boss o' everything."

Bo smiled. "You never did care for anybody who thought he was the boss. Reckon that's why you never spent much time working for wages."

"Huh," Scratch said. "I could say the same thing o' you, Bo Creel. Neither one of us was cut out for toilin' like regular folks."

"That's probably one good reason why we've wrapped up in our bedrolls hungry and without a roof over our heads so many nights."

"And you wouldn't'a had it any other way. You ain't foolin' me."

"I wouldn't even try, not after all these years," Bo declared.

They rode on, and as usual, their keen frontiersmen's senses were fully at work. Their eyes never stopped roving over the starlit landscape around them, and their ears were wide-open for the sound of hoofbeats pursuing them.

The night was quiet and peaceful, though, and the only sounds were the normal scurrying through the brush of nocturnal creatures, the swish of air as an owl swooped by in search of prey, and the faintly distant, long-drawn-out barking cry of a coyote.

Tom Harding probably knew by now that the Texans had killed two of his men; the cattle baron no doubt had cronies in town who would have ridden out to his ranch immediately to deliver the news to him. If Harding intended to come after Bo and Scratch, though, it appeared he wasn't going to do it tonight.

As for what the future would bring, there was no way of knowing, but the Texans would mosey across that bridge when they came to it.

Right now they were coming to a patch of shadow that was thrown across the trail by a stand of pines that crowded up alongside it. Bo kept an eye on that swath of darkness, knowing that it would be a good place for danger to lurk. Because of that alertness, he wasn't surprised when a man suddenly stepped out of the shadows into the trail, blocking their path as he lifted a long, sinister-looking object in his hands.

"Hold it, you two!" the man shouted. "Don't try anything funny, or I'll blow you right out of the saddle with this shotgun!"

CHAPTER 4

Bo knew that at this range, a double load of buck-shot from a scattergun's twin barrels would shred him and Scratch into something resembling raw meat. That was why, under normal circumstances, he would have reacted very carefully to a threat like that.

These weren't normal circumstances, though, and . . .

"That's not a shotgun," Bo said.

The stranger jabbed the object at them. "It damn sure is," he insisted, "and if you don't drop your guns and get down off those horses right now, you'll be sorry!"

Scratch looked over at Bo and asked, "Broken branch o' some sort, ain't it?"

"That's what it looks like to me," Bo answered with a nod.

The stranger tried to brazen it out. "I'm not fooling now!" he said. "I'm warning you—"

"Give it up, son," Bo said. "It's not going to work."

"Nice try, though," Scratch added. "That looks a little

like a shotgun, I reckon, in bad light. If you hold your mouth just right, tilt your head, and squint a mite."

The man uttered a disgusted curse and flung down the thing in his hands. It broke in two with a crack, confirming not only that it was a tree branch, but that it was rotten as well.

"All right, go ahead and shoot me," he said. "I tried to hold you up and steal your goods and horses, so I guess I've got it comin' to me."

"We're not going to shoot you," Bo said. "Come over here."

The man hesitated, then shrugged and walked closer to them. Bo had thought he recognized the would-be robber, but now he was sure of it. The man's dark suit and hat and fair hair revealed his identity. His voice was even a little familiar from the pleading he had done back in the settlement.

"We're the fellas who saved you from that mob, you know," Bo said.

"Son of a bitch!" Scratch exclaimed. "It *is* him!" He urged his horse forward a step. "What are you doin' out here, mister?"

"What do you think?" the swindler who had called himself Charles Wortham said. "I'm trying to stay as far ahead of those crazy bastards as I can. I don't want anything to do with hot tar and chicken feathers!"

Bo said, "They might not bother with that next time."

"They might just take you straight to the nearest hangin' tree," Scratch added.

"There's not going to be a next time," the stranger vowed. "I've learned my lesson. I follow the straight and narrow from now on."

"Sure," Bo said. "That's why you pretended to have a shotgun and threatened to kill us with it unless we gave you our horses."

For a moment, the man didn't say anything. Then he chuckled and said, "Well, you can't blame a gent for trying."

"Actually, you can," Scratch said. "You can even shoot him."

"I didn't actually do anything!" the man protested. "You said it yourself. That's not even a real shotgun."

"Son," Bo said, "even if it had been, I don't reckon we would've been in all that much danger." He paused. "What's your name?"

The swindler dusted off his clothes, straightened his coat, and tucked his thumbs in the lapels. "My name is Charles Wortham," he said. "I work for the—"

"Don't even try that," Bo warned him. "We heard all about it back in town."

"Oh." The stranger was abashed, but only for a second. "My name is really Jake Reilly."

"Are we supposed to believe that?"

"As it happens, it's true."

"You tried to cheat those folks back there," Scratch accused.

"I would have gotten away with it, too," Reilly said, and there was a note of pride in his voice. "That is, if Harding hadn't had to go and ruin everything."

"Don't you even feel the least bit ashamed?" Bo asked.

"Let me tell you something," Reilly said, "something that everybody in my line of work knows. Every single person on the face of the earth has at least a little bit of larceny in his or her soul. *That's* what you have to appeal to if you want to make the schemes work. A man who wants to get something for nothing is the easiest to cheat."

"But those folks back yonder weren't tryin' to get somethin' for nothin'," Scratch argued. "They just wanted the railroad to come to their town."

"So they could get rich. Everybody who handed over a deed to me would never have done it if he hadn't believed that he'd make a lot more money in the long run by doing it."

Bo shook his head. "We can go round and round all night arguing about this, and it won't accomplish a blamed thing." He extended a hand toward Reilly. "Are you coming or not? If you are, climb up here behind me."

Scratch and Reilly both stared at him. It would have been hard to say which of them was more surprised by Bo's offer.

Scratch found his voice first. "You're askin' the likes o' him to ride with us?"

"I won't leave any man afoot," Bo said. "Not even a swindler and con artist like our friend Jake here."

"He ain't my friend," Scratch said. "And I think you're loco for not leavin' him here."

Bo smiled. "Wouldn't be the first time you thought I was loco, would it?"

"Well . . . not hardly."

Grinning, Reilly came forward to reach up and clasp Bo's wrist. "I'm surely obliged to you for the ride, Mister . . . ?"

"Creel," Bo introduced himself. "Bo Creel. My partner is Scratch Morton."

"I'm sure pleased to meet you both." With a grunt of effort, Reilly lifted himself onto the back of Bo's dun and settled himself behind the saddle. "It was gonna be a mighty long walk to the next town."

"We won't get there tonight," Bo told him. "We'll have to find a place to make camp before too much longer. I wouldn't mind putting a few more miles between us and that settlement, though."

Reilly laughed. "You and me both, brother. You and me both."

Now that he appeared to be out of immediate danger and wouldn't be forced to wander through the night on foot, Reilly's natural, easygoing arrogance had returned. Bo sensed that it was as much a part of the man as his blond hair.

"What happened to your horse?" he asked. "I reckon you *did* have a horse?"

"I sure did. A fine little mare. She's back there in the livery stable, though . . . a livery stable co-owned by Tom Harding, I might add . . . so I don't think I'll be going back to get her."

"Not unless you want to risk a dose o' tar and feathers again," Scratch said.

"How about a gun?" Bo asked.

"I had a pocket pistol. They took it away from me when they stormed into my hotel room, the barbarians."

"So you don't have a thing?"

"The clothes on my back," Reilly answered. "And my charm."

Scratch made a disgusted noise in his throat to indicate just how charming he thought Reilly was. Bo said, "Well, maybe you can make a fresh start in the next town we come to. You can probably get a job in a store or a livery stable or some such."

Reilly reached around and held up a hand, wiggling the long, slender fingers. "Does that look like a hand that should be loading flour sacks or mucking out stalls? If you'll stake me to a dollar or two, Mr. Creel, and let me find a poker game in some saloon, I'll run that up to plenty of money in no time."

"By cheating?" Bo asked. "And call me Bo. Even as old as I am, Mr. Creel is still my father."

"I don't have to cheat," Reilly boasted. "I can take these yokels for plenty just by playing fair and square. Of course, if I need to shade the odds a little . . ."

Scratch exploded. "A damn tinhorn! You've got a blasted cardsharp ridin' with us, Bo!"

"Afraid he's going to get us into trouble?" Bo asked dryly. "It seems to have a way of finding us anyway."

"Maybe so, but that ain't no reason to give it a helpin' hand."

Scratch continued to mutter in disgust as Bo said to Reilly, "You don't need to get into any poker games, Jake. Some good honest labor will get you back on your feet again."

"I thought you just dressed like a sky pilot," Reilly said. "I didn't know you were going to start preaching at me, or I might not have accepted that ride."

Bo lifted the reins as if getting ready to bring the dun to a halt. "I'll let you get down right now, if you want."

"No, no," Reilly said hastily. "There's no need for that. We'll talk about what I'm going to do next once we get where we're going." He couldn't resist adding, "For a couple of saddle tramps, you two are sure full of advice about how a fellow ought to live."

That brought on a fresh round of muttering from Scratch, but Bo just ignored the comment. A few minutes later, he swung the dun off the trail and onto an even narrower path that led upward through the trees. Scratch followed, and a minute later they came out into a small clearing, just as Bo had expected.

"This'll do," he declared. He waited until Reilly had slid down from the dun's back, then dismounted as well. Scratch had already swung down from the saddle.

Not much light penetrated into the clearing since it was surrounded by tall pines, but the Texans had good enough eyes despite their age to let them see what they were doing as they unsaddled the horses. "Look around and find us some firewood, Jake," Bo told Reilly.

"Look around?" Reilly repeated. "How can I look around? I can't see a blasted thing!"

"Sure you can," Bo said. "Just relax and wait a minute. Open your eyes. Don't squeeze them half-shut like you would if you were in some smoky saloon."

"I wish I was," Reilly muttered. But after a few moments, he began moving around the clearing and bending over to pick up broken branches small enough to use as firewood.

"Careful you don't grab a shotgun by mistake," Scratch gibed.

A few minutes later, Bo had a tiny fire burning inside a circle of rocks he had carefully arranged so that they threw back the heat from the dancing flames. Reilly looked on skeptically and said, "You can't cook anything with a fire that small."

"Hide and watch," Scratch said.

"And you don't have to eat if you don't want to," Bo added.

"Now, I didn't say that . . ."

Bo fried bacon, made some fresh gravy with the grease, and heated biscuits left over from that morning's breakfast. Simple fare, but good and filling. Reilly pitched in and ate his share . . . a little *more* than his share maybe.

When the meal was over and the cleaning up had been done and the flames were burning down to redly glowing embers, Bo and Scratch walked over to check on the horses, leaving Reilly slumped on a log by the fire.

"We're gonna have to stand watch all night to keep that young coyote from runnin' off with our horses and all our gear," Scratch warned. "Wouldn't put it past him to try to murder us in our sleep."

"I don't think he's quite that bad," Bo said. "And we'd be standing guard anyway, in case Harding and his men come after us."

"Which we wouldn't have to be worryin' about if we hadn't stepped in to give Reilly a hand," Scratch pointed out.

Bo shrugged. "What's done is done. Now we make the best of it."

"We could cut him loose, let him fend for himself."

"It may come to that," Bo admitted. "But I reckon we can afford to see how the hand plays out."

Scratch gave an eloquent snort in response to that.

By the time the Texans came back to the fire, Reilly had slumped down off the log, stretched out on the ground, and was sound asleep, low-pitched snores coming from him. "I'll stand first watch," Scratch volunteered, and Bo nodded. It didn't really matter who took the first turn and who took the second. Both men were accustomed to making do with a minimal amount of sleep when they had to.

Contrary to Scratch's worries, the night passed peacefully. Reilly didn't budge from his spot beside the log, and he slept like a log, too. Nor was there any sign of Tom Harding and his men. As the sky lightened with the approach of dawn, Bo hoped that Harding had decided losing two of his gun-wolves was enough.

Bo had bacon frying and coffee boiling by the time the savory smells woke Reilly. The young man sat up, ran his fingers through his tousled blond hair, and yawned. "That sure smells good," he said with a grin.

Bo used a piece of leather to protect his hand as he picked up the coffeepot and filled an extra tin cup he had taken from his saddlebags. He held it out to Reilly, who took it and sipped gratefully on the strong black brew.

Scratch slipped into camp with a Winchester tucked under his arm. "Trail down below looks clear," he reported. He had gone down to have a look a few minutes earlier.

"I got to wondering about something," Reilly said. "Are there any Indians around here?"

"Hostiles, you mean?" Bo asked.

"That's right."

Bo shook his head. "Not to speak of. Most of the Indian trouble now comes from the Apaches over in Arizona Territory."

"Come to think of it, though," Scratch said, "there are still a few bands of renegade 'Paches in the mountains over west of here, and they come out to raid ever' now and then."

"Do you think we'll run into any of them?" Reilly asked with a worried frown.

"It's not likely," Bo told him.

"But if we do, you don't want to let 'em take you prisoner," Scratch added with a leering grin. "They can keep a poor devil alive for days whilst they're havin' their fun torturin' him."

Reilly shuddered.

When breakfast was finished, Bo and Scratch cleaned up the camp. Reilly helped grudgingly. Then they saddled the horses and rode back down the hill to the main trail, Reilly once again behind Bo on the dun's back.

The three men continued south, and around midmorning Scratch suggested that Reilly ride double with him for a while. "It ain't that I'm all that fond of you, mister," he informed Reilly bluntly. "But it ain't fair to Bo's horse to make him carry you all the time."

"It doesn't matter to me," Reilly said as he dismounted

and then climbed up behind Scratch. "As long as I'm not walking, I don't care who I ride with."

This was magnificent country through which they rode. Up ahead, a rugged slope littered with huge boulders loomed to the left of the trail. A mountain goat bounded from rock to rock with almost supernatural grace and agility.

Pretty though the scene might be, Bo was eyeing the slope with a wary frown when Scratch said, "Somebody up ahead of us."

Bo lowered his eyes to the trail and saw a lone man riding in the same direction they were. He said, "That fella ought to turn around and come back. I don't like the looks of those rocks up there. I can see a little dust, like they're trying to shift—"

At that moment, one of the boulders broke free of its precarious perch. It began to roll down the slope, striking another large rock with a crunching impact. That one moved, too, and suddenly, in the blink of an eye and with a mighty roar, an avalanche began sliding down the side of the mountain . . .

Straight toward the lone, luckless rider who found himself directly in the deadly, earth-shaking path of thousands of tons of rock and dirt.

CHAPTER 5

As Bo, Scratch, and Reilly watched in horror, the man on horseback ahead of them jerked his mount in a tight circle, his head whipping back and forth. Bo knew the questions that had to be going through the man's mind: *Can I outrun it? Which way should I go?*

He answered those questions by spurring his horse into a hard run back the way he had come, toward the Texans and Jake Reilly.

Looking over Scratch's shoulder, Reilly gasped, "He'll never make it!"

"He's got a better chance comin' this way than goin' straight ahead," Scratch said. "But it's gonna be mighty close. If that rock slide misses him, it'll just be by a whisker."

Reilly surprised Bo a little by asking, "Is there anything we can do to help him?" So far, Reilly hadn't struck Bo as the sort to care about anyone other than himself. Maybe seeing someone trapped and about to be overwhelmed by an unstoppable force of nature had touched something human inside Reilly.

"It's all up to him and his horse," Bo said. "Say a prayer for him if you like. That's about all we can do."

Reilly swallowed and asked nervously, "We're well clear of it, aren't we?"

Scratch nodded. "Yeah, it'll miss us by several hundred yards. We don't have to worry about being caught in it."

All three of them had been forced to raise their voices to be heard over the growing rumble of the avalanche. It was a terrible, awe-inspiring sight as it swept down the mountain, too powerful to be halted by anything any puny human could do. Dust billowed up in a huge cloud, obscuring the slope. Smaller rocks began to pelt down in the trail around the fleeing rider, who leaned far forward over his horse's neck and urged the animal on to its greatest speed.

"Son of a gun," Scratch breathed. "I think maybe he's gonna make it."

The lone rider might have escaped, just as Scratch said, if at that moment a rock the size of two doubled fists hadn't struck him in the head. It was only a glancing blow, but it was enough to knock the man out of the saddle. He pitched to the ground, rolling over and over as the now riderless horse raced on, caught up in a frantic, panic-stricken flight.

"No!" Reilly cried as he and the Texans saw the man fall. "He was so close!"

"He's not giving up," Bo said as the horse bolted on past them. The man had scrambled to his feet and now ran desperately toward safety, his arms pumping and his legs flying back and forth.

His valiant effort was doomed to fail, though. The

edge of the rock slide caught him. A rock the size of a loaf of bread crunched into his side and knocked him off his feet, sending him sprawling in the trail. A larger boulder rolled over the lower half of his body. His head and shoulders jerked up involuntarily, and his mouth opened wide in an agonized scream that was swallowed up by the avalanche's roar. More rocks crashed around him, and dust and dirt threatened to cover him up completely.

No more than two minutes had passed since the first warning rumble. That was how little time it took for devastation to occur. That was how quick calamity could pass, too, because as the rock slide reached the more level terrain west of the trail, it ground to a halt. Dust hung thickly in the air, billowing and swirling, but the roar diminished to a rattle as smaller rocks clattered down the slope in the wake of the avalanche.

Bo said, "Let's see if there's anything we can do for him!" and heeled his horse into a run toward the man who had been caught in the cataclysm. Scratch and Reilly were right behind him.

A breeze began to disperse the dust clouds, carrying them away from the trail. Bo spotted the man lying half-buried in the rubble that now covered the trail. He swung down from the dun while the horse was still moving and ran toward the man. When he reached the spot where the man had fallen, he began tossing rocks aside, trying to uncover him. Scratch and Reilly dismounted and hurried to help.

The man had a gash on his head where the rock that had knocked him out of the saddle struck him, and blood from the injury covered the right side of his face. Despite that, Bo could tell that the man was fairly young, and the hair that hadn't been stained crimson was the color of straw. Somewhat surprisingly, the man was still alive. A groan came from him as the Texans and their companion shifted rocks away from him and uncovered him.

Scratch stopped working suddenly and reached over to touch Bo's arm. He nodded grimly toward the man's lower body. Bo's jaw tightened as he saw the damage that giant boulder had done when it rolled over the man. Everything from just above the waist on down was crushed almost flat. The luckless hombre's legs appeared to be broken in dozens of places, and there was no telling what had happened to his insides. He was still alive, but he was doomed.

"Get that bottle from your saddlebags, Scratch," Bo said as he knelt beside the injured man's head. "We'll try to make him comfortable, maybe find out who he is. That's all we can do."

"Bottle?" Reilly repeated as Scratch trotted off toward the horses. "You've got a bottle of whiskey, and you didn't tell me?"

"Strictly for medicinal purposes," Bo said.

Reilly snorted. "I'll bet."

Actually, it was true, although Bo didn't waste any breath trying to convince Reilly of that. Whiskey worked about as well as anything else for cleaning bullet wounds, and you never knew when you might have to patch up an injury like that.

Bo got an arm under the man's head and shoulders and lifted him slightly while Scratch fetched the bottle. When he came back with it, Scratch knelt on the other side of the man and pulled the cork with his teeth, then put the neck of the bottle to the man's lips and tilted it up just enough to spill some of the liquor into his mouth.

The man coughed and choked, but he swallowed most of the fiery whiskey. His eyelids fluttered for a few seconds, and then he opened his eyes as the liquor's bracing effects took hold.

"Wha . . . what h-happened?" he managed to gasp.

"You got caught in a rock slide, mister," Bo told him. "But you're going to be all right. Just lay there and rest for a few minutes, before you try to get up and move around again."

It was a lie, of course, but Bo hoped it would be of some small comfort as the man slipped out of this life and into the next.

"W-whiskey . . ."

Scratch held the bottle to the man's lips again, but the man somehow found the strength to raise a hand and push it away.

"Whiskey . . . Flats," he went on. "Got to get to . . . Whiskey Flats . . . supposed to . . . be there . . ."

"What the hell's Whiskey Flats?" Reilly asked as he leaned over the injured man, hands on his knees.

"Sounds like the name of a town," Scratch said. "Don't reckon I've ever heard of it, though."

"Take another drink, fella," Bo urged the man. "It'll help you feel better."

"Got to . . . get there . . ." the man said again. "Whiskey Flats . . ."

"He's determined, isn't he?" Reilly said.

Scratch managed to get some more of the whiskey

in the man's mouth. His throat worked convulsively as he swallowed. He looked up at Bo and said, "Reckon I'll . . . be all right now . . . nothing hurts any—"

His eyes glazed over, and the breath came out of him in one long, last, despairing sigh. He was gone.

Bo sighed, too, and shook his head as he reached up to close the sightlessly staring eyes. "I reckon we can start digging a grave now," he said.

"With what?" Reilly asked.

"I've got a shovel that folds up wrapped in my bedroll," Scratch said. "Come on, Reilly. You can lend a hand with the diggin'."

Reilly didn't look too enthused about the idea, but he followed Scratch. The silver-haired Texan got the shovel from his gear and selected a nice, pine-shaded site on the far side of the trail for the grave. He and Reilly took turns digging while Bo went through the dead man's clothing in search of something that might tell them who he was.

The ground was hard and a little rocky, so it took time to scoop out a big enough hole. Reilly was down inside the grave when Bo walked over carrying a piece of paper in one hand. He appeared to be clutching something else in his other hand, something small enough that it couldn't be seen as long as Bo's hand was closed.

"Well, I found out who he was, and found out about Whiskey Flats, too," Bo announced.

"Is this deep enough?" Reilly asked. He had taken off his hat and coat, and his shirt was dark with sweat from his unaccustomed efforts.

Scratch told him, "Yeah, that'll do fine," and reached

down to offer him a hand climbing out. Reilly took it and clambered from the hole in the earth. He brushed himself off and frowned at the palms of his hands.

"I'm gonna have blisters," he complained.

Bo and Scratch ignored him. Scratch pointed at the paper in Bo's hand and asked, "What's that?"

"It's a letter from the mayor of a settlement called Whiskey Flats," Bo said. "Must be somewhere south of here, since that's the direction the fella was going. The letter is addressed to John Henry Braddock."

Scratch frowned. "Say, that name sounds familiar. Ain't he . . ."

Bo held his other hand out to reveal the gold-plated star that lay in his palm. "A lawman," he said. "Making quite a name for himself as a town tamer, like Bill Hickok. I guess this is his badge."

"Lawman, eh?" Reilly grunted. "Maybe I don't feel as sorry for him as I thought I did."

"I ain't overfond o' star packers myself," Scratch snapped, "but nobody deserves to go out like that hombre just did. Just like a certain four-flushin', swindlin' con man didn't deserve to be tarred and feathered and run outta town on a rail, I reckon."

Reilly grimaced and shrugged in acknowledgment of that point.

Bo went on. "This letter from Mayor Jonas McHale makes it clear that the town council of Whiskey Flats hired Braddock to come in and clean up the settlement. It doesn't say exactly what sort of trouble they're having there, but it must be something bad enough to need a tough, gun-handy marshal like Braddock to take care of it."

"Reckon they'll have to find somebody else now," Scratch said.

"Yeah, I reckon," Bo agreed, but a frown of thought creased his forehead for a moment before he went on. "Why don't you see if you can go catch Braddock's horse, Scratch, while I get one of our blankets and wrap up the body in it?"

"Sure thing," Scratch said. "That cayuse was still goin' hell-for-leather when he went past us, but I'll bet he didn't run too far."

Scratch rode off on his bay in search of the lawman's horse while Bo and Reilly walked back to the edge of the debris from the avalanche where Braddock's body lay. Bo brought a blanket from his war bag with him, but he handed it to Reilly and said, "Hang on to this for a minute." Then he knelt beside Braddock's body.

"What are you doing there?" Reilly asked with a frown.

Bo straightened with the dead man's gunbelt and holstered Colt in his hands. The gun had been lying under Braddock's hip when the boulder rolled over him, and it had escaped damage.

Bo held out the gunbelt and weapon toward Reilly. "This looks like it would fit you," he said. "Might as well get some use out of it, since Braddock doesn't need it anymore."

Reilly's frown deepened. He didn't reach for the gun. "I don't know," he said. "I told you I carried a pocket pistol. I've never used one of those big six-shooters."

"Just take it," Bo said. "You never know when it might come in handy."

After a moment, Reilly shrugged and took the gunbelt. He strapped it around his waist, and looked somewhat surprised as he buckled it in place.

"Yeah, it fits all right," he said.

Bo nodded. "I thought it would. Now, let's spread that blanket on the ground and lift Braddock onto it."

"That's gonna be an ugly job," Reilly said with a grimace. "He's pretty busted up."

"You'd want somebody to take care of you properly, if it was you lying there and not him."

"I suppose."

Reilly looked away as much as possible as they lifted the gruesome remains of John Henry Braddock out of the rocks and onto the blanket. He seemed relieved when Bo rolled the blanket around the corpse and it was no longer visible.

Just then, Scratch came trotting back on the bay, leading Braddock's horse by the reins. It was a good-looking buckskin, the sort of mount that a well-known lawman would ride. Reilly looked at the horse with keen interest and lightly slapped the holstered gun at his side.

"I'm carrying Braddock's Colt," he said. "Do I get to claim his horse, too?"

"Might as well," Bo said. "That's what I had in mind."

"Better'n you havin' to ride double with one of us," Scratch said. He dismounted and tied the reins of Braddock's horse to a pine sapling. His bay and Bo's dun didn't have to be tied up; they knew not to stray very far from the Texans.

Bo and Scratch took hold of Braddock's blanket-wrapped body, lifting it and carrying it over to the grave. They lowered it into the hole in the earth as gently and carefully as they could, then stepped back and removed their hats. Reilly had ambled over after them. Scratch nudged him in the ribs with an elbow and nodded toward his hat. Reilly rolled his eyes and took it off, holding it in front of him as Bo and Scratch held theirs.

Bo and Scratch bowed their heads. "Lord," Bo said, "we ask that You show mercy on this man and welcome him into Your kingdom. Grant him peace and rest from all the ills and troubles of this world, and let him dwell in Your house forever and ever. Amen."

"Amen," Scratch echoed.

"You really think that does any good?" Reilly asked as they all put their hats on again.

"There are some as don't believe in El Señor Dios," Scratch said as he picked up the shovel. "I don't hold that against 'em because every man's got to make up his mind about such things for his own self. But tell me this . . . what harm's it gonna do?"

Reilly didn't say anything, and Scratch laughed as he thrust the shovel into the young man's hands.

"That's what I thought. Get busy coverin' him up. The dirt'll go back in easier'n it came out."

CHAPTER 6

The rock slide completely blocked the trail and extended for a hundred yards or so beyond it on the other side. That presented no problem for horsemen, who could easily ride around the rubble, but the trail would have to be cleared before wagon traffic could get through again.

That wasn't the responsibility of Bo, Scratch, and Jake Reilly, so after they finished refilling the final resting place of John Henry Braddock, they mounted up and rode on, still heading south. Bo had slipped the letter from the mayor of Whiskey Flats into the inside pocket of his coat, along with Braddock's badge.

The badge itself didn't have any markings, so Bo assumed it could function as the symbol of authority no matter whether its wearer was serving as marshal, sheriff, constable, or in some other law enforcement position.

"How far do you think it is to this Whiskey Flats place?" Reilly asked. He was a decent rider, Bo noted, and handled Braddock's buckskin without much trouble.

"I don't know," Bo replied. "Scratch and I have been through this part of the territory before, but it was a long time ago."

"Thirty years or more, I reckon," Scratch commented. "Back then it was still part of Mexico." He chuckled. "Remember the big ruckus we got into in that cantina in Santa Fe?"

"You could ask a similar question about nearly every place we've been," Bo said dryly.

"Hell *does* have a habit o' poppin' wherever we happen to be, don't it?"

Reilly said, "Well, I guess if we keep riding, we'll come to it sooner or later."

"Hell," Scratch asked, "or Whiskey Flats?"

"With a name like that, and the way Mayor McHale talks about it in his letter, there may not be much difference," Bo said.

It was almost midday by the time they left the scene of the avalanche behind, but they rode on for a while before stopping to eat a little and rest the horses. The meal consisted of cold biscuits and a little jerky from Scratch's saddlebags.

Reilly said, "You know, you could break out that bottle again. A couple of swigs might make this food go down easier."

"That's all right," Bo said. "You need a clear head, Jake, for what's coming next."

"Oh? What's that?"

Bo gestured toward the Colt .45 on Reilly's hip. "Let's see how good you are at handling that smokepole."

Reilly frowned and said, "I told you, I never used a gun like this very much."

"Well, give it a try anyway." Bo pointed. "See that rock over there, about twenty feet away?"

"The one sitting on top of the bigger rock?"

"That's right."

Reilly squinted at the target Bo had chosen, a fist-sized rock resting on top of a stone about the size of a carpetbag.

"Seems like it's sort of far away."

"Just see if you can hit somewhere in the general vicinity," Bo told him.

"All right," Reilly said with a sigh. "If you're sure."

He positioned himself with his right side toward the rocks and reached down to draw the gun. He pointed the Colt toward the sky and then extended his arm to its full length so that he could squint down the barrel toward the target.

"Hold on," Scratch said. "You ain't fightin' a duel with them rocks. Stand facin' 'em."

Reilly lowered the gun and turned so that he was squared up toward the rocks. "Like this?"

"Yeah. Holster that gun and draw it again."

Reilly slid the weapon back into its sheath. "Shouldn't I have the holster tied down or something? Or be wearing it lower?"

"Why? You want to impress some pretty girl with what a gunfighter you are? I don't see no pretty girls out here."

Bo said, "Just wear the holster normally, Jake. You don't want it too low or too high. It needs to be where you can catch hold of the gun naturally as your hand comes up in your draw."

"All right." Reilly faced the rocks, took a deep breath, and drew. The gun came out of leather smoothly enough. He didn't fumble it. But he still stuck his arm straight out and aimed along the barrel for a second before he pressed the trigger. The bullet struck the bigger rock a few inches below the target stone and ricocheted off with a whine.

"Not bad," Bo said, impressed with Reilly's accuracy. "You won't always have time to aim like that, though. See how you can shoot from the hip."

"The key is keepin' your eye on what you're shootin' at," Scratch added. "Learn how to do that, and you'll hit what you're lookin' at more often than not."

"Sort of like knowing what card is gonna come out of the deck next, even when you haven't marked them," Reilly said with a grin.

"Yeah, something like that," Scratch said with a shake of his head.

Reilly holstered the Colt, took his stance again, drew, and fired, snapping off the shot from his hip.

"A clean miss!" Scratch called.

Reilly flushed. "Let me try again."

"Go ahead," Bo told him.

The next time, Reilly's bullet kicked up dirt a good twenty feet beyond the rocks. "Blast it!" he said, and stubbornly holstered the revolver and set himself to try again.

By the time he had emptied the Colt, only his first

shot had hit anywhere near where it was supposed to. The others had all missed by considerable margins.

"Son of a bitch!" Reilly exclaimed. "Nobody can hit anything shooting like that!"

"Is that so?" Scratch drawled.

Bo had a pretty good idea what was coming next, so he wasn't surprised when Scratch's ivory-handled Remingtons seemed to leap into his hands. Scratch held the guns waist-high and squeezed off round after round, the shots coming so closely together that the explosions formed one long, rolling roar. The fist-sized rock leaped into the air, then split in two as another bullet struck it, and then those pieces shattered as well as Scratch's slugs continued to find their targets unerringly. By the time Scratch's guns fell silent, the rock had turned into gravel pattering down to the ground.

Reilly stared, wide-eyed. "Son of a *bitch*!" he said again. "I never saw shooting like that!"

"There are men who can do better," Scratch said as he holstered the left-hand Remington and broke open the other one to begin reloading it. "And that ain't false modesty, just fact. But I'll admit that I'm pretty fair at gun-handlin'."

"And at wasting ammunition by showing off," Bo said, but his grin made it clear that he wasn't really annoyed with Scratch. "Load that Colt and try again, Jake. That's the only way you'll get any better."

"What'll I shoot at?" Reilly wanted to know. "He busted that little rock all to pieces!"

"Just try for the big one," Bo told him.

Reilly reloaded and continued to practice, and his

last two shots from that cylinder both hit the target. He turned to Bo and Scratch with a grin. "How about that?"

"Yeah, but the rock ain't shootin' back," Scratch pointed out.

"You show some promise, Jake," Bo said. "Keep it up, and you might be a pretty good hand with a gun like that."

Reilly shook his head. "Don't know why I'd ever need to be. I'm just carrying it because Braddock doesn't have any use for it anymore. When we get to Whiskey Flats, I'll probably sell it. Might get enough to buy a smaller gun and have some left over to stake me in a game of cards."

He appeared to have forgotten what Bo had said about him getting a job in a store or a livery stable. That was all right, Bo mused.

Because he had something else in mind for Jake Reilly now.

They hadn't reached Whiskey Flats by nightfall, if indeed the settlement lay in this direction. That seemed likely, considering that John Henry Braddock had been heading south, too. It might take several days to get there, or they might ride right into the place tomorrow. Only time would tell.

Bo and Scratch found another good place to camp, this one on top of a small hill with a view of the surrounding countryside. Considering the location, the Texans deemed it best not to have a campfire, which would have been more visible here than the place they had camped in the night before. It was still possible that Tom Harding and his gunhands might be coming after them, although Bo deemed that more unlikely with each day that passed.

Reilly groused about not having a fire, of course. "Cold food will fill your belly just as well as warm," Scratch told him. "And the weather ain't nippy enough at night to freeze off anything important."

"I just don't understand why you have to be so careful all the time."

"That's because we want to stay alive," Bo said. "And the best way to get dead in a hurry out here is to be careless."

"What about Braddock?" Reilly asked. "He wasn't being careless. He was just riding along the trail. And now he's as dead as he can be."

Bo shrugged. "Sometimes bad luck can't be avoided no matter what you do. But it doesn't hurt to try to tip the odds in your favor."

"I guess that makes sense," Reilly admitted. "Sort of like playing poker."

"Cheatin' at poker, you mean," Scratch said disdainfully.

"Anyway," Bo added, "you were the one who was worried about Indians, Jake. You wouldn't want to advertise our presence up here, just in case there *is* a war party anywhere around these parts, would you?"

Reilly shut up after that.

They made another meal on biscuits and jerky, washed down with cold, clear water from a nearby creek instead of the whiskey that Reilly would have preferred. Afterward, Reilly leaned back on a rock and took a cigar out of his pocket. He was reaching for a match when Bo said, "Might as well put it away, unless you want to chew on it unlit, Jake."

"Damn it!" Reilly said. "Now you mean to tell me that I can't even smoke either?"

"I'd like a pipe myself," Bo said, "but the smell of tobacco smoke can drift a long way. If anybody's looking for us, it'd be easy to follow the smoke right back here to us."

Muttering disgustedly, Reilly shoved the cheroot back in his pocket. "It's like traveling with a pair of damned old mother hens."

"These mother hens are tryin' to keep you alive, boy," Scratch said. "Seems to me like we've pulled your bacon outta the fire a couple o' times already. You ought to be a mite grateful."

"I am," Reilly said, although he didn't sound particularly thankful.

"If that's true, then maybe you'll consider an idea I have in mind," Bo said.

Suspicion was suddenly audible in Reilly's voice as he said, "An idea? What sort of idea?"

Bo thumbed his hat back on his head as he sat on the ground with his legs stretched out in front of him. "I've been thinking about what's going to happen when we get to Whiskey Flats," he said.

"I sort of figured we'd go our separate ways," Reilly said. "No offense, and like I told you, I'm grateful to you fellas for what you've done for me, but let's face it . . . we're just not cut from the same cloth. You're cramping my style."

"Crampin' your style?" Scratch repeated as he started to get up. "Why, you little pup—"

"Take it easy," Bo said. "Jake, how do you think the people of Whiskey Flats are going to feel when they find out that John Henry Braddock, the man they were counting on to bring law and order to their community, is dead?"

Reilly shrugged. "Disappointed, I suppose. But that's not my problem, and it's not yours either. Hell, you're doing them a favor just by bringing them the news that Braddock is never going to get there."

"But what if he does?" Bo asked. "What if John Henry Braddock rides into Whiskey Flats after all?"

A laugh came from Reilly. "That's gonna be pretty hard, seeing as how he's dead and buried."

Now it was Scratch's turn to be suspicious as he asked, "What sort o' crazy notion is floatin' around inside that noggin o' yours, Bo Creel?"

"It's really simple," Bo said. "John Henry Braddock can still take the job of marshal in Whiskey Flats and bring law and order to the settlement." He held out his hand, and the light of the rising moon glinted on the badge that rested on his palm once again. "All you have to do, Jake, is pretend to be Braddock. *You* can be the marshal of Whiskey Flats."

CHAPTER 7

Scratch and Reilly both stared at him for a long moment in the fading light, and then both exploded in surprise at the same time. "You're crazy!" Reilly exclaimed, and Scratch put it more colorfully by bursting out, "Bo, you've gone plumb loco!"

Bo shook his head and told them, "Not at all. It makes perfect sense. The letter from Mayor McHale makes it clear that neither he nor anyone else in Whiskey Flats has ever actually met Braddock. The town council arranged to hire him as marshal through correspondence. McHale says that they're all looking forward to meeting him for the first time."

"But maybe they've seen pictures of him, or at least know what he's supposed to look like," Reilly objected.

"You saw Braddock for yourself," Bo said. "He was about the same age and size as you, Jake, and your hair color is close enough to pass for his."

"But . . . but . . . you're forgetting one thing . . . *I'm not a lawman!*"

"But you could be," Bo insisted. "All you have to do is pretend to be Braddock."

"And bring law and order to some wide-open, lawless town! How in blazes am I supposed to do that?"

"That's simple, too." Bo smiled. "We'll help you."

"Now I *know* you're loco," Scratch said.

"Just think about it," Bo urged. "Jake here tells the folks in Whiskey Flats that he's John Henry Braddock. They'll believe him. And to help him restore order, he's brought a couple of deputies with him. That would be you and me, Scratch."

Deep trenches appeared in Scratch's weathered face as he frowned in thought. He reached up and rubbed his jaw.

Reilly looked over at him. "You can't actually be considering this insane scheme!" he said.

"You know, it just might work," Scratch mused. "It'd take a heap o' luck, but it might work."

"It would take me agreeing to go along with it, too," Reilly said, "and I'm not gonna! Do I *look* like a lawman to you? Do you really think I'm cut out for that sort of thing?"

"You pretended to be a railroad man," Bo pointed out. "All you'd have to do is pretend to be a marshal." He paused. "Unless you think you couldn't convince anybody that's who you were."

Reilly laughed. "I can convince anybody of anything! Hell, I once persuaded a little gal in Kansas that I was Jesse James! If I wanted to, I could put it over. I could—"

He stopped short and glared at Bo.

"You see, Jake," the Texan said quietly, "you've just got to have confidence."

Reilly stood up and paced back and forth across the campsite. He took off his hat and ran his fingers through his tousled blond hair. Finally, he stopped to look at Bo and Scratch and asked, "What's in it for me?"

"In a town as grateful as Whiskey Flats is bound to be when the man they believe to be John Henry Braddock shows up . . . well, it seems to me that a fella could get just about anything he wanted in a town like that."

Reilly stared at Bo for a moment. He still held his hat in his hand, and he abruptly lifted it and pointed it at the Texans as he exclaimed, "Yes! That's exactly right! All I'd have to do is pretend to be the marshal for a little while, and they'd open up the town wide for me!" He threw his head back and laughed. "It's brilliant! Good Lord, Bo, I never realized you had such a streak of larceny in you, too!"

"Just don't forget your faithful deputies when it comes time for the big cleanup," Bo said.

Reilly clapped his hat back on his head. "Don't worry about that," he assured them. "You boys will get your share. Maybe not quite as big as my share, of course, since I'll be the marshal and you'll just be deputies, but we'll all come out of this rich men. Rich men, I tell you!"

He capered around the campsite a while longer, then finally sat down again to turn over all the potentially lucrative possibilities in his mind. Scratch climbed to his feet and said, "Reckon I'd best have a look around 'fore we turn in, just to make sure there ain't nobody lurkin' in these parts. Bo, why don't you come with me?"

"I can do that," Bo agreed as he stood up. "You'll be all right here, Jake?"

"Huh?" Reilly glanced up distractedly. "Oh, yeah, sure. You fellas take your time. I've got plenty of thinking and planning to do."

Bo and Scratch nodded and moved off into the darkness, carrying their Winchesters with them. They moved with the silent grace of born frontiersmen and didn't stop until they were well out of easy earshot of the camp.

"Now," Scratch said as he turned to his trail partner. "How about tellin' me just what the hell is *really* goin' on here?"

"Maybe some of Reilly's shady nature has rubbed off on me," Bo suggested.

Scratch shook his head. "Not hardly. You got somethin' else in mind. I can tell."

Bo laughed softly and said, "All right, you've got me. I knew I couldn't put it over on you. Jake was easy. All I had to do was make him think that we're as crooked as he is, and he went right along with the idea."

"Like he said about swindlin' somebody," Scratch replied as understanding dawned in him. "Make a fella think he might get somethin' for nothin', and he'll do whatever you want him to."

"Exactly. Jake thinks he's going to Whiskey Flats to swindle the people there, but he's actually going to be their marshal and do some growing up."

Scratch grunted. "I'll believe *that* when I see it."

"Think about it," Bo urged. "He's a smart kid, you've seen that for yourself. And he's got some sand, too. He's in the habit of running away from trouble, but back him into a corner and he might actually grow a backbone and become a man."

"And you're plannin' on backin' him into that corner."

"If Whiskey Flats is as full of trouble as Mayor McHale's letter indicates, it'll do the job for us. Jake won't have any choice but to grow up in a hurry while he's pretending to be the marshal."

"Either that or get himself killed," Scratch said gloomily. "And us right along with him."

"Well," Bo said with a faint smile in the darkness, "there's that possibility to consider, too."

In the end, Scratch went along with the idea, of course, just as Bo knew he would. Scratch might not have a very high opinion of Reilly, but he trusted Bo's instincts.

Anyway, Bo had figured out why Scratch and Reilly didn't get along all that well. They were just too much alike, at least as far as their devil-may-care natures went. It was no wonder they sometimes rubbed each other the wrong way.

The Texans took turns standing watch again that night, and early the next morning they were on their way again. Reilly was still excited and full of talk about how they would carry off the deception once they reached Whiskey Flats.

"I've seen plenty of big-city police," he said, "but not that many frontier marshals."

"Don't worry," Bo assured him. "We've run into plenty of small town star packers, so we know how they act. You can just follow our lead."

"But it'll have to look like I'm giving the orders," Reilly pointed out. "After all, I'm the marshal—"

"And we're just the deputies," Scratch finished for him. "We ain't forgot."

Bo said, "We'll make it look like you're in charge, Jake. That's what the people in Whiskey Flats will be expecting, so that's what they'll see."

After the three riders made their way by a twisting trail over a couple of ridges, the terrain began to flatten out more as the valley they were following once again spread out between mountains to east and west. The countryside took on the look of cattle country, with broad, lushly grassed pastures interspersed with creeks and bands of trees. Scratch spotted some cows grazing in the distance and pointed them out.

"This is prime range," he commented. "Whoever owns it has got himself a mighty nice spread."

"How far do you think we are from Whiskey Flats?" Reilly asked.

"No way of telling yet," Bo said. "But there's bound to be a settlement pretty close by. The ranches in these parts will need a supply center."

Scratch grinned and added, "And a place for the cowhands to raise hell on Saturday night and payday."

Reilly licked his lips in anticipation. "Man, I'd like to spend some time in a saloon! Some good whiskey, a game of cards, a few pretty little gals in spangled dresses to choose from . . ."

"You're supposed to be cleanin' the place up," Scratch reminded him, "not addin' to the general debauchery."

"But I can at least have a drink, can't I?" Reilly asked, starting to sound a little desperate.

Bo smiled and said, "I reckon even a famous lawman can be allowed a drink now and then."

Reilly heaved a sigh of relief. "For a minute there, I was afraid you were gonna say I can't have any fun at all—"

His words were cut off by the sudden crackle of gunfire up ahead.

The three men reined their mounts to a halt as shots blasted through the midday air. Up ahead, the trail twisted through some trees, so they couldn't see very far along it. The reports sounded like they were coming from handguns, and they drew closer as Bo, Scratch, and Reilly listened. After a moment, they heard the rumble of hoofbeats, too. A desperate pursuit was under way—and coming straight at them.

"What do we do?" Reilly asked. He looked and sounded nervous.

"Take that badge I gave you out of your pocket and pin it to your lapel," Bo told him. "We don't know what's going on here, and until we do I don't want there to be any question about you being a lawman."

"Keep your eyes and ears open," Scratch added. "The way those hombres are ridin' hell-for-leather, they'll be here any minute."

Sure enough, a rider soon swept around the bend in the trail up ahead and pelted toward them, leaning

over the neck of his horse and kicking it in the sides
to get all the speed out of it that he could. Bo couldn't
tell anything about the man other than that he was
riding for his life.

It quickly became apparent why the lone horseman
was fleeing. Half a dozen more riders thundered
around the bend. Puffs of gun smoke spurted from the
revolvers they brandished as they fired after the madly
galloping rider.

"Six-to-one odds, Bo," Scratch said. "I don't cotton
to that, no matter what that lone fella's done."

"Neither do I," Bo agreed. "Let's put a stop to it and
see if we can find out what's going on here."

Reilly swallowed. "What do I do?"

"Let's move aside and let him pass," Bo said. "Then
we'll stop those men who are chasing him."

The three of them pulled their mounts to the side of
the trail. Mere seconds later, the fleeing rider flashed
past them. Bo caught only a glimpse of him. He appeared to be small and fairly young, maybe just a boy.
He wore fringed buckskins and a battered old brown
hat with the brim pushed up in front. Foamy sweat
covered the heaving flanks of the horse, which was
clearly on its last legs.

As soon as the rider had gone by, Bo urged the dun
back out into the trail. Scratch and Reilly followed suit
with their horses. They sat in the middle of the trail,
blocking the pursuit. Of course, the gang of gunmen
could have gone around them, but instead they stubbornly came straight on, although they ceased shooting as soon as Bo, Scratch, and Reilly got in the line

of fire. Bo glanced over at Reilly and saw that the young man looked scared but determined.

"Just remember," Bo said. "You're a famous fighting marshal. You don't have any reason to be scared of these hombres. *They* ought to be scared of *you*."

Reilly nodded and looked a little more resolute. As long as he had a role to play, he was more confident.

The stocky, gray-bearded man who seemed to be leading the charge hauled back on his reins with one hand and lifted the other in a signal for his companions to stop. As the horses slowed, dust swirled around them for a moment. As it cleared away, Bo could see that the men were all hopping mad.

"What the hell do you think you're doin'?" the gray-bearded man shouted, his voice fairly shaking with rage. "You're lettin' that damned rustler get away!"

Bo glanced over his shoulder. The buckskin-clad rider had slowed. Well out of handgun range now, he brought his mount to a stop before the poor, exhausted horse collapsed.

"He doesn't look like he's going anywhere right now," Bo said. "How do you know he's a rustler? Did you catch him with a running iron, or driving off some of your stock?"

"He was skulkin' around on Rocking B range, lookin' over our herd!" the leader of the group said. "Mr. Bascomb's been losin' stock right and left, and anybody who ain't got no business here is suspect! For that matter, who the hell are you?"

Bo looked at Reilly, who was hanging back a little. Reilly urged his horse forward, so that the badge pinned to his coat was more visible.

"This is John Henry Braddock, the new marshal of Whiskey Flats," Bo announced. "We're his deputies."

That took the men by surprise. They were all rugged-looking hombres in range clothes, but even though they had been blazing away at the fleeing rider, it was clear to Bo's experienced eye that they were cowhands, not hired gunmen. Faced with confronting a representative of the law, they were suddenly a little nervous.

"Marshal?" blustered the gray-bearded man. "I heard somethin' about a new marshal comin' to town."

"Whiskey Flats is close by then?"

The man jerked a thumb over his shoulder. "About five miles on down this trail." He glared past them. "What about that thievin' son of a bitch? I'll bet he works for that damned North!"

"Well, it's pretty obvious that he doesn't have any cows in his pockets," Bo said dryly, "so I don't think he's done any rustling today. We'll question him and find out what he's doing on Rocking B range. I reckon this Mr. Bascomb you mentioned is the owner?"

"That's right. Chet Bascomb. As fine a man as you'll find in these parts . . . not like that no-good polecat Steve North."

Bo let that pass. Not being familiar with the situation or the folks involved, he wasn't going to waste time getting involved in an argument about the relative merits of either Chet Bascomb or Steve North, who was evidently a rival cattleman.

Instead, he said, "You hombres can go on back about your business. We'll take care of this matter from here."

The gray-bearded man frowned. "Mr. Bascomb ain't gonna like it. Around here we stomp our own snakes. We don't depend on no lawdogs to do it."

"Things are different now," Bo said, his voice and his gaze firm. "You can start spreading the word, friend. Law and order have come to these parts."

Graybeard grumbled some more, but then he turned his horse and profanely told the men with him to get back to work. They rode off, casting a few hostile glares back over their shoulders as they did so.

"I thought for sure they were going to start shooting again," Reilly said.

Bo shook his head. "Not cowboys like that. They may be pretty rough around the edges, but they're generally law-abiding. They respected that badge you're wearing, Jake."

"People really do that?" Reilly sounded like he couldn't quite grasp that concept.

"Honest ones do," Scratch said. "I don't reckon you'd know."

Reilly grinned as they turned their horses toward the buckskin-clad rider. "Honesty's like beauty, boys," he said. "It's only skin-deep. Put enough temptation in anybody's way, and they'll forget all about being honest fast enough."

Bo didn't agree with that, and he hoped that in time Reilly would come to realize that it wasn't true, too. For now, though, he wanted to find out more about what was going on around Whiskey Flats, and the "rustler" seemed as good a place as any to start.

As they rode toward the man, Scratch said, "From the sound o' what that varmint with the beard was sayin', there's a range war brewin' in these parts, too, Bo, to go along with the other trouble the mayor o' Whiskey Flats told Braddock about in that letter."

Bo nodded. "Yeah, I'd say you're right. Get a couple of fellas who fancy themselves cattle barons locking horns and you can have a real problem on your hands."

"But not me, right?" Reilly said. "I mean, I'm the town marshal. I don't have anything to do with what happens outside of the settlement."

"According to the letter of the law, you're probably right. But a good lawman will poke his nose into anything that has an effect on what goes on in his town, and if a range war breaks out this close to Whiskey Flats, it's bound to spill over into the settlement, too."

Reilly grimaced. "I think you're taking this whole marshal business too seriously. I'm not really John Henry Braddock."

"But you've got to act like him for a while," Bo said. "Otherwise, people won't believe what we want them to believe. From what I've heard about Braddock, he wouldn't allow a shooting war to break out so close to any town where he was the marshal."

Reilly sighed and shook his head. "All right, all right. We'll get to the bottom of the rustling. Or try anyway."

Bo nodded and said, "I think that would be best."

They had almost reached the rider who had been fleeing from the Rocking B hands. His shoulders slumped and his head hung low, just like his horse's. Both of them were clearly exhausted.

Even so, Reilly and the Texans were taken slightly by surprise when the buckskin-clad figure suddenly swayed in the saddle for a moment and then pitched loosely to the ground to lie there motionless.

"Good Lord!" Scratch exclaimed. "Maybe he was hit after all!"

Bo was already moving, swinging down from the saddle and hurrying forward. He knelt at the side of the senseless figure, grasped his shoulders, and rolled him onto his back. As Bo lifted the man's head, the battered old hat fell off.

Long, red, luxuriously thick hair spilled out. Bo found himself staring down into the unconscious, unmistakably female face of a young woman . . . . and an undeniably beautiful one at that.

CHAPTER 8

"Son of a gun!" Reilly exclaimed. "That's a girl!"

"And a mighty pretty one, too," Scratch said. "Is she hurt, Bo?"

"I don't see any blood on her clothes," Bo replied. "Don't think she stopped a slug, but I can't be sure yet . . ."

Reilly had dismounted by now. He hurried over, knelt on the redhead's other side, and said, "Let me see if her heart's beating," as he slipped a hand inside the buckskin shirt.

Bo started to tell him that it wasn't proper for him to be feeling around in that area on a woman he wasn't married to, but before he could say anything to Reilly, the redhead's eyes snapped open. She gasped, and one small but evidently hard fist shot up and smacked cleanly into Reilly's jaw. Reilly yelped in surprise and pain and went over backward.

Scratch guffawed. "That's showin' him, little missy!" he called.

The young woman jerked free from Bo, who

wasn't really trying to hold her. She rolled over, came up agilely on one knee, and emptied the holster on her hip in a smooth, swift draw. The nickel-plated .38 revolver in her hand swung back and forth as she covered Bo, Scratch, and Reilly at the same time.

"What happened?" she demanded. "Who are you men?"

"It appears that you fainted, ma'am," Bo told her. "As for us, that fella you punched is Marshal John Henry Braddock, and we're his deputies, Bo Creel and Scratch Morton."

"Marshal?" she said as she glared at Reilly. "What's a marshal doing pawing me like that?"

Reilly sat on the ground a few feet away. He glared back at her as he lifted a hand, grasped his jaw, and moved it back and forth to see if it still worked right. Then he said, "I was trying to make sure you weren't hurt. Excuse me for wanting to help you!"

"It felt to me like you were helping yourself," she snapped. "You can see that I'm all right. And I *don't* faint!" she added vehemently.

"Suit yourself, ma'am," Bo told her. "When you toppled off that horse, we were worried that you'd been hit by one of those slugs flying around you."

She turned her head to gaze back along the trail. "What happened to Bill Cavalier and the rest of those Rocking B hands?"

"They weren't happy about it, but they decided to leave it to the marshal to question you about some suspicious behavior."

The redhead snorted. "Suspicious behavior, my hind foot! That bunch is so trigger-happy they were

ready to shoot at anybody they ran into, even
somebody like me they should have recognized.
Idiots must've seen me a dozen times or more in
town!"

"I reckon they just didn't get a good look at you,"
Bo said.

"No, they started blazing away as soon as they
came in sight, without even waiting to find out who I
was. And then they were too blinded by their own
powder smoke to recognize me, I reckon."

"I take it you're saying that you're *not* a rustler?"

"Do I *look* like a rustler to you?" the redhead demanded, unknowingly echoing what Reilly had said
the night before about looking like a lawman.

"Well, ma'am," Bo said mildly, "I reckon rustlers
can come in all sizes and, uh, shapes." He continued
trying to be a gentleman and averted his eyes from the
enticingly rounded breasts that poked out the front of
the buckskin shirt.

"I'm not a rustler," she said. She got to her feet, and
while she didn't pouch the iron she held, she lowered
it to her side so that it wasn't pointing at the Texans
and Reilly anymore. "As a matter of fact, I was taking
a look around to see if I could find anything that
would put me on the trail of whoever's been stealing
Rocking B stock. Chet Bascomb blames Steven North,
of course, but I don't believe North is behind the
widelooping."

"North being the other big rancher around here,"
Bo guessed.

The young woman nodded. "That's right."

"And North and Bascomb don't get along."

She shook her head. "Never have. Probably never will."

She paused. "You ask questions like a lawman, all right." She looked at Reilly, who had gotten to his feet and taken off his hat. He slapped it against his clothes to get some of the dust off of them. "You didn't say anything in your letters about bringing any deputies with you, Marshal."

"Well, a, uh, lawman's got to have good help," Reilly said. "Somebody he can trust to watch his back whenever there's trouble." He frowned. "How do you know about the letters?"

"I keep up pretty good with what goes on in the settlement," she said with a defiant thrust of her chin. "My grandfather founded it nearly forty years ago. My name's Rawhide Abbott."

"Rawhide? What sort of name is that for a girl?"

"It's mine, all right?" she snapped. The gun in her hand started to come up. "You got a problem with it?"

Reilly held up both hands, palms out in surrender. "No, no, no problems at all, Miss Abbott."

She gave an unladylike snort. "I didn't think so." Finally, she holstered the gun, picked up her hat, and tucked her hair under it, snugging the hat in place with the chin strap. "Let me get my horse, and I'll ride on into town with you fellas."

"I can get him for you—" Reilly began.

"I've got him! No offense, Marshal, but I don't need no fancy-pants tin star to fetch a horse for me."

Reilly shrugged and stood back while she got her own horse. Then he and Bo mounted up as well, and along with Scratch, they started down the trail toward Whiskey Flats.

"You said your grandfather founded the town, Miss Abbott," Bo said. "Can you tell us about it?"

"Well, first of all, you can forget that stuffy Miss Abbott business," she said. "I'm Rawhide, and don't you forget it."

Reilly said, "I don't think you'd let us do that."

She glared at him for a second, but otherwise didn't dignify his comment with a response. To Bo and Scratch, she said, "Grandpap was a trader. He brought wagon trains of supplies up and down the Santa Fe Trail, back in the days when all this part of the country still belonged to Mexico. You two look old enough to remember that time."

Scratch grinned. "We sure are, ma'am. We're Texans, born and bred, and fought in the war to free our land from General Santy Anny."

Rawhide went on. "One time when Grandpap was coming through these parts, he found himself a pretty spot with good water and decided that he wanted to stay, instead of traipsin' up and down that long, hard trail all the time. He started a trading post, and a little settlement grew up around it. After the Mexican War in '48, when this became American territory, the settlement grew even faster."

She told the story as if she had heard it many times. Bo supposed that she had, since it was part of her family history.

"How'd the place get a name like Whiskey Flats?" Reilly asked.

"Well, it had always been called Abbottville, after

my grandpap and my pa, who took over the trading post and turned it into a general store and built a lot of the other businesses in town. But when the community leaders got together and petitioned the government for a post office by that name, they were turned down. Seems that there's already a town called Abbottville in New Mexico Territory, somewhere down along the border. Nobody up here knew that. Some of the rowdy element in town had always called it Whiskey Flats, because it has the only saloons in these parts. Somebody—and nobody was ever willing to take the blame—sent the name to the folks in Washington as a joke, and they accepted it. The post office was officially named Whiskey Flats, and so was the town. My pa raised hell with the government, but it didn't do any good."

"It never does," Scratch commented dryly.

"So we were stuck with the name," Rawhide went on. "It always bothered Pa, right up until the day he passed away a couple of years ago."

"What about your grandfather?" Bo asked.

The young woman waved a hand. "Oh, it never bothered Grandpap. He'd always been sort of a hellraiser, even after he settled down and started the settlement. He thought it was funny. To tell you the truth, Mr. Creel, it wouldn't surprise me a bit if *he* was the one who sent the Whiskey Flats name to Washington. Having a town named after him would've been a mite too stuffy for him anyway."

"That explains the town's name," Reilly said. "How'd you come to be called Rawhide?"

Her temper flared again. "What the hell business is it of yours?"

"None at all, I guess. I'm just curious. You're the first girl I've ever met who wore buckskins and packed a shooting iron, too."

"Then maybe you been hangin' around with the wrong sort of girls," she shot back at him. She sneered as she looked up him and down. "I'll bet your taste in women runs more toward painted-up saloon floozies in spangled dresses."

That was pretty perceptive of her, Bo thought. She had Reilly's personality pegged, even though she seemed to have accepted his pose as Marshal John Henry Braddock.

"You're just as touchy as all get-out, aren't you?" Reilly said. "A fella can't even talk to you without getting his head bitten off."

"I don't ever bite off more than I can chew. Best you remember that, Marshal."

That seemed to settle the question, but when they had ridden on for a while longer, she said, "My grandpap tagged the Rawhide handle on me. He did most of the raising where I was concerned. My ma died when I was a baby, and my pa was always too busy with the store and all his other responsibilities around town to spend much time with me. I reckon Grandpap was more suited for grandsons than granddaughters, because he taught me how to ride and hunt and fish and whittle and cuss. Pa didn't know what to do with a little hellion like I turned out to be, so after a while he just gave up, I reckon. He knew I wasn't ever gonna be no lady."

Scratch said, "It looked like you can handle that Colt pretty good. Your grandpa must've been a fair hand with a gun." He frowned. "Wait a minute. Abbott . . . your grandpa wasn't Hawk Abbott, was he?"

Rawhide nodded. "That's right. Did you know him?"

Scratch shook his head and said, "No, but we heard tell of him, didn't we, Bo?"

"Hawk Abbott was one of the old-time mountain men," Bo said with a nod. "Trapped all over the Rockies with that fella called Preacher and his friends. I remember hearing rumors that he retired from trapping and went to hauling freight. I reckon they were true."

"Hawk Abbott was one tough hombre," Scratch said. He grinned. "I can see now where you get your, uh, salty nature, ma'am. No offense."

Rawhide returned the grin. "None taken. Bein' compared to Grandpap is a compliment as far as I'm concerned."

"Has he passed on, too?" Bo asked.

"Yeah, a couple of years before my pa died. A fever got him." Rawhide squared her shoulders and lifted her chin. "I'm the last of the Abbotts, at least in these parts."

"What about the general store and the other businesses your father was involved in?"

"The store's still operating. Pa left half of it to me and half to the fella who'd been helpin' him to run it for years. He keeps it going and gives me my share of the profits. Same with the newspaper Pa started. The editor he hired runs it and owns half of it now. Pa had already sold all his interests in other businesses before he passed away. He hung on to the store and paper so

I'd be taken care of when he was gone." Rawhide smiled sadly and shook her head. "Pa didn't know what to make of me, but he loved me, I reckon."

"Sounds like it, all right," Bo agreed.

For the past several minutes, they had been riding up a long, gradual slope. Now, as they reached the top, the ground on the far side fell away at a steeper slant, with the trail angling back and forth down it to a broad, green valley. A stream twisted through the valley. About a mile from where Bo, Scratch, Jake Reilly, and Rawhide Abbott reined in, the buildings of Whiskey Flats were visible.

The settlement had one long main street that crossed the creek on a wooden bridge that divided the town neatly in half. The northern part, closest to where the riders sat their saddles, had a number of businesses along the main street, with nice-looking houses lining a couple of cross streets. Bo saw a church steeple and another building that he pegged as a schoolhouse in that section of town.

The other part, south of the bridge, also had a number of false-fronted businesses along the main street, but instead of homes, they were surrounded by adobe hovels, tarpaper shacks, and buildings of raw, hastily slapped-together lumber that probably served as cribs. It wasn't hard to tell, even from a distance, that the part of Whiskey Flats lying south of the bridge was the less-reputable section.

"That'd be the red-light district, on the other side o' the creek?" Scratch asked anyway.

"That's right," Rawhide confirmed. "There's not much over there except saloons, gambling dens, and, uh, houses of ill repute." Surprisingly, given her seemingly brash nature, she blushed a little at those words.

"So that's the part of town I'm supposed to clean up," Reilly mused, playing the part of John Henry Braddock.

"Hardly a day goes by without a gunfight, a knifing, or some back-alley murder," Rawhide said. "The town fathers don't want all the places shut down, just the worst ones. They just want the killing to stop."

"Of course they don't want all the saloons and cribs shut down," Reilly said with a grin. "Chances are, most of the respectable citizens in town sneak over there one or two nights a week for a little discreet hell-raising of their own."

Rawhide shook her head. "You might be right about that. I wouldn't know."

They had continued riding and were drawing closer to the settlement now. It was a nice-looking place, Bo thought. He vaguely remembered hearing about a town called Abbottville when he and Scratch had passed through this area years earlier. He hadn't made the connection between that town and the one called Whiskey Flats until Rawhide had cleared it up with her little history lesson. The Texans' last visit had been before the official name change.

The trail they had been following turned into the northern end of Main Street. In the middle of the day like this, quite a few people were on the board-walks, the hitch rails were full, and wagons and buckboards were parked in front of many of the businesses. Whiskey Flats was a bustling place. Bo saw some of the townspeople looking at them curiously. Rawhide would be known to them, but he, Scratch, and Reilly were strangers, and strangers always provoked a lot of interest in frontier towns.

As they drew closer to a large livery stable and wagon yard, a man stepped out from the barn and looked like he was about to hail them. Bo saw that he was tall, well built, and had a close-cropped brown beard. He also wore a brown tweed suit, which meant he probably didn't work in the livery stable. He might own it, though.

Just as the man lifted a hand to signal them to stop, gunshots roared not far away. Blast after blast ripped out, shattering the peaceful street scene. It sounded like a small-scale war had broken out south of the bridge, because that was where the shots were coming from.

"Sounds like a job for you right away, Marshal!" Bo called as he heeled his horse into a run.

Scratch, who was always ready for a ruckus, let out a whoop and followed right behind Bo. "Come on, Marshal!" he shouted over his shoulder to Reilly. "Let's bring some law and order to Whiskey Flats!"

Reilly hesitated before charging after them, but only for a second, Bo noted. As the fusillade of shots continued to slam out, he thought wryly that the entrance of "Marshal John Henry Braddock" into Whiskey Flats was certainly going to be a dramatic one.

CHAPTER 9

The horses thundered over the wooden bridge separating the two sections of the settlement, steel-shod hooves ringing against the planks. Bo glanced over his shoulder and saw, not entirely to his surprise, that Rawhide Abbott was riding with them, whipping her reins back and forth as she lashed her horse in an attempt to keep up.

As they entered the southern part of town, clouds of powder smoke rolled from two buildings, one on each side of the street. It appeared that half a dozen or more gunmen were holed up in the buildings, blazing away at each other. The street had cleared, pedestrians on the boardwalks scurrying to get out of the line of fire, but there might be innocent bystanders in those buildings, and there was no telling where stray bullets might ricochet or who they might hurt. Bo, Scratch, and Reilly had to put a stop to this battle royal as quickly as they could.

It looked like Rawhide intended to help, because she swung down from her saddle, too, as the men reined in and dismounted to crouch behind a parked wagon loaded with hay bales. The hay would stop any wild slugs that came in this direction.

"I reckon those must be rival saloons," Bo said to Rawhide over the continuing gunfire.

The young woman nodded. "Yeah. That's Tilden's Top-Notch on the left, the Lariat Saloon on the right. The hardcases who hang around each place don't like the ones across the street. I don't know what set off this free-for-all, but it was bound to happen sooner or later." She looked at Reilly. "What are you going to do, Marshal?"

Reilly was wide-eyed and didn't look much like the cool-headed lawman he was supposed to be. Bo said quickly, "We'll do what the marshal always has us do in a situation like this. We'll split up and come at them from behind. Right, Marshal?"

Reilly managed to nod. "Uh, yeah, that's right, Deputy." He was obviously trying to look and sound more decisive as he went on, "You take the saloon on the left, Bo. Scratch, circle around behind the one on the right."

"Which deputy are you going with, Marshal?" Rawhide asked.

"Well, uh . . ." Reilly nodded toward Bo. "I'll go with Deputy Creel, I reckon."

"Then I'll go with Deputy Morton," Rawhide declared.

"Now hold on, ma'am," Scratch said. "No offense, but I ain't in the habit o' goin' into a shootin' scrape with a female backin' my play."

"And I'm not your ordinary female," Rawhide snapped as she drew her gun. "Seems like you boys should've tumbled to that fact by now."

Bo could tell that she wasn't going to be talked out of it, and even though he didn't like the situation much more than Scratch did, they didn't have any time to waste arguing about it.

"Go ahead, ma'am," Bo told her. "Just be careful."

Rawhide gave a snort that clearly indicated how she felt about that warning to be cautious.

The hay wagon was parked on the left side of the street, so Bo and Reilly didn't have as far to go. Bo said, "We need to hit 'em as close to the same time as possible, so we'll give you a couple of minutes to get in position, Scratch."

The silver-haired Texan nodded curtly as he filled his hands with the ivory-handled Remingtons. "Good luck, partner."

Bo returned the nod and said, "To you, too, amigo."

Scratch would need the luck. No matter how tough and competent Rawhide was—or *thought* she was— Scratch's very nature would force him to try to look out for her while at the same time dealing with the threats to his own hide. Might as well try to get the sun to come up in the west as to change that.

The two of them took off at a run toward an alley mouth across the street, while Bo and Reilly waited a minute behind the hay wagon. Reilly asked nervously, "Are you sure we're doing the right thing?"

"As sure as an hombre can be when he's about to charge right into the big middle of a gun battle," Bo replied with a tight smile.

"I, uh, never did anything like this before."

"Just follow my lead," Bo told him. "Those fellas inside the Top-Notch will likely be clustered up at the front of the building. We'll go in the back and try to get the drop on them before they know what's going in. Cover them as best you can, and maybe they'll decide to give up the fight and drop their guns."

Reilly swallowed hard. "And if they don't? If they start shooting at *us* instead?"

"You're the law," Bo reminded him. "You'll be justified in shooting back at them, Jake . . . or should I say, Marshal Braddock." The Texan hefted his Colt. "Scratch and the girl ought to be ready by now. Let's go."

The two of them ducked into an alley on this side of the street. Reilly looked a little like he was about to be sick, Bo thought.

But it was too late for either of them to back out now. They had a job to do.

Bo just hoped that luck would smile on Scratch and Rawhide across the street.

In a way it was lucky that he had the gal along, Scratch reflected as he and Rawhide hustled along the narrow, trash-littered lane behind the buildings. She knew the town, knew which of the rear doors led into the Lariat Saloon.

Unfortunately, that door turned out to be locked. Scratch knew that he could shoot it open or kick it down, but if he caused a commotion like that, it would warn the men inside the saloon that a new threat was on its way in from the rear.

He looked around and spotted a window not far

away. It was closed, though, and the sill was too high to reach easily.

Rawhide saw where he was looking and seemed to read his mind. As she holstered her gun, she said, "Give me a boost and I'll see if it's open."

"A, uh, boost," Scratch repeated.

"That's right, Deputy." Rawhide's tone was acerbic as she went on. "I reckon you're a mite too big for *me* to boost *you* up there."

"Yeah, yeah." Scratch pouched his irons, moved over to the window, and bent over, lacing his hands together to form a stirrup. "Hurry up. We don't want Bo and the marshal gettin' too far ahead of us."

Rawhide put her hands on Scratch's shoulders and placed a booted foot in his hands. That brought her bosom level with his face and made his ears start to warm up. With a grunt of effort, he lifted her as she pushed down on his shoulders. That embarrassed him even more, because now his face was practically shoved up against her lady parts. Luckily they had some nice thick buckskins covering them. Scratch loved women, but his tastes ran more toward widow ladies and the occasional unsatisfied wife—although he never pursued a gal he absolutely knew to be hitched. But he felt downright uncomfortable being this intimate with a girl young enough to be his granddaughter.

Thankfully, the experience didn't last long. Rawhide grabbed the sill, shoved the pane up, and clambered through the window, her weight departing from Scratch's grip. She turned around and stuck her hand back out, whispering urgently, "Come on!"

Scratch shook his head. "I'm a mite too old for acrobatics like that. Why don't you just unlock the door?"

"Oh," she said. "Yeah, I guess I could do that. Hang on."

The shooting hadn't let up any. Those old boys were wasting enough powder and shot to have stood off an attack by Comanch', Scratch thought as he hurried through the door that Rawhide swung open for him. He drew his guns again as he saw that they were in a back room used for storage. From the sound of the shots, one flimsy door was all that stood between them and the combatants.

Rawhide had her nickel-plated revolver in her hand again, too. Scratch looked at her and asked, "Ready?"

She nodded but didn't say anything. She didn't seem to be afraid, but her mouth was tight. She knew as well as he did that they might be just about to bull their way into a hornet's nest.

Scratch gestured toward the door. "You open it, and I'll go through first."

"Why you and not me?"

"Because I got two guns and you got a free hand," Scratch answered. It seemed like a simple, practical matter to him.

Rawhide understood and nodded. She reached for the doorknob.

A simple twist opened it. She flung the door back and Scratch rushed into the saloon's main room, brandishing the twin Remingtons. Rawhide was right behind him.

"Hold it!" Scratch bellowed, raising his voice to be heard over the shots. His keen eyes took in the scene in a heartbeat. A couple of poker tables had been overturned and moved up to the front windows to serve as cover behind which crouched six gunmen, three on each side of the batwinged entrance. Those batwings were riddled with bullet holes, but they still swung back and forth a little under the impact of fresh slugs. The reek of spilled liquor filled the air, along with the sharp tang of powder smoke, because most of the bottles that had been arrayed along the back bar in glittering ranks had been busted all to hell by flying lead. A couple of heavily made-up soiled doves peeked nervously over the bar from where they crouched behind the relative safety of the thick hardwood, and with them was a little bald man with bulging eyes and a prominent Adam's apple. At the unexpected entrance of Scratch and Rawhide, the man's fish-eyes rolled up in their sockets and he disappeared from sight.

The hardcases at the windows whirled around to meet this new threat. They found themselves staring down the barrels of Scratch's Remington and Rawhide's nickel-plated Colt. That didn't stop one man from snarling and jerking up his own gun in an attempt to get off a shot.

Scratch's left-hand Remington roared and bucked. He was almost as good a shot with his left hand as he was with his right, and at this range he didn't have any trouble hitting what he shot at. The gunman was thrown back against the overturned table behind him as Scratch's bullet shattered his upper right arm. The gun he had tried to use went flying from nerveless fingers.

Another man clearly thought about trying to get a shot off, too, but Rawhide told him coldly, "Just try it, mister."

The man grated a curse, but he lowered his gun.

"Drop 'em!" Scratch ordered. "Now!"

One by one, the guns hit the floor. The eerie silence that followed the end of every battle filled the room.

It wasn't *too* quiet, though, because shots still blasted from across the street, and one of the few surviving bottles behind the bar shattered. Scratch heard the whine of a ricochet through the room and knew that he and Rawhide were still in danger, even though they had disarmed the hardcases in the Lariat.

If Bo and Jake Reilly didn't put a stop to all the shooting from the Top-Notch, and mighty damned soon, Scratch thought, he and Rawhide still stood a good chance of getting ventilated.

Bo and Reilly didn't encounter anyone as they hurried along the alley and then turned into the lane behind the saloon. Everyone in this part of town was lying low while the bullets flew, and wisely so. Most of the buildings had a similar ramshackle look from behind, but Bo was able to pick out the one that housed Tilden's Top-Notch Saloon. The barrage of gunshots coming from inside it was a dead giveaway, so to speak.

Bo tried the back door and found it unlocked. He looked over at Reilly and asked, "You ready?"

Reilly swallowed nervously and nodded. "Ready as I'm gonna be, I guess," he said. "I can tell you now, though, I'm not cut out for this law-and-order business."

"You'll be fine," Bo assured him. "And think how

much more willing the townspeople will be to accept you as Marshal John Henry Braddock once you've put a stop to this ruckus."

Reilly brightened a little. "Yeah, you're right," he said. "Nobody will doubt that I'm who I say I am after this."

Bo hoped it worked out that way. He nodded and grasped the doorknob again, then smiled and nodded at Reilly. "Let's go."

Bo twisted the knob and eased the door open. Since it wasn't locked, he and Reilly didn't have to charge in. They could take their time and see what the situation was. Motioning for Reilly to take it as quietly as possible, Bo catfooted into a narrow little passageway with doors opening off both sides. The door to the left was ajar and revealed a small office, while the other door was closed. Bo and Reilly slipped past them to a door at the far end of the corridor. The shots were louder now, so Bo knew the saloon's main room was right on the other side of that door.

Still moving stealthily, he opened that one as well and stepped out into the barroom. The thunder of gunfire was almost deafening as seven men crouched at the front windows poured lead at the saloon across the street. No one was in sight behind the bar.

Bo and Reilly moved forward, their guns trained on the murderous hardcases. Suddenly, movement flickered to their right. A burly man in a tight tweed suit popped up behind the bar, a shotgun in his hands.

"Look out behind you, boys!" he shouted as he swung the Greener toward Bo and Reilly.

Reilly was between Bo and the bar, and in that shaved second of time, the Texan realized there was no way he could fire around Reilly in time to stop the man from pulling the triggers and unloading both barrels. At this range, a double load of buckshot would blow Reilly in half and probably kill Bo, too.

That dire thought barely had time to flash through Bo's mind before Reilly's gun arm came up in a blur and flame gouted from the muzzle of his Colt. John Henry Braddock's Colt, to be precise, but in this perilous moment, Reilly wielded it with speed and precision worthy of the famous fighting marshal.

The man behind the bar twisted around as the slug plowed into him. The barrels of the shotgun tilted up as they discharged with a volcanic blast, blowing a hole in the ceiling. The man in the tweed suit disappeared as he collapsed behind the bar.

The shouted warning had alerted the gunmen by the windows, though, and as they jerked around Bo yelled, "Freeze! Drop those guns!"

A couple of the men ignored the command. One of them triggered his gun, sending a slug whipping past Bo's head. Bo fired twice. Both bullets punched into the man's belly and doubled him over.

At the same time, another man fired and knocked splinters off the back of a chair just inches away from Reilly. The young man pulled the trigger again. This time the bullet plowed into the floor right at the gunman's feet. That was enough to upset the man's balance as he crouched and sent him toppling forward. Bo took a fast step forward and brought the barrel of his gun down across the man's head, laying him out senseless on the floor. Bo moved back just as swiftly and covered the remaining hardcases. The fight seemed to have gone out of them.

"In the name of the law, drop those guns!" Reilly called. Bo thought that was a nice touch. Maybe Reilly was getting more enthusiastic about posing as John Henry Braddock. At any rate, it worked, because guns began to hit the floor as the other men let go of them and put up their hands.

"What about the man behind the bar, Marshal?" Bo asked as silence descended on the room. "Want me to check on him?"

"I'll do it," Reilly said. He leaned over to look behind the bar and paled. "I can't tell if he's alive or not. There's an awful lot of blood back there."

"Important thing right now is that he's not going to get up and take a hand in this game again."

Reilly shook his head. "It'll be a medical miracle if he does."

Bo herded the captured hardcases away from their guns and out through the bullet-shattered batwings, leaving behind the man Bo had shot. It had taken only a quick check for the Texan to confirm that he was dead.

Across the street, Scratch and Rawhide Abbott marched their prisoners out of the Lariat Saloon. Scratch grinned at his trail partner and said, "Looks like we got the job done."

Bo said, "That's right." He turned to Reilly and added, "Your plan worked perfectly, Marshal."

If Rawhide remembered that it had actually been Bo who suggested the strategy, she didn't say anything. Bo's comment was overheard by people who were starting to poke their heads out of nearby buildings now that the shooting had stopped, just as he'd intended. He couldn't think of a better way to introduce "Marshal John Henry Braddock" to the citizens of Whiskey Flats. Already, folks were pointing at Reilly and talking to each other in hushed voices. The new marshal was making quite an impression.

Bo turned to the young woman and went on. "Since you seem to know everything there is to know about this settlement, Rawhide, can you tell us if there's a jail?"

"There sure is," she said, pointing toward the bridge. "Just north of the creek, so it's handy to where most of the trouble is. The town council had it built a couple of years ago, got a marshal's office in it and everything. But nobody held the job long enough to even get the place dirty."

"Why's that?" Reilly wanted to know.

Rawhide looked at him and said, "Either they saw how impossible it was and gave up . . . or they got themselves dead."

Judging from the expression that passed across Reilly's face, he wished that he hadn't asked the question.

"Well, Marshal," Bo said, "what do you want us to do with these prisoners?"

Reilly gave a little shake of his head, as if trying to forget what Rawhide had just told him. He summoned up a weak smile and said, "What else, Deputy? Take 'em to jail and lock 'em up!" His voice strengthened as he looked around and added for the townspeople's benefit, "It's time folks know that law has come to Whiskey Flats!"

CHAPTER 10

The man whose arm had been busted by Scratch's bullet complained mightily about needing a doctor as the prisoners marched at gunpoint across the bridge.

"We'll see that you get medical attention," Bo promised.

"So quit your bitchin'," Scratch added. "Anyway, I wouldn't'a shot you if you hadn't been tryin' to shoot me first."

There was no arguing with that logic, so the wounded man fell into a sullen silence, broken only by the occasional moan. Bo turned to Rawhide and asked, "I reckon you *do* have a sawbones in this town?"

"Sure." She called to a sag-jawed bystander, "Tooney, run and fetch Doc Summers!"

While the townie ran off up the street, another man hurried toward the group. Bo recognized him as the fella who had stepped out of the livery stable as they were coming into the settlement. He thrust out a hand toward Reilly and said, "Marshal Braddock?"

"Uh, yeah, that's right," Reilly said.

"I'm Mayor Jonas McHale!" The mayor grabbed hold of Reilly's hand and began to pump it enthusiastically. "It's an honor to meet you, Marshal! An absolute honor!"

"Well, the, uh, pleasure is all mine, Mayor," Reilly said.

"We weren't expecting your arrival in Whiskey Flats to be accompanied by such excitement," McHale went on. "What happened down there on the other side of the bridge?"

Rawhide answered, "The feud between the hardcases who hang out at the Lariat and the ones at the Top-Notch finally boiled over into a shootin' war, Jonas. But the marshal and his deputies put a stop to that quick enough."

"Deputies?" McHale frowned at he looked at the Texans. "Marshal, I don't recall you saying anything about bringing deputies with you."

"I just assumed I'd be able to hire whoever I needed to help me do the job," Reilly said. His confidence appeared to be growing again. Any time the situation called for fast, glib talk, he was right at home.

Of course, he had done surprisingly well with the gun-handling inside the Top-Notch, too, Bo reflected. He had known when he saw Reilly practicing with Braddock's revolver that the young man had the makings of a decent Coltman. Facing danger had brought out that ability even more. Now, if only the masquerade as John Henry Braddock would bring out some of Reilly's other good qualities as well . . .

"Of course, of course," McHale said quickly. "It's just that the town council didn't make any provision for extra wages . . ." He moved his hands rapidly from side to side. "But don't worry about that, I'm sure we can come up with something that'll be agreeable. We want you to have whatever you need, Marshal."

Reilly smiled. "Well, right now, I'd say that a good place to stay would be in order."

"Naturally, we've got the best room in the hotel reserved for you, for as long as you want it," McHale said. "Of course, you might decide to settle down here and want something more permanent . . ."

"The hotel room will be fine for now," Reilly said.

"And there are cots in the marshal's office where your deputies can stay," the mayor added.

Scratch glanced at Bo, who knew what his old friend was thinking. Reilly got the comfortable hotel room, while all they got were cots in what was probably a drafty old marshal's office. Bo just smiled, and Scratch shook his head, trying not to look too disgusted.

The hardcase with the busted arm said, "Are you gonna stand around here jabberin' all day, or are you gonna get me to the doctor before I plumb bleed to death?"

"Doc Summers will be here in just a minute," Rawhide told him. "Take it easy."

"Actually, Miss Abbott," Reilly said, sounding more authoritative now as he warmed to his role, "why don't you and Deputy Morton take the wounded man to the doctor's office? Deputy Creel and I can jail these other fellows. Oh, and by the way, the undertaker will be needed for at least one man there in the Top-Notch, maybe two. Someone should check on the man behind the bar."

"A big fella in a flashy suit?" Rawhide asked.

"That's right. I was forced to shoot him when he jumped up from behind the bar and threatened us with a shotgun."

"That's Big Mickey Tilden, the owner of the Top-Notch. Did you kill him?"

Reilly shook his head. "I don't know. He didn't give me a lot of time to place my shot."

"Someone had better check on him, too," Bo suggested.

"Here comes Ed Chamberlain," McHale said, adding by way of explanation for the newcomers, "Ed's our local coffin-maker and undertaker."

Chamberlain was a short, cherubic hombre with a pink scalp and a high-pitched voice, not at all like the cadaverous undertakers usually found in frontier towns. He grinned pleasantly as he asked, "Got some new business for me, Jonas?"

"There's at least one dead man in the Top-Notch," McHale told him. "Mickey Tilden's shot, too, and may be dead."

Chamberlain rubbed his hands together gleefully. "I'll go see about that right now."

"Make sure he's actually deceased before you haul him off to your place," McHale called after him as the undertaker hurried toward the bridge.

Chamberlain laughed as he asked over his shoulder, "Did you ever know me to plant a live one?"

"Ed is a member of our town council," McHale said to Reilly. "I'll introduce you to him formally later, Marshal, along with all the other members of the council. I'm sure they'll all be glad to meet you."

"And I'll be glad to meet them," Reilly said heartily. "Meanwhile, let's get these prisoners behind bars where they belong. We'll talk later, Mayor."

Scratch and Rawhide took the wounded man up the street to the doctor's office, while Bo and Reilly marched the rest of the prisoners over to the squat, stone-and-log building that served as the marshal's office and jail for Whiskey Flats. Despite the fact that no one had been able to occupy it for very long so far, the building had a solid look about it. The walls were thick, and the windows in the rear part of the building were all small and closed off with iron bars, so Bo knew the cell block had to be located back there.

When they went inside, he saw that he was right. The office was rather sparsely furnished, with a rolltop desk and chair, a gun rack on the wall with a couple of Winchesters and a shotgun in it, a black potbellied stove in the corner, and an old armchair. A couple of cots were folded and leaned in a corner. Directly across from the entrance door was the heavy door to the cell block, which stood open at the moment because the four cells—two on each side of a short corridor—were empty.

Not for long, though, because Bo and Reilly herded the prisoners into them, splitting them up so that the hardcases from the Top-Notch were on one side, the men from the Lariat on the other.

"I saw the keys on a ring hanging from a nail beside the desk," Bo told Reilly as he closed the cell doors with a clang.

One of the prisoners complained, "If you're gonna lock us up in here, you gotta feed us. It's the law."

"Shut up," Reilly said. "It's a long time until supper, and if you cause any trouble, we'll just see if you get anything to eat."

Another prisoner started to protest. "You damned high-handed badge toter! You can't—"

"Shut up, I said!" Reilly roared at him.

The prisoners subsided, still muttering among themselves.

Reilly grinned as he and Bo went back out into the office and Bo swung the cell block door shut. It closed with a solid thump. Bo took down the ring, found the right key, and locked it as well.

"That was fun," Reilly said, keeping his voice pitched low enough so that only Bo could hear. "Maybe I'm starting to understand why some fellas want to be lawmen."

"It's a good job to have if you like bossing folks around," Bo agreed. "But mainly, you should want to help folks, too."

"Yeah, sure." Reilly looked keenly at the Texan. "You seem to know a lot about this marshal business, Bo. You sure you and Scratch haven't worn badges before?"

"As a matter of fact, we have, on a few rare occasions," Bo admitted. "Most of the time, though, our encounters with the law have been from the other side of the bars, like those hombres back there in the cell block now. You see, whenever trouble breaks out, most star packers look for the nearest stranger to blame it on. And since Scratch and I are strangers just about everywhere we go . . ."

"Yeah, I know the feeling," Reilly said. "I've been blamed for a few things I didn't do, too." He chuckled. "But mostly for things that I did do."

Bo checked the drawers of the desk and found them empty except for a stack of reward dodgers that one of the previous occupants had left there. He flipped through them curiously, checking to see if he and Scratch were on any of them. They weren't actually wanted anywhere at the moment—that he knew of—but at times in the past their pictures had turned up on reward posters as the result of misunderstandings or overzealous lawmen. He didn't find any in this batch, though.

He didn't find any with Reilly's picture on them either, although to tell the truth, he wouldn't have been surprised if he had.

"You know," Bo said as he replaced the reward dodgers in the desk, "that hombre back there was right. We'll have to feed them. That means making arrangements with a café or hash house and getting the town council to pay for it. Now that I think about it, there are probably a lot of little details to running a law office that aren't apparent right off."

"You mean it's not all fun and games like nearly getting our asses shot off?" Reilly asked with a smile.

Bo chuckled and said, "No, there's likely some actual work involved, too."

Reilly tugged his hat brim down. "Well, since you're the deputy, I expect you'll be handling most of that. I think I should go out and introduce myself to the townspeople. You know, let them see that there's a new marshal in these parts."

"That's not a bad idea. You might want to let one of us go with you, though. I'm sure Scratch will be back soon."

Reilly looked like he wanted to argue, but before he could do so, the office door opened and Scratch came in, no longer accompanied by Rawhide Abbott.

"That fella you shot is still alive, Rei—" Scratch checked himself as he realized that the prisoners back in the cell block might overhear if he referred to Reilly by name. "Right enough," he went on quickly in an attempt to cover the near-slip. "The doc came down to the Top-Notch to check on him and said he might pull through; then that pink-cheeked little undertaker hauled him down to the doc's office in his meat wagon. Said it was a nice change havin' a live one in there, but I didn't really believe him. I reckon he was disappointed he only gets to plant one stiff, not two."

"The fella I shot didn't make it then," Bo said.

"Not hardly. Not with two slugs in the gut."

Bo shook his head, a solemn expression on his face. He didn't particularly cotton to killing, but sometimes there just wasn't time to do anything else.

Scratch thumbed his hat back and went on. "Anyway, I left that feisty redheaded gal down at the sawbones' place keepin' an eye on the fella whose wing I busted. Doc Summers said he'd patch it up and set it. He gave the fella a little morphine to tide him over whilst he tended to Tilden, so I don't think he's goin' anywhere for a while. He looked about as groggy as a Chinaman in an opium den when I left. I'll go back and get him later."

Bo nodded. "That sounds fine. We probably won't be able to charge those fellas with anything except disturbing the peace anyway. Somebody will have to set a fine for them. We'll talk to the mayor about that."

"See?" Reilly said with a smirk. "I told you you were good at all these little details, Bo. Now, let's go take that walk around town, why don't we?"

Bo asked Scratch, "You mind staying here with the prisoners for a while?"

Scratch shook his head. "Nope. 'Specially not if I can put my feet up for a spell."

"Go to it, old-timer," Bo told him with a smile.

"Old-timer!" Scratch snorted. "I ain't but a couple months older'n you, Bo . . . *dis*provin' that old sayin' about age before beauty."

There was nothing Bo could say to that, so he

just chuckled, shook his head, and left the office with Reilly.

The boardwalks were crowded with pedestrians now, and the whole settlement was buzzing about the brief but violent gun battle between the two groups of hardcases and the way the new marshal and his deputies had galloped into town and put a stop to it with some fast gunplay. As Reilly made his appearance and began strolling along with Bo at his side, well-wishers crowded around him, eager to shake his hand and introduce themselves. Reilly grinned widely, pumped every hand that was thrust at him, and tipped his hat to all the ladies, who seemed quite taken by his dashing good looks.

Bo stayed in the background, letting Reilly bask in the glory. This was the part that Reilly was good at, glad-handing and showing off for the towns-people. Bo was happy to let him do it, since he wasn't comfortable with such things himself.

Mayor McHale must have been alert for any commotion, because he emerged from the livery stable again and came over to Bo and Reilly. Laughing, he raised his voice to be heard over the commotion and said, "Let our new marshal breathe, folks! There'll be plenty of time for all of you to get to know him, because John Henry Braddock is going to be around Whiskey Flats for a long time! Isn't that right, Marshal?"

"We'll be here until the job's done, that's for sure," Reilly declared.

McHale took hold of his arm. "I was hoping I'd

get the chance to show you around. Come with me, Marshal."

Bo trailed a couple of steps behind as McHale guided Reilly up the street, pointing out all the businesses. The mayor himself owned the livery stable and wagon yard, as well as a freight line that ran between Whiskey Flats and Santa Fe.

The settlement had just about everything such a frontier cattle town needed: two general stores (one of them, Abbott & Carson, would be the one that had grown from the trading post started by old Hawk Abbott, Rawhide's grandfather, Bo noted), a butcher shop, a blacksmith shop, a saddlemaker, a gunsmith, a barber (HOT BATHS 50¢, ALSO TEETH PULLED, a sign next to the striped pole announced), a hotel, a café, the local newspaper, *The Whiskey Flats Clarion* (which Rawhide's father had started, Bo recalled), an apothecary, the undertaking parlor run by Ed Chamberlain, the house where Dr. Edwin Summers's medical practice was located, even a millinery shop that catered to the ladies in town. There were a couple of churches, a school that was open part of the year whenever the town could get a teacher, and a meeting hall where dances, political rallies, and town meetings were held.

And that was just *north* of the bridge.

Mayor McHale didn't say anything about the part of the settlement south of the bridge, and when Reilly pointed that out, the mayor paused and frowned.

"To tell you the truth," McHale said, "it would

be all right with most of us in this part of town if everything south of the bridge disappeared."

Bo knew good and well that wasn't true. Respectable folks liked to make a lot of noise about getting rid of the undesirable elements in a settlement, but as Reilly had pointed out earlier, the saloons and gambling dens and brothels south of the bridge probably couldn't stay in business if it weren't for the customers who slipped across the creek in the dark of the moon to patronize them.

"I don't reckon we can run them out entirely," Reilly said. "But we can certainly do our best to clean them up and stop all the violence down there. Give me and my deputies a chance, Mayor, and we'll make a big difference here in Whiskey Flats."

McHale nodded and looked relieved. "I'm sure you will. Anything we can do to help you, you just ask."

"Well," Reilly said with a smile, "if you could point me toward that hotel room you mentioned, I wouldn't mind freshening up. We've been on the trail for quite a few days, and it's been a long, dusty ride."

"Of course," McHale said quickly.

Bo spoke up. "Our horses need taken care of, too." He wasn't surprised that Reilly had forgotten about their mounts, since he wasn't a true frontiersman . . . yet. There was still hope for him, though.

"I've already thought of that," McHale said with a nod. "Just a little while ago, I told my hostlers to see to them, to give them the best stalls in the barn, a good rubdown, and plenty of grain and water."

Bo nodded and said, "We're much obliged."

McHale had already turned away, though, and was saying to Reilly, "Come on, Marshal, and I'll introduce you to Warren Macready, who owns the hotel."

"That's exactly the man I want to meet." Reilly glanced over his shoulder at Bo as he started to walk away with McHale. "Keep an eye on the town while I see about that hotel room, won't you, Deputy Creel?"

"Sure, Marshal," Bo said dryly. "You don't have to worry about a thing."

CHAPTER 11

Once Reilly had gone off with Mayor McHale, Bo found that the citizens of Whiskey Flats weren't nearly as interested in him. In fact, they pretty much left him alone to amble around the town and continue looking it over. He paused when he found himself on the boardwalk outside the Morning Glory Café.

That was an interesting name for an eatery, he thought, and since Reilly was counting on him to take care of the mundane details of running the marshal's office, Bo decided to go on in and see if he could make arrangements for the feeding of current and future prisoners in the jail.

At this time of day the place was fairly busy, and Bo's stomach reminded him that he hadn't eaten since breakfast. The tables, covered with blue-checked cloths, were all occupied, but there were empty seats at the counter. As Bo took one of them, brushing back the long tails of his black coat as he did so, a woman emerged from the kitchen through a swinging door behind the counter. She carried a tray containing several plates heaped with steak and potatoes and other fixin's.

Bo was immediately struck by how handsome she was, with dark hair only lightly threaded with silver done up in a bun on the back of her head. Her eyes were a dark, piercing blue. She wore a white apron over a gingham dress, and the dress was snug enough to reveal that she was a fine figure of a woman. Bo looked at her left hand, checking for a wedding ring, and felt a little odd for doing so, since that was usually Scratch's reaction to a good-looking woman of a certain age. No ring. Bo was pleased by that, which was even odder, but then he reminded himself that she could still be married and just not wearing her ring at the moment because she was working.

She saw him sitting there on the counter stool, gave him a smile and a brief nod, and said, "I'll be right with you, mister, as soon as I deliver this food."

"No hurry," Bo told her. "I'll study the menu while you're gone." He nodded toward a board on the wall behind the counter which read simply: BREAKFAST 25¢, LUNCH 50¢, SUPPER 40¢.

That brought a laugh from her, and he liked the sound of it. She moved out from behind the counter with the tray and carried the lunches over to one of the tables where several hungry-looking men waited impatiently. Judging by the delicious aromas in the air and the eager reactions of the customers, the food at the Morning Glory Café had to be pretty darned good, Bo thought.

Carrying the empty tray, the woman came back behind the counter and asked, "What can I do for you?"

"Reckon I'll have lunch."

"Good choice," she said with a smile. "New in town, aren't you?"

"Yes, ma'am. Name's Bo Creel."

Finely arched eyebrows rose a little. "You're one of the new marshal's deputies. I heard some of the men talking about you and that big shoot-out south of the bridge."

Bo shrugged and nodded. "Guilty as charged, ma'am."

"Goodness, don't call me ma'am. Everybody just calls me Velma." She extended a hand across the counter. "Mrs. Velma Dearborn." She paused just a second as Bo gripped her hand, then added, "My late husband started this café, and now I run it."

"So it's your place then?"

"That's right." She laughed as she slipped her hand out of his. "You figured I was just the waitress, didn't you?"

"I didn't think about it one way or the other, ma'am . . . I mean Velma." That was because he'd been too busy taking note of the fact that she was a widow, he thought. He'd definitely have to introduce Scratch to her, since she was the sort of gal he really liked.

Or maybe he wouldn't . . . just yet.

"I've got an old Swede who cooks for me," Velma

Dearborn said, tilting her head toward the swinging door that led into the kitchen. "Otherwise, I do just about everything around here, including sweeping out the place. And right now, I'd better see about getting your food for you."

She went out to the kitchen, the door flapping shut behind her, and when she was gone, the whiskery old-timer sitting next to Bo dug an elbow in his ribs and said, "Mighty pretty filly, ain't she?"

"That she is," Bo agreed.

"I reckon half the fellas in this town'd eat here even if the food wasn't so good." The old man laughed. "Not that it does 'em any good. Velma's friendly to ever'body, but she don't get close to nobody. Not since her husband passed away a few years ago. Durn shame, if you ask me, a good-lookin' gal like that a-witherin' on the vine, but what can you do? It's up to her what she does."

Bo nodded in agreement with the garrulous townie. It sounded like any man who got interested in Velma Dearborn would have a challenge on his hands if he tried to court her.

Which meant it was good that he wasn't looking to do such a thing.

Velma came back a couple of minutes later with a plate for Bo. The steak was a little tough, but nothing compared to some of the buffalo steaks he had eaten in his time. And it had a fine flavor to it to compensate for the added chewing required. The potatoes were fried just right and seasoned with a little wild onion. A couple of fluffy biscuits worked mighty fine for sopping up gravy. Bo dug in with gusto and thoroughly enjoyed the meal, especially when Velma placed a glass of buttermilk in front of him. The buttermilk was cold enough so that drops of condensation formed on the glass and trickled down the sides.

"What'd I tell you?" the whiskery old man asked. "Best grub in the territory, if you ask me."

"I reckon you might be right at that," Bo said.

He lingered over his meal until the lunch rush was over; then, after wiping up the last of his gravy with the final piece of biscuit and popping it into his mouth, he said to Velma, "Mrs. Dearborn, I have a question for you."

She paused in cleaning up the counter and asked, "It's not another marriage proposal, is it? No offense, but I'm not looking to get hitched again."

"Neither am I, ma'am," Bo responded without hesitation. He had been married once, back in the days when Texas was a republic, but sickness had taken his wife and children. That tragedy had marked the beginning of his wandering days with Scratch, and he had never considered starting a family again. Bo was the sort of man who loved once in his life, with great and enduring passion . . . although he got some enjoyment out of whirling a pretty gal around a dance floor from time to time and suchlike as that.

He went on. "What I had in mind to ask you was if you'd be interested in providing meals for the prisoners over at the jail. Your food is better than what they deserve, no doubt about that, but you'd, uh, be feeding the deputies on a regular basis, too, meaning me and my pard Scratch . . ."

Velma laughed. "Do you plan on having many prisoners over there, Deputy Creel?"

"Call me Bo," he said. "We've got nearly a dozen hombres locked up right now, and there's no telling how many there'll be in the future. Marshal Braddock intends to clean up the town. That's what he was hired for."

"And about time, too, if you ask me. The goings-on south of the bridge give the whole town a bad name . . . as if calling the place Whiskey Flats wasn't bad enough to start with. And then, too, the violence spills over into this part of town some-times. When bullets start to fly over there, they don't stop at the creek."

"No, ma'am, they wouldn't," Bo agreed.

"Would I get paid for providing meals to the jail?"

"Of course," Bo answered without hesitation. "You'd be paid a fair rate. I'd see to that."

"Talked it over with Mayor McHale, have you?"

"Well . . . no," Bo admitted. "Not yet. But he seems ready to give Marshal Braddock anything he needs to help bring law and order to the settle-ment."

"The whole town council feels that way, I expect, or they wouldn't have hired such a famous lawman." Velma nodded. "All right, if you can work the pay-ment out with the mayor, I'll take the job. I warn you, though, sometimes Jonas McHale can be pretty tight with a dollar."

Bo smiled. "I'll have Marshal Braddock ask him about it. That ought to smooth the way." He picked up the glass and drank the last of the buttermilk, then licked his lips in appreciation and satisfaction. "That was the best meal I've had in a long time, Velma." He took four bits from his pocket and placed the coins on the counter. "I'm much obliged."

"Come back any time, Bo," she said with a smile as she picked up the money. "Pot roast for supper tonight."

Bo managed not to lick his lips in anticipation. "I'm looking forward to it already," he said as he tipped his hat to the lady.

Scratch was probably wondering where he had gotten off to, he thought as he moseyed back toward the marshal's office and jail. The inhabitants of Whiskey Flats had settled back into their normal routines after the excitement of the gun battle and the arrival of "Marshal John Henry Braddock." Nobody paid much attention to Bo.

When he came into the office, he found that Scratch had gotten some water and coffee from somewhere and started a pot of Arbuckle's boiling. Bo had noticed the battered old coffeepot on a shelf near the stove when he was there earlier. Scratch sat to one side of the rolltop with his chair leaned back and his feet propped on the front corner of the desk.

"Careful of those spurs," Bo warned him. "You'll gouge holes in the desk."

"Won't be the first ones," Scratch said as he sat up straight. He leaned over and put the tip of his right little finger in a hole in the top of the desk. "Looks like a bullet hit here, and there's three or four more like it. The way they're arranged, I'd say one o' the fellas who had this job before was sittin' here when somebody opened up on him from the window and blew his lights out. What sort o' damn fool would have his desk sittin' so that his back was to the window?"

"That's a good question. We'll move that desk around . . . or just not use it."

"Best warn the marshal about it, too," Scratch said, obviously being careful not to refer to Reilly by his real name. He jerked a thumb toward the cell block. "Say, those varmints in there are still cater-waulin' about bein' hungry."

"I'm working on that," Bo said. "Why don't you go down to the doctor's office and fetch that fella with the busted arm back here, then go try out the food at the Morning Glory Café."

Scratch grinned. "Good eats, are they?"

"Mighty good. And the proprietor is a mighty fetching widow woman, too."

Scratch's eyes lit up, and he practically bounded out of his chair. "Why didn't you say something sooner?" he demanded. "I'll have that wounded hombre back here and locked up in a hurry, and then I'll go see about gettin' some lunch."

"I'm going to try to get the town to hire Mrs. Dearborn to provide meals for the jail."

"Mrs. Dearborn, eh?"

Bo nodded. "Velma Dearborn."

Scratch repeated it. "Pretty name," he commented.

"I ain't surprised that a pretty lady goes with it." He cocked his cream-colored Stetson at a rakish angle. "If I ain't back by suppertime, you'll know where to look for me."

"Oh, you'll be back before then," Bo said. "You've got a prisoner to fetch, remember?"

"Oh, yeah, dang it!" Scratch hurried out, eager to be finished with this chore so that he could check out the food at the café . . . and the lady who was dishing it out.

A little later, Reilly came in, whistling a merry tune. "Get settled in at the hotel, Marshal?" Bo asked him.

"I sure did. It's a pretty nice place for a town like this. Got a big bed with a nice soft mattress."

"Tried it out already, did you?" Bo asked dryly.

"Well, it's been a hectic day. I just caught a little nap, that's all, then had a late dinner in the hotel dining room."

Bo would have been willing to bet that whatever Reilly had eaten, it hadn't been as good as the meal he'd had at the café.

Reilly looked around. "Where's Scratch?"

"Picking up the other prisoner at the doctor's office. He ought to be back with the fella pretty soon. Then we'll have the whole bunch locked up except for Tilden and the one I had to shoot. You'll need to talk to the mayor about scheduling a hearing for the prisoners and an inquest for the dead man. Is there an actual judge in town?"

"Hell if I know. Can't you find out about things like that?"

Bo lowered his voice and said, "It might look better if you did. You don't want folks to get the idea that you're not in charge."

Reilly frowned and nodded. "Yeah, you're right. Got to put the act over for a while. You have any ideas on how we're gonna fleece these suckers?"

"I've always got ideas," Bo said, "but it'll be better if we let things sort of percolate for a while."

"I suppose," Reilly said with a sigh. "I just don't want to have to keep this up for too long." He added in a worried voice, "As long as I'm wearing this badge, somebody's liable to start shooting at me again!"

CHAPTER 12

The rest of the afternoon was busy, but peaceful enough. No more trouble broke out south of the bridge, or anywhere else in Whiskey Flats, for that matter. Scratch brought the wounded prisoner back from Doc Summers's place and locked him up, then had plenty to say to Bo about how pretty Velma Dearborn was and how good the food at the Morning Glory Café was, too.

"By God, it's almost enough to make a man think about settlin' down," Scratch declared. "If a fella could find hisself a woman who looks like that, and can *cook* like that, he'd be a plumb fool to pass up the chance."

Bo just smiled and nodded. Scratch said pretty much the same thing every time he was enamored of some lady. Bo knew that when the time came to make a decision, though, Scratch would choose the open trail rather than a placid life in some settlement. Once a man got used to answering the siren call of the frontier, it was hard to ignore for very long. The mountains, the prairies, the magnificent blue arch of the sky with an eagle soaring through it, all exerted a powerful pull on a fella . . .

Scratch stayed at the jail while Bo and Reilly went to see Mayor Jonas McHale again. McHale wasn't very happy about having to cover the expense of the prisoners' meals, but he sighed and nodded in agreement to the proposal Bo made.

"One thing you can say about Velma Dearborn, she's as honest as the day is long," the mayor declared. "She won't try to cheat the town when it comes time to settle up with her."

Bo thought he could say a lot more for Velma than just that she was honest, but he kept that to himself. Anyway, honesty was important . . . leastways, except to hombres like Jake Reilly, and Bo still had hopes that the responsibility of being the settlement's lawman would force the young man to grow up and see things a mite differently.

As far as judicial matters went, McHale admitted that he had served as the community's magistrate as well as mayor, ever since being elected. "I'm not sure that such an arrangement is really proper, but nobody else wanted the job. Of course, when we didn't have a marshal, it didn't matter who was the judge, because there weren't any cases to try. Lawlessness ran rampant around here." He smiled proudly. "That's not the case now. You've already proven that, Marshal, with your swift and decisive action earlier today."

"Well, if you want to schedule a hearing for the prisoners and an inquest for the dead gent in the town meeting hall tomorrow morning, I reckon that would be all right," Reilly said. "We'll get it out of the way. No point in waiting."

McHale nodded. "I couldn't agree more. What will the prisoners be charged with?"

"Uh . . ." Reilly glanced at Bo, who hoped it wasn't too obvious that he was trying to remember what he had been told earlier. "Disturbing the peace, I suppose."

"Is there a law against firing a gun in the town limits?" Bo asked.

McHale frowned and shook his head. "Not that I know of."

Reilly picked up quickly on the hint, saying, "Maybe that's something the town council ought to take up at its next meeting. You've got to enact some laws around here if you want me and my deputies to enforce them."

"That's an excellent idea. I'll sure bring it up with the council. For now, I'll fine those boys as heavy as I can for disturbing the peace. I don't suppose we can keep them locked up for a while?"

"Depends on whether or not they pay their fines," Bo said, speaking from experience. He and Scratch had been locked up more than once facing either a fine or a jail sentence.

McHale tugged at his close-cropped beard. "I don't suppose we can make the fines unreasonably heavy. We have to be fair about this, even though our goal is to clean up the town by any means necessary."

Reilly slapped him on the back affably and said, "Don't worry, Mayor. You'll get the hang of all this. We do things by the book now in Whiskey Flats."

Bo managed to keep a straight face at the idea of Reilly saying they were going to do things by the book . . . but it wasn't easy.

A short time later, they were on their way back to the marshal's office when they ran into Rawhide Abbott. She had cuffed her battered old hat back so that it hung on the back of her neck by the chin strap and let her auburn curls spill freely around her shoulders. Bo thought she looked mighty pretty, and judging by the semi-stunned expression on his face, so did Jake Reilly.

Reilly snatched his hat off and held it in front of his chest as he said, "Hello, Miss Abbott. It sure is nice to see you again."

"Put your hat back on, Marshal," she told him. "You don't have to fall all over yourself bein' polite to me."

"A gentleman should always be polite to a lady."

"I never claimed to be a lady." She turned to Bo. "What are you gonna do with those prisoners you've got locked up?"

The fact that she asked him about the prisoners instead of Reilly was a little troubling, Bo thought. Was she starting to suspect that Reilly wasn't actually calling the shots?

"We'll hold them tonight and then have a hearing tomorrow morning," Bo told her. "Mayor McHale will fine them, and if they pay up, we'll let them go."

"Oh, they'll pay up," Rawhide said. "Or rather, Dodge Emerson will."

"Who's Dodge Emerson?" Reilly asked. "I don't think I've heard mention of him until now."

"Emerson owns the Royal Flush Saloon, the biggest and best place south of the bridge. He's got it in his head that if he can get all the business owners down there to work together, they can stop the law from running them out of town. He'll pay the fines, just to get those roughnecks in debt to him."

"We don't want to close the saloons down or force the men who own them to leave town," Reilly pointed out. "All Bo and Scratch and I are supposed to do is enforce the law and put a stop to all the killing and thievery."

Rawhide shook her head. "You don't think Jonas McHale will stop at that, do you? He's like any reformer. He wants anything he doesn't agree with gone, and he wants the law to do the dirty work for him. Wait and see if I'm not right."

"Well, I don't take orders from McHale, and neither do my deputies," Reilly responded with a touch of bluster in his voice.

"Actually, you do," Rawhide said. "You were hired to enforce the laws the town council passes, and they do pretty much whatever McHale wants them to. So he *is* your boss."

Reilly looked at Bo, who shrugged. It was a fact of life. Even a lawman had to answer to somebody.

"We'll just see about that," Reilly said. "The mayor strikes me as a reasonable man. I'm sure he won't overstep his boundaries."

"He already had the town council appoint him

judge," Rawhide pointed out. "Seems to me that's grasping pretty tight to power."

Bo ran a thumbnail along his jaw as he frowned in thought. "You don't like the mayor very much, do you?" he ventured.

Rawhide shrugged. "He and my father were always rivals, I guess you'd say. McHale never had as much say as he wanted around here until after Pa was gone."

"He told us nobody else wanted the job of magistrate. Was that true?"

"Nobody wanted it bad enough to go up against him," Rawhide said. "And I don't reckon there is anybody in town who's qualified to be the judge . . . unless it's Harry Winston."

"Who's Harry Winston?" Reilly asked. "There sure are a lot of names to learn in this town."

"Harry used to practice law here," Rawhide explained. "He gave it up a few years ago after his wife was attacked by a bronco Apache who left the reservation and went on a one-man raid and killing spree. Harry came in just as the varmint was . . . molesting his wife. They fought, and the Apache knocked Harry out. Probably thought he'd killed him. He did kill Mrs. Winston before he took off to look for more victims. I think the hombre wanted to go out in a blaze of glory, and he got his wish when a cavalry patrol caught up to him and shot him to pieces. But that didn't help Harry . . . or his wife. After that, Harry sort of went to pieces, too."

Bo could understand that. He remembered the depths to which he had fallen following the deaths of his wife and children. Without Scratch's help, he never would have clawed his way out of that black hole, which was just one more debt Bo owed to his trail partner.

"Where is this fella now?" Bo asked. "Is he still here in town?"

"Oh, he's here, all right," Rawhide said. She inclined her head. "Come with me. I'll introduce you."

She led Bo and Reilly up the street, and after a minute it became obvious that she was taking them to McHale's livery stable.

"Wait a minute," Reilly said. "You're supposed to be taking us to see this Winston fella, not the mayor."

"He's here," Rawhide said as she led them into the big barn's cool, shadowy interior. As they started down the wide central aisle, a bandy-legged hostler came out to greet them.

"Howdy, Rawhide," he said to the young woman with the easy familiarity of one who had known her ever since she was a little girl. Bo suspected that Rawhide had been sort of a mascot for the whole town while she was growing up. "Somethin' I can do you for?"

"We're lookin' for Harry, Ike."

The old-timer's bushy eyebrows rose in surprise. "Harry? Why, he's back yonder muckin' out that last stall on the right. What'n blazes do you want with Harry, Rawhide?"

"We've got a question to ask him," Rawhide replied. She motioned for Bo and Reilly to follow her.

They went along the aisle until they reached the final set of stalls. In the one on the right, a tall, sandy-haired scarecrow of a man in ragged work clothes was using a pitchfork to heap up a mound of soiled straw. His hands were dirty, and he had smudges on his face. Bo didn't want to think about what those dark brown streaks might be.

At first, the man didn't realize the visitors were there, but when he became aware of them, he looked up and blinked bleary eyes behind thick, smeared spectacles that perched on his thin nose. He said, "Hello, Miss Rawhide. How are you?"

"I'm fine, Harry," she said with an unaccustomed note of tenderness in her voice. "How about you?"

"Oh, doing fine, doing fine, I suppose. Are you looking for Mayor McHale?"

"No, actually, Harry, we were looking for you." She gestured toward Reilly. "This is John Henry Braddock, the new marshal of Whiskey Flats. You may have heard about him."

Winston shook his head, confusion evident on his narrow face. "No, ma'am, I'm afraid I haven't. I don't pay too much attention to what goes on in town these days. I just do my job. I haven't done anything wrong, have I?"

Rawhide smiled. "No, not at all. We just want to talk to you for a minute. This other fella is Bo Creel, one of Marshal Braddock's deputies."

Winston nodded to Bo and Reilly. "I'm pleased to meet you gentlemen. I can't think of what you'd want to talk to me about, though, if I'm not in any trouble."

"No trouble at all, Harry," Bo assured him. "Miss Abbott tells us that you used to practice law here in town."

A slight look of panic appeared in the watery eyes behind the smeared lenses. "Oh, that was . . . a long time ago. I don't do that anymore."

"But you remember the law, don't you?" Bo persisted. He had thought at first that Winston was drunk, but then he decided that something else was wrong with the man. He wasn't quite sure what it was, though.

"Certainly, I remember the law. I practiced for more than ten years. A man doesn't forget something like that."

"So you'd know how to rule fairly in a court case if, say, you were the judge?"

"Of course." Winston smiled sadly. "But I could never be a judge."

"Why not?" Rawhide asked.

"Well . . ." Winston blinked again. "I . . . I don't know why. But I'm sure I couldn't . . ."

"That's why we're here, Mr. Winston," Bo said. "We'd like to know if you'd be interested in assuming the position of magistrate here in Whiskey Flats."

Ike, the hostler, let out a low whistle of surprise. "Well, what do you know," he said. "I never would'a suspicioned *that*."

Winston had to lean on the pitchfork to support himself. There was a faraway look in his eyes and a tremor in his voice as he said, "Me? A judge? Really?"

"You're not drunk, are you?" Bo asked sharply.

Winston's words were those of an intelligent, educated man, but there was definitely something wrong with him. Bo had to make sure what it was before they could go on with this conversation.

With a solemn expression on his narrow face, Winston shook his head and said, "No, sir. I don't touch liquor."

Rawhide leaned closer to Bo and Reilly and said in a low voice, "He keeps a bottle of opium in his pocket that he takes a nip from every now and then."

"Opium!" Reilly exclaimed. "And you didn't figure you needed to tell us about that?"

"It's my medicine," Winston said. "It helps me forget . . . things."

Bo said, "But you don't want to forget things like the law, do you?"

"Well . . . no, I suppose not. But I don't know how to . . . remember some things . . . and not the others . . ."

Reilly said to Bo, "This isn't going to work. You can see for yourself he can't do it."

"Hold on a minute," Bo urged. To Winston, he said, "Harry . . . you don't mind if I call you Harry, do you?"

Winston shook his head. "Not at all. That's my name."

"Harry, would it be worth it to you to give up your medicine if you could be a judge?" Bo knew that giving up opium would be rough on the man, but it could be done. They might have to find a good sturdy place to lock him up for a few days while it was going on, but if they could do that . . .

"What's going on back here?" a new voice asked.

Bo, Reilly, and Rawhide turned to see Jonas McHale coming toward them, a frown on his face. Trailing behind him was Ike. Obviously, the hostler had slipped off to tell his boss about the conversation the three visitors were having with Harry Winston.

"I'm sorry, Mayor," Winston said hastily. "I'll get right back to work."

"No, that's all right, Harry," McHale told him. "I just want to know what these folks are talking to you about." He looked at Bo and Reilly. "You can't be serious about asking him to take over as judge."

"According to Mr. Winston, he practiced law for over a decade," Bo said. "Most places on the frontier, that makes a fella eminently qualified to serve as a judge."

"And you said yourself that it wasn't really proper for one man to be both mayor and magistrate," Reilly put in. Bo was grateful for that. Reilly might think the idea was loco, too, as McHale clearly did, but at least he was willing to play along with Bo's plan.

"Well, yes," McHale agreed grudgingly. "But I hardly think that Harry is the right man for the job. I mean . . . look at him."

It was true that Harry Winston was about the most unimpressive specimen of humanity that Bo had seen in quite a while, but there was something about him . . . possibly the intelligence that lurked deep in those bleary eyes, behind the terrible pain of memory and the opium that served to partially deaden it . . . Bo just had a hunch that he was doing the right thing here, and he had learned over the years that his hunches were correct more often than not.

"I could do it," Winston said suddenly. "I think I could anyway."

"Are you sure?" Bo asked.

"I . . . I . . ." Doubt appeared in Winston's eyes and made him look toward the floor, but after a second, he used the pitchfork to steady himself as he straightened, and he looked up and nodded. "I can do it." He reached into the pocket of his filthy trousers and pulled out a small brown bottle of the sort that came from apothecary shops. He held it out to Bo and went on. "Here. You take my medicine right now before I change my mind."

"Loco," Ike said. "Plumb loco."

Bo didn't think so at all. He took the bottle of opium from Winston and said, "You're doing the right thing, Harry."

McHale shook his head. "You'll never get the town council to go along with this. And they'll have to appoint him, you know."

Reilly slapped him on the shoulder, operating in his element again. "I think you underestimate your influence, Mayor. Give us a few days and let us work with Harry. If you see that he can do the job after all, I'm sure the council will go along with whatever you recommend."

"Well . . . I suppose I could keep an open mind on the matter . . ."

"Of course you can! Even though we haven't been acquainted for long, I can tell that's the sort of fellow you are. Fair-minded, and willing to give a man a chance."

McHale nodded. "That's true." He frowned again as he went on, "But we're supposed to have a hearing tomorrow about those prisoners who are locked up in the jail, as well as that inquest."

"You can go ahead and preside over those," Bo told him. "It doesn't matter a whole lot, because according to Rawhide, an hombre named Dodge Emerson is just going to pay their fines anyway."

McHale grimaced. "That's true. Dodge Emerson takes a particular delight at being a thorn in the side of the respectable citizens of Whiskey Flats. So I suppose the hearing is just a formality. The inquest will be, too, since the dead man was killed by a peace officer in the lawful course of his duties." The mayor nodded. "All right. I'll handle those matters tomorrow, and then we'll see what happens with Harry here. I warn you, though . . . I still think it's a crazy idea."

"Sometimes crazy ideas work out," Reilly said. He grinned. "Look at me. Who'd have ever thought that a handsome devil like me would turn out to be a marshal?"

CHAPTER 13

Scratch's eyebrows rose as Bo introduced Harry Winston to him. Winston had cleaned up a little at the livery stable's water trough, but he was still pretty dirty. He didn't offer to shake hands, just ducked his head in a nod and said, "I'm pleased to meet you, Mr. Morton. I just hope I can live up to the confidence you and Marshal Braddock and Deputy Creel are showing in me."

"Uh-huh," Scratch said dubiously. He looked at Bo. "This fella is gonna be Whiskey Flats' new judge, eh?"

"That's the plan," Bo said with an emphatic nod. "He'll be staying here with us for a while before he takes over the court."

"You *are* gonna have the barber bring a tub and some hot water up here, ain't you?"

Bo chuckled. "We'll go down there. Marshal, you mind staying here for a while and keeping an eye on the prisoners?"

Reilly pulled the chair back from the desk. "Nope. Not as long as you're back before suppertime."

Before the young man could sit down, Scratch

took hold of the chair and turned it so that it faced the windows. "You might want to put it like that," he told Reilly. "Always best to have a wall at your back, as Bill Hickok learned to his regret up in Deadwood a few years back."

"Oh." Reilly glanced nervously at the windows as if bushwhackers were lurking there this very minute. "I see what you mean."

Bo and Scratch took Winston and headed down the street to the barbershop. The former lawyer shambled along between the Texans. He licked his lips, and his hands shook a mite. Bo figured Winston was getting thirsty for a swig of his "medicine" along about now.

The barbershop was run by an affable, muttonchop-whiskered man named McCormick. He was a big man, well over six feet and probably over three hundred pounds, but like a lot of big men, he had a friendly, gentle demeanor to him. He wrinkled his nose as Bo and Scratch came in with Harry Winston.

"Let me guess," McCormick said. "You boys want a hot bath for poor Harry here."

"How'd you know?" Scratch asked.

"Ike from the livery stable was already over here, spreading the word about how you intend to make Harry the local judge." McCormick shook his massive head. "I like you, Harry, always have. You know that. But I ain't sure you're up to being a judge."

Winston smiled slightly. "Then we're of one mind, Jerry, because I'm not sure about it either."

McCormick shook his head. "Well, I wish you all the luck in the world. Lord knows you deserve a break, for a change." He jerked a thumb over his shoulder. "Go on back. I keep a tub heated up most of the time, and it just so happens I got one goin' now."

A door in the back wall of the barbershop led into a canvas walled rear area where several large galvanized tin tubs were sitting. A small fire burned under one of them, the flames just large enough to keep the water in the tub warm. Off to one side sat a massive iron pot where a larger flame could be kindled to heat the water that was then dumped into the tubs with pitch-lined buckets.

"Shuck those duds and climb in, Harry," Scratch told Winston. "Bo and me will see to it that you don't drown."

Winston looked reluctant. "It's been a while since I had a bath."

"We can tell," Bo said. "Go ahead, Harry. It'll be all right."

"Well . . . all right." Winston took his spectacles off, folded the stems carefully, and handed them to Bo. "You'll take care of them for me, won't you? I don't see very well without them."

"Sure," Bo told him. "Don't worry about them."

While Winston began taking off his filthy work clothes, Bo held the spectacles up to the light that came through the entrance into the bath area. The lenses were so smeared it was hard to believe that Winston could see anything *with* the spectacles, let alone without them. Bo pulled a handkerchief from his pocket, breathed on one of the lenses to fog it up, and began cleaning it.

Without his clothes on, Winston was so pale and scrawny, he looked like a fella on the verge of starving to death. He climbed awkwardly into the tub and sank down in the warm water.

Scratch used the toe of his boot to prod the pile of clothes Winston had left on the ground and said, "We should've got him some more duds before bringin' him down here. If he puts these back on, he'll be almost as dirty as he was when he climbed in there."

Bo regarded his handiwork with the spectacles. He wasn't sure if he was improving the situation or just making it worse. He said, "I can walk over to the general store and pick up a few things for him, if you don't mind staying here and watching him by yourself."

"I reckon I can handle that chore," Scratch said dryly.

Bo refolded the spectacles and slipped them into his coat pocket. "I'll be back in a few minutes then." He left the bathing area and walked back through the barbershop.

A ladder-back chair sat to one side in the bathing area. Scratch picked it up, reversed it, and straddled it. He reached into his buckskin jacket, pulled out the makin's, and with a satisfied sigh began to roll himself a quirly.

"Doin' all right in there, Harry?" he called to Winston.

"Yes, I . . . I think so," the former lawyer replied. "The water's awfully hot, though."

Scratch doubted that. The tub hadn't been steaming. The water was probably only lukewarm, but that might feel hot to somebody who hadn't had a bath in a long time.

"There's some soap there on the edge of the tub," Scratch said as he spilled tobacco from his pouch onto a paper. "Get it and give yourself a good scrubbin' all over."

"All right . . . Uh, Deputy Morton . . ."

Scratch heard the footsteps behind him at the same time as Winston spoke with a warning tone in his voice. The silver-haired Texan grimaced. He had made the same sort of mistake that he had cautioned Jake Reilly against only a short time earlier. He had sat down with his back partially toward the entrance from the barbershop. Not only that, he had his hands full at the moment.

"Hey there, mister," a harsh voice said.

Scratch turned his head to look over his shoulder. Three men had just stepped out of the barbershop into the canvas-walled bathing area. They were roughly dressed, hard-faced men, all three of them gun-hung. In fact, one of the men packed two irons, just like Scratch. And all of them looked like they knew how to use those weapons.

"If you're lookin' for a bath, boys, you'll have to wait," Scratch said, keeping his tone light.

"What we're lookin' for are the sons o' bitches who shot up the Top-Notch and the Lariat earlier today and killed one o' our pards," the two-gun hombre said. He had an ugly face topped by carroty hair under a squashed-down hat. "You're one of 'em, ain't you? One of those bastards who calls hisself a lawman?"

"What do you aim to do if I am?"

Ugly Face snarled. "We aim to kill you, that's what! And then we'll finish settlin' the score with your pards!"

"Well, then, boys," Scratch said with a sigh, "I guess you got it to do. Duck, Harry!"

And with that he erupted up off of the chair.

* * *

After leaving the barbershop, Bo walked up the street to the Abbott & Carson General Mercantile Emporium. It was a big frame building that took up an entire block by itself, with a long loading dock out front where wagons could pull up and supplies could be stacked in their beds. This bustling enterprise had grown from a tiny frontier trading post, according to Rawhide. That was the way of civilization, Bo reflected. Things always got bigger.

Sometimes they even got better . . . but not always.

He climbed the steps to the loading dock and walked through the double doors that stood open. The store was high-ceilinged and somewhat cavernous inside, with wooden shelves full of merchandise taking up most of the area. More merchandise was in glass-fronted counters along the side walls, and farm implements, tools, rope, and other goods hung on hooks and pegboards on the walls behind those counters. Toward the rear of the store were huge barrels of sugar, flour, salt, crackers, and pickles. Another glass-fronted counter that ran from one side of the store to the other contained rifles, handguns, shotguns, bowie knives, axes, and hatchets. As far as Bo could tell, a fella could get almost anything he needed to survive on the frontier here, but there were things for the ladies, too, such as bolts of cloth, colorful beads and other notions, and shelves full of canned goods. Considering the selection of merchandise available, Bo wasn't surprised that the store was doing good business.

At least a dozen customers were in the place, being helped by three white-aproned clerks.

Rawhide Abbott was there, too, which surprised Bo a little. Not too much, though, because he recalled that the young woman owned a half interest in this emporium. She struck Bo as being canny enough to keep a sharp eye on her holdings. She stood at the rear counter talking to a man in a gray suit who stood behind it.

Rawhide noticed Bo and motioned him back to join them. "This is my partner, Thatcher Carson," she said as she nodded toward the man in the gray suit. "Thatcher, meet Deputy Bo Creel."

"I've heard a lot about you lawmen," Carson said as he reached across the counter to shake Bo's hand. He was a little below medium height, clean-shaven, with sleek, iron-gray hair and the face of a terrier. His brisk accent marked him as not being a native Westerner. Bo pegged him as being from Massachusetts or somewhere else in the Northeast. Carson went on. "I'm glad to see that someone is finally going to make Whiskey Flats a decent place to live."

"The town strikes me as already being a decent place to live, Mr. Carson," Bo said. "It just needs a few of the rough edges sanded off."

"Indeed. And all of those rough edges are south of the bridge. You've made a good start, Deputy. Keep up the good work."

"Were you looking for me, Bo?" Rawhide asked.

"No, as a matter of fact, I came to get some new clothes for Harry Winston. He's over at the barbershop getting a bath, and those rags he was wearing aren't fit for man nor beast to put back on."

"Amen to that," Rawhide agreed. "Thatcher can fix you up."

"I certainly can, Deputy," Carson said. "What did you have in mind?"

"Maybe a white shirt and a plain black suit?" Bo suggested. "And a tie and some socks and underwear, of course. A couple of shirts, I guess. We want Harry to look like a judge once he's himself again."

Carson frowned. "You've acquired yourself quite a project, Mr. Creel. I always liked Harry Winston and wish only the best for him, but it may be too late."

"Somebody's got to bet on the long shots," Bo said, thinking not only of Winston but also Jake Reilly. Bo had gotten mixed up in this because he wanted to help Reilly, and now he had another lost soul to help out in Winston. Bo knew that he looked a mite like a preacher in his sober garb, and now he was starting to act like a sky pilot, too. He warned himself not to get too carried away. It wasn't his job to help all the lost sheep in the world find their way home.

"I suppose so," Carson said. "I'll gather up those clothes myself."

He bustled off to take care of that. Once Carson was gone, Bo said, "Seems like a nice fella. Probably pretty efficient, too."

Rawhide laughed. "You got that right. Thatcher's a regular eagle eye when it comes to watchin' the pennies and makin' sure that the store is run right. There's no way I could've kept it going by myself. I reckon my father knew that, and that's why he set things up the way he did." She paused. "How's Harry?"

"Getting cleaned up," Bo replied. "And that's liable to take—" He was about to say "a while," but he didn't get to finish his sentence.

Because at that moment, gunfire erupted somewhere down the street, filling the late afternoon air of Whiskey Flats with the sounds of violence once more.

Scratch dropped the tobacco pouch and paper as he exploded into action. His right hand flashed to the ivory-handled grips of the Remington on that hip. As he spun toward the gunmen, his left hand reached down and grabbed the top rung of the chair's back. He dropped into a crouch as he slung the chair at them.

The gun-wolves had already begun to howl. The roar of shots pounded against Scratch's ears as flames jetted from the muzzles of the revolvers wielded by the would-be killers. A bullet whistled past the silver-haired Texan's ear, and more of them clawed through the air near his head.

But then the chair crashed into the man who was firing two guns and knocked him backward. That gave Scratch just enough respite to plant a slug in the middle of Ugly Face's chest. The carrot-topped gunman rocked back and then forward, pain and disbelief etched on his face as he realized he was dying. He tried to raise his gun for another shot, but instead his knees unhinged and he pitched forward.

By then Scratch had filled his left hand, too, and that Remington blasted twice. The first shot narrowly missed the third gunman. The second shattered the man's elbow on his gun arm. He grabbed at the injury with his other hand as he let out a high-pitched, keening wail of agony and staggered to the side.

That left the two-gun hombre who'd been knocked off balance by the chair, which had also busted his nose, from the looks of the blood streaming from it now. As he caught himself and started to raise his guns again, he found himself alone, facing a grim-visaged Texan who also had two guns. Unwilling to match his Colts against Scratch's Remingtons, the man did the only sensible thing.

He turned and ran.

Scratch could have shot him in the back as the man galloped out through the barbershop. He considered the idea very seriously for a second before lowering the Remingtons. He'd never been a backshooter, and was too danged old to start now, he told himself.

A little splash came from behind him as Harry Winston stuck his head up from the water in the tub. Winston was gasping a little because he had held his breath and gone under when the shooting started. Now that the blasts had stopped, he blinked soapy water out of his eyes and asked, "Is . . . is it over?"

"I reckon," Scratch said. He was pretty sure Ugly Face was dead, and the man with the shattered elbow had fallen to his knees and was whimpering as crimson rivers continued to flow down his arm. Scratch stepped over to Ugly Face and toed the hombre over onto his back, just to make certain.

He was looking into the glassy, lifeless stare in

Ugly Face's eyes when Harry Winston yelled, "Look out, Deputy!"

Scratch jerked his head around and saw that the other man had managed to get to his feet. In his left hand was a long-bladed knife he must have plucked from a sheath worn behind him, because Scratch hadn't seen it earlier. The man howled curses as he lunged at Scratch and started to bring the knife down in a killing stroke.

Scratch still had both guns in his hands. He tilted up the barrel of the right-hand Remington and fired. The bullet caught the man in the throat at a rising angle, tore through the jugular so that a crimson fountain spurted from his neck, and then bored through his brain to explode out the back of his head in a grisly spray of blood, gray matter, and bone fragments. The varmint dropped like a puppet with its strings cut, the knife falling harmlessly to the ground beside him.

"Now it's over, right enough," Scratch said. "For these two stupid bastards anyway."

"What . . . what about the other man?" Winston asked.

More shots thundered in the street.

Scratch turned to look in that direction. "Sounds like somebody's dealin' with him now."

As Bo ran out the double doors of the emporium, he could tell that the shots came from the barbershop where he had left Scratch and Winston. He couldn't see any reason why anybody would want to hurt the drug-addicted former lawyer, but some of the lawless element in Whiskey Flats might have seized this opportunity to try to rid themselves of one of the new lawmen. Three or four different guns were firing. It was a regular battle, and Bo cursed himself for leaving Scratch alone to face that ambush attempt.

But he was still a block from the barbershop when a running man burst out the front of the place and the guns fell silent. The man carried two revolvers, but didn't look like he had any more interest in using them. He looked around frantically for a second, then pouched the irons and started to walk away as if he hadn't had anything to do with the gun battle behind the barbershop.

Bo felt a little better now. The man had dashed out of the barbershop as if the Devil himself were behind him. It hadn't been the Devil that had chased him out of there, Bo knew . . . although the fella responsible *was* called Scratch.

If the hombre thought he could fool anyone by his casual pose, he was sadly mistaken. The townspeople who were near the barbershop had seen him run out, and so had Bo. The Texan strode toward him determinedly. Bo was going to arrest the man and find out if there was anything behind this gunplay besides mere vengeance.

Suddenly, a single shot rang out behind the barbershop. Bo didn't know what that was about, but he thought the report sounded like one of Scratch's Remingtons going off. Whatever it was, it galvanized the gunman on the street into action again. He clawed his Colts out as he broke into a run and craned his neck to look over his shoulder, clearly afraid that somebody was going to come after him.

He should have been looking in front of him. Bo planted himself in the street and called, "Hold it!"

The man jerked toward him and swung the guns up. Bo had no choice but to pull his own Colt. He fired just as the other two guns erupted, and the three shots were so close together they sounded almost like one.

A slug kicked up dust at Bo's feet, and he heard the wind-rip of the other as it passed by his head. Both of the gunman's shots had been close, but clean misses anyway.

Bo's bullet found its target, though. Dust puffed out from the breast pocket of the gunman's shirt as the deadly piece of lead punched through it and on into the man's chest. He swayed drunkenly as both guns slipped from his fingers and thudded to the street. For a long moment, he managed to stay on his feet, but then his eyes rolled up in their sockets and he collapsed.

Bo shook his head in disgust. He had wanted to take the hombre alive.

Scratch emerged from the barbershop while Bo was walking over to the man he had just killed. The Texans met at the corpse, looking at each other over the gunman's body.

"You all right?" Scratch asked.

"Yeah. You?"

Scratch nodded. "Fine as frog hair. Can't say the same for the two fellas lyin' dead behind the barbershop, though."

"What about Harry?"

"He was still in the tub when I left, a mite shook up but not hurt."

"So there were three of them, eh?"

"Yep. Claimed to be friends of the hombres we shot earlier in the day."

Bo nodded. "I suspected as much. I would have liked to question one of them, though, just to be sure."

Scratch gestured toward the corpse between them and asked, "Why'd you kill this one then?"

"Wasn't time not to," Bo said.

CHAPTER 14

Quite a crowd gathered around the Texans as everybody wanted to know what the shooting was about. Rawhide and Thatcher Carson appeared, having followed Bo out of the general store.

"Where's Harry?" she asked.

"Still back yonder behind the barbershop, takin' a bath," Scratch told her with a nod of his head in that direction. "I reckon one of us better get over there and keep an eye on him, Bo. With all the shootin' goin' on, I wouldn't put it past him to run off and try to hide somewhere."

"Not Harry," Rawhide insisted. "He's not a coward. He's just had some bad luck and made some bad decisions."

Scratch headed for the barbershop again. Bo was about to ask Rawhide to fetch Ed Chamberlain, the undertaker, when Jonas McHale pushed his way through the crowd.

"Good Lord!" the mayor exclaimed at the sight of the dead man. "Now there are gun battles on *this* side of the bridge! I expected Marshal Braddock to put a stop to this sort of thing."

"It's all connected," Bo told him. "This hombre, and the two Scratch killed over at the barbershop, were friends with the men we shot earlier. You'll find that bringing law and order to a town isn't an easy process, Mayor. One thing leads to another, and then another and another."

McHale's bearded jaw was tight with anger. "Where is the marshal anyway?" he wanted to know.

"I'm right here," Jake Reilly said as the crowd parted to let him through. He carried a rifle that he had brought with him from the marshal's office. "I heard the shooting. What happened, Bo?"

Bo sketched in the bloody events of the past few minutes for Reilly, musing as he did so that the young man had been careful to wait until all the shooting seemed to be over before emerging from the marshal's office. No one else seemed to have noticed that, however, and Bo certainly wasn't going to bring it up.

"Scratch and I would have arrested them," he concluded, "but they didn't give us that choice."

McHale shook his head in dismay. "Four killings in less than a day."

"That's the sort of thing you have to expect when you bring in a fighting marshal like me, Mayor," Reilly said, unknowingly echoing what Bo had told McHale a few minutes earlier. "Things are liable to get worse before they get better, too."

"I wish you hadn't told me that," McHale said. "I suppose you're right, though. Progress doesn't come cheap."

The curious crowd spread out even more as Ed Chamberlain arrived, driving his meat wagon. The little undertaker looked as cheerful and cherubic as he had earlier. "Business is booming in Whiskey Flats today," he all but chortled.

"Your business," McHale muttered. With another shake of his head, he walked off toward the livery stable. Bo watched him go, thinking that the mayor's reaction was all too typical. Folks wanted their messes cleaned up, wanted justice done, but usually didn't want to have to see the bloody price that was often paid to do such work.

Bo, Scratch, and Reilly left Chamberlain and his helpers to do their grim work. Reilly headed back to the marshal's office while the Texans returned to the barbershop. Jerry McCormick, the proprietor, was sitting in his own chair when they came in, gingerly massaging a swollen lump on his forehead.

"Did you get all three of the bastards?" he asked, wincing as the sound of his own voice obviously made pain shoot through his head.

"We did," Scratch replied. "Glad to see that you're all right. I saw you slumped in the chair when I went out, and hoped that those varmints hadn't stove your head plumb in."

"The ugly one buffaloed me with his six-shooter as soon as they came in. I reckon they didn't want me calling out a warning to you."

"Ever see any of them before?" Bo asked.

The barber's broad shoulders rose and fell in a shrug. "I don't know. There are always lots of hardcases like that around town. It's hard to tell one from another."

Bo nodded. "Well, there are three of them who won't be causing any more trouble." Something occurred to him. "Son of a gun. I forgot to get those clothes for Harry. I was just about to do that when the shooting started."

He went to the door, intending to return to the general store and get the new garments Thatcher Carson had been gathering for him, but when he stepped outside he saw Rawhide walking toward him, carrying a paper-wrapped package.

Bo smiled and asked, "Is that what I think it is?"

"Harry's new duds," Rawhide replied as she hefted the package. She tossed it to Bo. "Here you go. I'll wait out here."

Bo took the clothes inside, and he and Scratch walked back to the bathing area. The bodies of the two gunmen still lay there, with flies starting to buzz around them. Harry Winston peered nervously over the edge of the tub. His sandy hair was plastered to his head by the water.

"You clean?" Scratch asked.

"I . . . I think so. It was hard to wash up with . . . with those two lying there like that."

"Why? They can't hurt you or anybody else now. Anyway," Scratch went on as he eyed the now-brownish water in which Winston sat, "you got to be cleaner now than when you got in there. Haul them spindly shanks o' yours outta there, get dried off, and put these duds on."

A few minutes later, Winston was dressed. Thatcher

Carson had thought to include a pair of shoes in the package, which Bo had neglected to mention. Winston didn't wear the tie, but he donned the white shirt and the dark suit and looked considerably different from the filthy, ragged scarecrow he had appeared to be in the livery barn.

"Where are my spectacles?" he asked Bo. "Like I told you, I can't really see much without them." A shudder ran through him. "I was sort of glad of that, so I didn't have to look too close at those corpses."

Bo took the spectacles from his pocket and handed them to Winston. "I tried to clean them a mite," he said, "but I don't think I did a very good job."

"That's all right," Winston said as he unfolded them and put them on. "The world has looked rather blurry to me for a long time now. That was always . . . the way I liked it."

They left the barbershop, with McCormick saying, "Sorry for the trouble, Harry," as they went out. Winston just gave him a little smile and a wave.

"What now?" Winston asked. The former lawyer was licking his lips again, Bo noticed, and tiny beads of sweat had begun to pop out on his forehead.

"It's getting close to supper time. Let's get you something to eat, and maybe some coffee."

Winston shook his head doubtfully. "I don't know . . . I'm not very hungry. I'm not sure I can eat anything."

"You'll feel better if you do," Bo assured him.

"'Specially if you eat at the Morning Glory Café," Scratch added. "Miz Dearborn's got the best food in town."

"I . . . I seem to remember that. Velma Dearborn was friends with . . . with my wife." Winston pushed his spectacles up his nose. They slid back down. "She made . . . really good biscuits."

"She still does," Scratch said. He took Winston's arm. "Come on, Harry. Time to start putting some meat back on them bones of yours."

Ike the hostler must have continued running around town spreading the news, because when Winston and the Texans went into the café, Velma came out from behind the counter to greet Winston with a hug.

"Harry, I think it's just wonderful that you're going to be the judge," she told him. "You're cut out for something a lot better than mucking out stalls, and the town will be better off with a real judge, too."

Winston smiled. "I just hope I can live up to that."

Bo said, "We came to get something to eat for Harry."

"And I reckon we could do with a surroundin', too," Scratch said. "It's a mite early, but it's never too early for a good meal."

Velma laughed. "Come on, then, all three of you. We'll go out in the kitchen. Won't have to carry the food as far that way."

They sat around the table where Velma and her cook, a handlebar-mustachioed Swede named Borglund, took their meals. Borglund's accent was so thick that Bo and Scratch could understand only the occasional word he spoke, but they gathered that he was glad to meet them, that it was good to see Winston looking so respectable again, and that he would be more than happy to serve them all the pot roast, new potatoes, and boiled carrots that they could eat. He said that he would fix them something that sounded like lutefisk, too, but behind his back Velma made a face and shook her head, so Bo and Scratch declined the offer as graciously as possible.

Velma seemed able to communicate with the Swede just fine, so she got him busy cooking while she poured coffee for Winston and the Texans. Winston expressed his doubts about being able to eat, but Velma just said, "Hush up with that, Harry. You know you never could turn down my food."

"No offense, ma'am," Bo said, "but it appears that Mr. Borglund there is the one who's doing the cooking."

"From *my* recipes," Velma answered with hesitation. "I think I have some biscuits left over from lunch that haven't gone stale yet. Would you like to start out with one of those, Harry?"

"Well, I . . . I'll try." He took out a handkerchief that Carson had tucked in the breast pocket of his coat and blotted sweat off his forehead.

Velma took a biscuit from a basket that was covered with a piece of linen and handed it to him. Harry nibbled on it, not seeming to take much interest in the food. Velma looked at him for a moment, then said, "I think we could use a little more firewood for the stove. Mr. Creel, would you mind stepping out back with me to bring some in from the woodpile?"

"It would be my honor, ma'am," Bo said. He caught the quick frown that Scratch sent in his direction. Scratch would have liked it if Velma had picked him to perform that little chore.

Bo had a feeling that Velma was interested in more than getting some firewood, though, and once they were outside she confirmed that by saying in a low voice, "You know that Harry's been drinking that damned opium almost ever since his wife died, don't you?"

"Yes, ma'am, we do," Bo replied. "He says he's willing to give it up, though, if he can be Whiskey Flats' judge."

"That stuff's harder to give up than liquor, from what I've heard."

Bo shrugged. "Depends on how much booze a fella's accustomed to putting away, I reckon. I know it'll be a rough next few days for Harry, that's for sure."

"You can't leave him alone," Velma warned. "If you do, he'll find a way to get some of the stuff."

"Yes, ma'am, I expect he will." Bo frowned. "We've been thinking about that very thing. What we need is someplace to lock him up—"

She swatted him on the arm. "You can't do that. Harry's got a sensitive nature. Lock him up and he's liable to go plumb loco, as the cowboys say. You need a place where somebody can look after him all the time . . . and I don't think you can do that while you're busy being lawmen."

"No, ma'am, probably not. If you've got any suggestions . . ."

"Leave him here with me," Velma suggested.

"With you, ma'am?" Bo couldn't keep the doubt out of his voice.

Velma nodded. "My living quarters are here in the same building as the café, and I've got a spare room. Harry couldn't leave without coming out through the café, and either Ole or I would see him and stop him. He wouldn't fight us."

"I don't know, Velma. I've seen men do some mighty bad things when they've really got a hankering for that stuff."

She smiled. "You don't know Harry Winston. He wouldn't hurt anybody, no matter how bad a shape he was in. I tell you, he's got the gentlest soul of anybody you ever met . . . but there's a core of steel somewhere inside him, too. I'm convinced that it's still there. If he wants to lick this thing, he can do it. At least, he can with a little help and Ole and I can give it to him."

Her words were mighty convincing, and Bo had to admit to himself that she knew Harry Winston a lot better than he did. But he wasn't ready to agree just yet.

"It wouldn't do much for your reputation, a man that you're not married to staying here with you."

Velma laughed. "You think I give a fig about my reputation? Anybody who knows me very well will know that there's nothing improper going on. And those who don't know me . . . well, they're the same sort who came sneaking around after my husband died, hinting about how they'd be happy to help out, me being a widow and all and having *cravings* . . ." She snorted. "People like that can just go to hell, as far as I'm concerned."

"You make a mighty strong case, ma'am." Bo nodded. "I reckon if it's all right with Harry, it's all right with Scratch and me."

"Can you speak for Mr. Morton that way?"

"Oh, I think I can."

In actuality, Scratch would probably be a mite peeved that Winston was staying with Velma. Having the former lawyer around would be a distraction when and if Scratch decided to pay court to the proprietor of the Morning Glory Café.

Scratch would just have to put up with it, though, because the solution Velma offered was better than anything Bo had been able to think of. He gathered up an armload of wood from the woodpile, since that was the excuse Velma had used for calling him out here, and they went back inside.

Winston had managed to eat about half of the biscuit Velma had given him, and he had taken a few sips of the strong black coffee. Bo thought he looked a little better. Not much, but a little.

Bo postponed breaking the news until after the three of them had eaten. The pot roast was excellent, moist and tender, and the potatoes and carrots were savory. Winston only picked at his food, but he ate some and managed to drink a whole cup of coffee.

When the meal was over, Bo said, "Harry, how would you feel about staying here at Mrs. Dearborn's place for a few days?"

Winston's still-watery eyes blinked behind the spectacles. "But . . . I have a place to stay at the livery stable. Mayor McHale didn't just give me a job. He lets me sleep in the loft, too."

Velma reached across the table and patted his hand. "You'll be more comfortable here, Harry," she told him. "And Ole and I can help you out if you get to feeling bad."

"Well . . . you don't think the mayor would mind?"

"I don't think he would." Velma added, "I don't

care all that much what Jonas McHale thinks anyway, do you?"

"He's been good to me . . ." Winston took a deep breath. "But if you think it would be all right . . ."

"We all do," Bo said, even though Scratch was frowning at him from across the table. Winston didn't seem to notice that, and Scratch stopped frowning when Bo kicked him lightly in the shin.

"Uh, yeah, you go right ahead and do that, Harry," Scratch said. "Heck, I'd jump at the chance to eat Miz Dearborn's cookin' three times a day."

"You can do that anyway," Velma pointed out. "You don't have to live here."

"Yes'm," Scratch said.

"It's settled then," Bo said. He scraped his chair back. "Scratch and I will leave you here, and if you need anything, Harry, anything at all, you just send somebody to find us."

"All right. Thank you." Winston ducked his head bashfully. "It's been a long time . . . since anybody really trusted me to do anything. I'll try not to let you down."

Bo patted him on the shoulder. "I don't expect you will."

As they were walking away from the café a minute later, Scratch asked, "Was that your idea?"

"Nope," Bo replied. "Velma came up with it all on her own. She and her husband were friends with Harry and his wife. I expect she just wants to help him."

Scratch sighed. "Lucky fella, gettin' to spend all his time with a woman like that . . . while me, I'm stuck with an ol' mossyhorn like you."

"That goes both ways, pard," Bo said with a grin.

CHAPTER 15

After all the excitement of the Texans' action-packed first day in Whiskey Flats, the next forty-eight hours or so were relatively quiet. They made their rounds along with Reilly, who only occasionally made some impatient comment to Bo about wanting to start figuring out some way to cash in on this sweet deal they had stumbled onto. Bo kept putting him off, saying that they had to build up more trust from the townspeople first.

The next morning after the shoot-out between the Top-Notch and the Lariat, Mayor McHale held a hearing in the town meeting hall and fined each of the participants in the fracas fifty dollars, including the ones who were still laid up at Doc Summers's place. A lawyer named Carrothers represented all of the men and paid their fines for them.

Instead of one inquest, there were four that morning, following the hearing. Ed Chamberlain was the local coroner as well as the undertaker, which was only logical, and the jury he appointed wasted no time in finding that the deceased had met their ends in an entirely legal manner, that is, being gunned down by the very star packers they were trying to kill. The proceedings were short and simple, with no lawyers to complicate and prolong them.

"Carrothers works for Dodge Emerson," McHale explained to Bo, Scratch, and Reilly later. "Emerson's the one who provided the money for those fines, I'm sure of it."

Emerson himself seemed to be keeping a low profile. Even though the three lawmen had visited the Royal Flush Saloon several times during their rounds, they had seen no sign of the owner, and the bartenders always responded with head shakes when asked if Emerson was there.

The Top-Notch and the Lariat remained closed, the former because the owner, Big Mickey Tilden, was still recuperating from the serious bullet wound he had suffered at Reilly's hands. According to Rawhide, the Lariat's proprietor, Fred Byrne, was a nervous sort of gent and might have decided to pack it in after the big shoot-out. Or, she speculated, it was possible that he just didn't have enough of a liquor stock left to open again, hundreds of bottles having been blasted to pieces while the bullets were flying around.

In fact, everybody south of the bridge seemed to be on their best behavior. There were only a few minor fights in the saloons, and no shootings or stabbings. It was the quietest stretch that section had seen in months, McHale told Bo, Scratch, and Reilly as he chatted with them in the marshal's office.

"I don't know whether to be thankful," the mayor said, "or hold my breath waiting for the real storm to break. Because that's what it feels like, the calm before a bad thunderstorm."

"I guess folks are behaving themselves because my reputation has preceded me," Reilly responded with a cocky grin. Scratch rolled his eyes at that, but Bo was the only one who saw the reaction.

"If this keeps up, we may not need Harry Winston to take over as judge," McHale said. "We may not need a judge at all. How's Harry doing, by the way?"

"He's getting there," Bo said, not wanting to go into the details. "I expect he'll be fine in another day or two."

As a matter of fact, though, Winston had been going through pure hell, and Bo knew it. He went to the café a couple of times a day to check on the former lawyer, as well as take his meals there. The first twenty-four hours, Velma had been grim-faced when Bo asked her about Winston.

"It's the torments of the damned he's suffering, Bo," she told him as they shared a cup of coffee in the kitchen. "He can't keep any food down, and he shakes and sweats all the time. I never saw a man so miserable. And every time I think he's starting to do a little better, it gets worse again."

"Has he tried to get out?" Bo asked.

Velma shook her head. "He told Ole to tie him to the bed in the spare room, so that's what we did. We only let him loose when he tries to eat. Poor man. He's weaker than a kitten. I'm not sure he could walk, even if he was loose."

"Don't let him fool you," Bo warned. "I've seen fellas who were just as weak and sick as Harry is toss grown men around like they were kid's dolls. When that sickness comes on them . . ."

"Maybe it won't," Velma said. "I'm praying that it won't get that bad."

Bo nodded. "I'll put in a good word with El Señor Dios myself."

With the prisoners having been released, there was no need for someone to stay at the jail all the time. Eventually, though, that problem was bound to come up again, and Bo had been thinking about it.

"I've got an idea," he told Scratch and Reilly as they sat in the office early in the evening of their third day in Whiskey Flats. "We need a jailer so we won't be stuck here every time we have to arrest somebody. How about Rawhide Abbott?"

Reilly's eyebrows jumped up in surprise. "That loco redhead?"

Scratch was equally dubious. "A woman jailer? I never heard of such a thing!"

"You've seen for yourselves that she's plenty tough," Bo said.

Reilly reached up and felt of his jaw. "Yeah, I remember that punch that laid me out. For a little thing, she packs a hell of a wallop."

"And she can handle a gun, too," Bo added. "Got steady nerves."

Scratch nodded. "She showed that when she went into the Lariat with me." His naturally chivalrous nature came to the forefront. "But dadgum it, Bo, just think about the sort o' things prisoners would be liable to say to her!"

"From what I've seen of her, she'd probably just cuss right back at 'em," Bo said with a smile.

"Yeah, I reckon that's true, too," Reilly said. "Maybe it's not as far-fetched an idea as I thought it was at first."

"Well, then, if we're in agreement, should we go find her and ask her if she'd be interested in the job?" Bo suggested.

Scratch grunted. "I still got reservations, as the old chief said . . . but I reckon we can give it a try."

They left the office and went looking for Rawhide. She lived in a comfortable, good-sized house on the edge of Whiskey Flats that her father had built many years earlier, when he first married Rawhide's mother, who had also been a redheaded beauty. Since both the general store and the *Clarion* brought in money for her, she didn't have to worry about a living. From the gossip Bo had heard, most of the unmarried young men in town had tried to court her at one time or another, but none of them had had much luck. She seemed content with her life the way it was.

Bo had a feeling that a challenge would appeal to her, though, and that was what the job as jailer would represent. She didn't need the wages, and might even refuse to take them, but he felt like she would accept the job.

Abbott & Carson was still open, so the three lawmen went there first. Rawhide was in the store talking to Thatcher Carson, as they had thought she might be. She greeted them by asking almost eagerly, "Is there some sort of new trouble?"

"No trouble," Reilly assured her. "But we have a proposition for you."

Her eyebrows drew down in a frown. "I've heard *that* before."

"No, no," Reilly said quickly. "I'm talking about a job."

Now Rawhide was really surprised. "You want to hire me? To do what?"

"To be the jailer and keep an eye on the marshal's office whenever none of us can be there," Bo explained.

Thatcher Carson said in disbelief, "You want a *woman* to be the jailer?" When Rawhide's head snapped toward him and she gave him an angry glare, he went on hurriedly. "Not that there's any reason a woman couldn't be the jailer—"

"Forget it, Thatch," she told him. "I reckon most men would say the exact same thing if they heard what Deputy Creel just said." She turned back to Bo, Scratch, and Reilly and went on. "I've got just one word for you, boys. No, I take that back. I've got two words . . . Hell, no."

"You won't take the job?" Reilly asked. Somewhat to Bo's surprise, he looked and sounded disappointed.

"As jailer?" Rawhide shook her head. "Nope. Not interested." She paused. "But if you want to make me a deputy, then maybe we can talk about it."

"A deputy!" Carson exclaimed. "I—" He shut up and started to back away as Rawhide glared at him again. "I think I should go over the books before we close down for the night."

He went through the door behind the counter that led into the store's office.

That left Rawhide standing there with the Texans

and Reilly. She looked at them squarely and said, "Well? How about it?"

Reilly was starting to look confused again. He had grown in confidence in his pose as John Henry Braddock over the past couple of days, but Rawhide's suggestion clearly had thrown him for a loop. Bo stepped in to buy some time, saying, "Well, I don't reckon that occurred to us. What do you think, Marshal?"

"I couldn't pay you," Reilly told her. "Mayor McHale complained enough about having to come up with wages for Bo and Scratch."

Rawhide waved off that objection. "I don't care about the wages. I've got plenty of money. But I think it would be fun to be a deputy. Shoot, that's pretty much what I was that first day, when we had to break up the war between the Lariat and the Top-Notch."

Bo had brought up that very point earlier, when he made his initial suggestion to Scratch and Reilly, so he couldn't very well argue against it now. "You know it's liable to be dangerous?" he said.

Rawhide laughed. "The day you got here, when all that hell started poppin', was the most entertaining day in Whiskey Flats in a long time. Don't worry, I'll take my turn guarding the prisoners, whenever we have any. I just don't want to be stuck there in the office all the time, while the rest of you are out where the excitement is."

"Well . . ." Reilly shook his head, not in negation but in acceptance. "You seem to have an answer for everything. I guess I'm within my rights as marshal to appoint you as a special, volunteer deputy."

"With all the powers of a regular deputy," Rawhide said. It wasn't a question, but rather a statement.

Reilly shrugged. "With all the powers of a regular deputy, leastways until somebody in higher authority says different. I can't give you a badge, though. Don't have any except the one I'm wearing."

"That's all right. Just make sure everybody knows that I'm a peace officer now, too."

Reilly nodded. "I've got a feeling you'll take care of that anyway."

Rawhide thumbed her hat back and grinned. "Deputy Abbott," she said. "I like the sound of it."

"Just don't get any ideas about makin' it Marshal Abbott," Reilly muttered. "I'm still the marshal around here."

"For now," Rawhide said, still grinning. "For now."

She insisted on making their evening rounds with them, and since there were now four of them, Bo suggested that they split up, two taking each side of the street. Before Reilly could suggest that Rawhide go with him, Bo said, "Rawhide, you're with me." He didn't want the two of them spending a lot of time alone together. Rawhide was a smart girl; she might tumble to the fact that Reilly wasn't actually who he was pretending to be without either Bo or Scratch around to cover for him.

Reilly looked a little disappointed. Bo knew that he was still attracted to Rawhide, despite the fact that she had given him absolutely no reason so far to think that she might ever be interested in him in a romantic way. Just the opposite, in fact. But Reilly didn't protest, and so the foursome split up, Bo and Rawhide taking the left side of the street, Scratch and Reilly the right.

They made their way south along Main Street and crossed the bridge. That section of town was quiet again tonight.

It didn't stay that way, though. As Bo and Rawhide approached Emerson's Royal Flush Saloon, which like the Abbott & Carson Emporium on the other side of town took up the front of an entire block by itself, glass suddenly shattered ahead of them. Bo and Rawhide instinctively reached for their guns as the man who had just been thrown through the saloon's front window sailed across the boardwalk, crashed through the railing, and landed hard in the street, rolling over a couple of times before coming to a stop.

"Sweet Lord of Mercy!" Rawhide burst out, a pretty mild exclamation for her. "Who could have tossed a fella hard enough to do *that*?" She answered her own question a second later as a realization obviously hit her. "*He's* back in town, blast it!"

"Who?" Scratch asked, but before Rawhide could answer, a massive, shaggy head was poked out through the broken window and a voice like the rumble of a stampeding buffalo herd spoke up.

"Did I kill him? Did I bust him to pieces? Damn tinhorn tried to cheat me!"

Men crowded around the batwings inside the saloon to peer out curiously as Bo hurried to the side of the man who had been tossed through the saloon window like a rag doll. Having heard the commotion, Scratch and Reilly came running from the other side of the street.

The unfortunate victim had come to a stop on his belly. Bo knelt beside him and rolled him over. The man groaned in pain, confirming that he was still alive.

The giant looking out through the busted window snorted in disgust and withdrew, evidently disappointed that the hombre he had manhandled so roughly was still alive.

The man's face was already swelling and turning dark with bruises. His attacker must have cuffed him around some before flinging him through the window. He cried out in pain as Bo tried to lift him into a sitting position.

"He probably busted a few ribs when he went through that railing," Bo said as he carefully lowered the man to the ground again. "We'll need to get the doc down here, as well as a wagon to load him in, more than likely."

Reilly looked at the crowd on the boardwalk just outside the saloon's entrance and snapped, "One of you men fetch the doctor. Now!"

None of them budged, though, until another man stepped through the crowd and said in a quiet, powerful voice, "Do what the marshal says. Rance, you take care of it."

"Yes, sir," the man said as he broke into a run toward the other end of town.

"That's Dodge Emerson," Rawhide breathed to Bo, nodding toward the man who had given the order. "Reckon the commotion finally drew him out of his hidey-hole."

There was nothing Bo could do for the injured man, so he straightened and turned toward the boardwalk. The man Rawhide had indicated was only medium-sized, but the body in the light-colored suit was muscular enough so that he seemed a mite bigger than he really was. He wore a silk vest and cravat as well as the suit. His hair was dark and sleek in the light that spilled from the saloon, and a thin mustache adorned his upper lip. The corners of his mouth quirked as if he smiled frequently.

"I'm sorry about this," he drawled. "Looks like one of my customers was celebrating, and it got a mite out of hand. I'll be glad to pay that poor man's medical bills." He paused and looked a little surprised as he noticed who was with Bo, Scratch, and Reilly. "Is that you, Miss Abbott?"

"It is," she snapped. "And that's *Deputy* Abbott to you, Emerson."

Dodge Emerson cocked one eyebrow. "Really? As of when?"

"Tonight. And don't you forget it."

Emerson chuckled and said, "Oh, I'm not likely to forget something like that. You know me . . . I keep close tabs on what goes on in this town."

"Yeah, so I've heard." Rawhide glanced at Bo. "I'll tell you about that later."

Bo nodded and gestured toward the injured man, who was still moaning softly. "We want to talk to whoever's responsible for this. He's going to have to come down to the jail with us and be locked up to face charges of assault and attempted murder."

"I don't think any murder was intended—" Emerson began.

"That's where you're wrong, friend," Scratch said. "We all heard the big galoot who flung him out the window askin' if he'd killed the poor son of a gun. Sounds like attempted murder to me."

Emerson shrugged. "You're welcome to come in and talk to whoever you like. This is a public place, after all, and you folks are the law."

Rawhide caught hold of Bo's sleeve. "I'm not sure this is a good idea," she whispered.

"Why not?" Bo asked, surprised that anybody could put the fear of God into Rawhide Abbott.

"See that mule at the hitch rack?"

Bo looked and saw probably the biggest mule he had ever seen in his life. It was so tall and massive he was surprised he hadn't noticed it before now . . . but he'd been a little distracted when that hombre came flying through the window.

"I see it," he said. "Are you saying that mule belongs to the fella who did this?"

"That's right. He lives alone up in the mountains and doesn't come down to town very often, but whenever he does, there's usually trouble. Folks have learned to steer well clear of him." Rawhide looked at the man lying in the street. "I guess that gambler's new in these parts and didn't know any better than to try to cheat Chesterfield Pike."

"Chesterfield?" Reilly repeated with a laugh. "The man we're after is named Chesterfield? How much trouble can it be to arrest him?"

With that, Reilly stepped onto the boardwalk, strode past a clearly amused Dodge Emerson, slapped the batwings aside, and disappeared into the saloon.

CHAPTER 16

"Oh, Lord!" Rawhide exclaimed. "Bo, Scratch, go after him! He doesn't know what he's getting into."

"Neither do we, ma'am," Scratch muttered, but he and Bo hurried after Reilly anyway. Rawhide brought up the rear, looking unaccustomedly anxious.

The crowd inside the big barroom was still buzzing about what had happened. The first thing Bo noticed, though, was that everyone in the Royal Flush was giving one gent standing at the bar a wide berth.

He needed that room, because his shoulders seemed as broad as an ox yoke. He towered over everyone else. Jerry McCormick over at the barbershop was a big man, but next to this fella McCormick would have seemed puny and undersized. The man wore a homespun shirt that was stretched dangerously tight over the bulging muscles of his arms and shoulders. Crammed down on his head was an old brown hat that had seen much better days. Nicks had been cut from the brim, and in one place Bo would have sworn that someone had taken a bite out of it. A couple of bullet holes decorated the crown.

The man wore no gun, but a long, heavy-bladed knife was thrust behind the length of thick rope that he had tied around his waist to serve as a belt. With his reach, if he ever started flailing away with that pig-sticker, he could lay waste to a large area around him. Bo imagined that blood would flow like water in a fight like that.

Not that the giant probably had to resort to his knife very often. He could probably win most fights just by swinging those long arms with the hamlike fists on the end of them.

Of course, when you got right down to it, neither prodigious strength nor a razor-sharp blade were any match for six bullets from Colonel Colt's great equalizer. But if you ever went to shoot that big fella, you'd want some distance between you and him, because Bo had the feeling he could absorb several lead pills and keep right on a-comin'. It wouldn't profit a man to fill Chesterfield Pike with slugs if Pike still got his hands on the shooter. Even dying, Pike could choke a man to death in a matter of seconds, or break him in half.

There was no time to explain any of that to Reilly, because the young man had planted himself in the middle of the room and called out over the hubbub, "Chesterfield Pike! In the name of the law, I'm looking for Chesterfield Pike!"

Scratch cast a glance toward Bo, who knew very well what his trail partner was thinking. For a smart man, Reilly could be pretty damned dumb at times. There was only one man in here big enough to have picked up that gambler and tossed him so casually through the front window, and that was the giant at the bar.

Scratch leaned toward Bo and said under his breath, "You seen a beanstalk growin' anywhere around here?"

"Big as he is, that fella's real," Bo said. "He's not something out of a fairy tale."

"Damn it," Reilly demanded when no one responded to his question, "somebody tell me where I can find Chesterfield Pike!"

The man at the bar had a large, full schooner of beer in front of him. When he picked it up, it looked sort of like a thimble in his sausagelike fingers. He downed the whole schooner at one gulp and lowered the empty to the bar with a sigh that threatened to shake the rafters. Then he turned slowly and brushed at his ear.

"Sounds like a gnat buzzin' in here," he rumbled. "Anybody hear that same annoyin' little noise?"

Reilly took an angry step toward the bar, but then it finally dawned on him just what a behemoth he was facing. He stopped and swallowed, but he couldn't back down now, not in front of a whole saloon full of people, many of whom heartily disliked him because he had a lawman's badge pinned to his coat.

"Are you Chesterfield Pike?" he asked, and he managed not to have a quaver in his voice.

"I am. Who are you, and why're you lookin' for me?"

Reilly took a deep breath and reached up to tap the badge on his lapel. "I'm the law in Whiskey Flats, that's who I am. Marshal John Henry Braddock. And

I've got another question for you. Did you throw a man through the front window a few minutes ago?"

"You mean that tinhorn gambler who tried to cheat me?" Pike shook his head ponderously. "I wouldn't call him a man. More like a puny little bug. He's lucky I didn't just squash'm underfoot."

Bo stepped forward, figuring it was time he gave Reilly a hand. "He'll be lucky if he doesn't have more than three or four broken ribs, and if the swelling in his face goes down so that he starts to look human again in a week or so."

"Nobody cheats Chesterfield Pike."

"Well, then," Reilly said, "how would it be if I arrested him for being a crooked gambler?"

Pike's bushy eyebrows, which looked two giant caterpillars crawling across his face, pulled down as he frowned. "You'd do that?" he asked.

"I'm told that you spend most of your time up in the mountains, Pike," Reilly said, surprising Bo a little now that he had regained his composure. "You probably didn't know that we've got law and order here in Whiskey Flats now. But we do. Me and my deputies are responsible for enforcing it. So, yeah, we'll arrest that fella, just as soon as Doc Summers says he's healthy enough, and see that he pays a proper fine for what he did."

Pike took a step toward Reilly, and that one step seemed to carry him halfway across the room. "Why, that's mighty decent of you, Marshal," he boomed as he slapped Reilly on the shoulder. The friendly gesture knocked Reilly a couple of steps to the side.

Reilly caught himself, grimacing at the pain in his

shoulder, and said, "There's just one thing, Mr. Pike. Since I'm the marshal, I have to enforce the law fair and square for everyone."

Pike nodded. "That makes sense, I reckon."

Reilly swallowed again. "That's why I have to arrest you, too. You see, what that gambler did was wrong, but what you did was just as wrong. Maybe more so, because you're so big."

Pike frowned darkly again and said in an ominous tone, "I never have cottoned to bein' put in jail. Fact o' the matter is, I never seen a jail that could hold me."

Bo could believe that. Someone as massively strong as Pike could probably wrench the iron bars right out of the windows in the jail. Of course, Pike's shoulders wouldn't go through one of those windows, but he could just kick himself a new doorway in the wall.

Reilly wasn't going to give up. He said, "I know you don't like it, but it's the only fair thing to do."

The saloon was quiet as everyone watched this confrontation. Probably most of the bystanders expected Pike to start ripping Reilly limb from limb at any second.

But then Dodge Emerson stepped forward and said, "You know, Chesterfield, what the marshal is saying makes sense."

"It does?" Pike said, still frowning.

Emerson nodded. "I'll tell you what . . . you trust me, don't you, Chesterfield?"

The big head bobbed up and down. "You ain't never steered me wrong, Mr. Emerson."

The saloon keeper reached up to rest a hand on Pike's shoulder as he suggested, "Why don't you go with the marshal and his deputies and spend the night in jail? I know for a fact that if you do, you'll get breakfast tomorrow from the Morning Glory Café."

"Miz Velma's place?" A big grin wreathed Pike's rough-hewn face. "I do like Miz Velma's food, that's a plumb fact."

"All you'll have to do is get a good night's sleep, have a good breakfast, and then go to a hearing and pay a little fine. And I'll take care of that for you. How does that sound?"

"It don't hardly sound like bein' in jail a'tall."

"You'll do it then?" Emerson persisted.

Pike nodded again. "I sure will. You got my word on it."

Emerson turned to Reilly and said, "There you go, Marshal Braddock. Chesterfield's word is his bond."

"Yeah, well, how do I know that?" Reilly asked skeptically.

Emerson's genial features hardened slightly. "Because *my* word is *my* bond, and I say you can trust him. That ought to be good . . . unless you want to call both of us liars."

Bo said, "I don't reckon anybody wants to do that. Mr. Pike, would you come with me?"

Pike pointed, "I'd rather go with Miss Rawhide. Didn't I hear her say that she's a deputy now, too?"

Rawhide nodded. "That's right, Chesterfield, I am. You're not gonna give me any trouble?"

Pike smiled sheepishly and shook his head. "No'm. My ma raised me to be a gentleman round ladies, and Mr. Emerson, he says you're a lady even if you don't dress like one and don't always talk like one."

Rawhide shot a glance at the saloon keeper. "He says that, does he?"

Emerson slid a cigar from his vest pocket. "I always try to tell the truth," he said with a suave smile.

Rawhide just grunted. She said to Pike, "Come on, Chesterfield. You'll have the jail to yourself tonight, unless there's any more trouble."

Pike went peacefully, lumbering along behind Rawhide. Bo nodded for Scratch to follow them, and then he and Reilly lingered for a moment in the saloon.

"I'm obliged to you for your help in handling that big fella, Emerson," Reilly said. "Things could've gotten ugly if you hadn't stepped in like you did."

Emerson chuckled. "You don't know the half of it, Marshal. But Chesterfield has always liked me and trusted me, so I thought I could get him to be reasonable. A man as big and short-tempered as he is, people just expect him to be loco all the time. But if you stay calm and treat him fairly, he's generally not much trouble."

Bo said, "He's not right in the head, is he?"

"I wouldn't think of it like that," Emerson replied with a frown. "Have you ever known a really smart kid? I mean, a youngster who's as smart as a whip?"

Bo nodded. "I reckon I have."

"Well, that's Chesterfield for you. He's smart enough, but he just doesn't know as many things as somebody his age usually would. Anybody who takes him for dumb would be making a big mistake . . . and it might just backfire on them."

"What about you?" Reilly asked.

Emerson grinned. "Now, I never claimed to be smart."

"No, I mean why did you help us out? You're supposed to be the one who's getting together all the saloon owners and such south of the bridge to keep law and order from coming to Whiskey Flats."

Emerson's grin went away. "Someone's misinformed you," he said in a flat, hard voice. "Sure, I think all of us down here could do better if we quit trying to cut each other's throats all the time. There's nothing wrong with some healthy competition, but gun battles like the ones between the Top-Notch and the Lariat the other day don't do anybody any good. Mickey Tilden's laid out with a gunshot wound, Fred Byrne's slunk out of town with his tail between his legs, and four other men are dead." Emerson looked at Bo. "Killed by you and your partner, I hear."

"They didn't give us any choice in the matter," Bo said.

"I'm sure they didn't. But if you lawdogs think I'm behind any of that, you're dead wrong." Emerson smiled again, but his eyes remained chilly. "I'm just a mostly honest businessman trying to get along the best I can. I don't have any quarrel with you or your deputies, Marshal."

"That's good to know," Reilly said, but his tone made it clear that he didn't fully believe Emerson's claims. "Come on, Bo."

They left the saloon, and as they went through the batwings Bo glanced back and saw Emerson watching them with hooded eyes as he lit his cigar. Bo didn't know what to make of the saloon keeper. If Emerson was telling the truth, he might not be as much of an enemy as Bo had expected him to be. On the other hand, the man could be a slick liar. He could have even been behind the attempt on their lives a few days earlier.

"What do you think?" Reilly asked as they walked back across the bridge.

"I don't know," Bo replied honestly. "I'm not sure what to make of him."

"I am. Sometimes it takes a crook to know a crook, and believe you me, Dodge Emerson is as crooked as a dog's hind leg."

"I reckon we'll see," Bo said. "Right now, I want to make sure that Scratch and Rawhide got that Pike fella locked up all right. His night isn't going to be as comfortable as what Emerson made out it would."

"Why not?"

"You've seen the bunks in those cells," Bo said. "Pike's going to hang off both ends!"

CHAPTER 17

Despite Bo's prediction, the sound of raucous snoring came from the cell block as he and Reilly entered the marshal's office a short time later. Scratch grinned from the chair, which he had tipped back against the wall as usual.

"That big boy didn't give us a lick of trouble," he said. "Went right into one of the cells, told us to be sure and wake him up for breakfast, curled up on the floor like a big shaggy dog, and went off to sleep."

"On the floor?" Bo said.

"That's right. Didn't seem to bother him at all."

Rawhide was over at the stove pouring herself a cup of coffee. As she turned toward the others, she lifted the cup and said, "I reckon since I'm a deputy now, I'm entitled to drink your coffee, too."

"Help yourself," Reilly said. "Oh, that's right, you already did."

She made a face at him, then perched a hip on a corner of the desk. "Now that I've got some authority, I want to do some more investigating about the rustling that's been going on up at the Rocking B and the Star."

Bo poured himself a cup of Arbuckle's and said, "The Rocking B would be Chet Bascomb's spread, I take it?"

Rawhide nodded. "And the Star belongs to Steve North."

"The North Star?" Scratch said.

"Yeah," Rawhide said with a smile. "Pretty bad, isn't it?"

"Fella's got a right to name his ranch whatever he wants to, I reckon."

Reilly said, "You're going out there to poke around by yourself?"

"Why not?"

"The last time you did that, you wound up being chased by a bunch of cowboys who were trying to shoot you, remember?" Reilly reminded her.

"That won't happen this time," Rawhide insisted. "By the time I ride out there in a day or two, Bascomb and North will have heard that I'm a deputy now, and they won't let their men shoot at an officer of the law. Both of those old-timers are rough as cobs, but they won't want the trouble that would come down on their heads if some of their hands killed a star packer. They're basically law-abidin' gents, which is why I think somebody else is behind the widelooping, even though they've been blaming it on each other."

"You're putting a lot of faith in a badge you don't even have," Reilly argued.

"Why, Marshal, you sound like you don't want anything bad to happen to me." Rawhide grinned. "I didn't think you cared."

Reilly flushed angrily. Bo thought he might be a

little embarrassed, too. "If something happens to one of my deputies," Reilly said, "it reflects badly on me, too, as well as on the office of the marshal. We're trying to get people around here to respect the law, and it won't help if you get yourself shot up."

"I'll be careful," Rawhide promised. "I know these parts, and the folks who live here, better than any of you three. I stand the best chance of finding out what's really going on out there."

Reilly gave in with a reluctant nod. "All right. You might take Bo or Scratch with you, though, just in case."

"I reckon if I have to," she said with a mock sigh.

Bo took a sip of coffee and then said, "You know, we didn't quite finish making our rounds."

"I plumb forgot about it after that fella came sailin' through that plate-glass window," Scratch said. "How do you reckon he's doin'?"

"One of us ought to go down to the doc's and check on him."

"I'll do that," Rawhide volunteered. She left the office and headed for Dr. Summers' place. Reilly stayed to watch the prisoner, while Bo and Scratch walked down Main Street to the bridge and resumed making sure that the town was quiet and settled in for the night . . . or at least, as quiet and settled in as this section of the settlement was going to get. Laughter and tinkling music would be coming from some of the saloons and other "dens of iniquity" all night.

The two lawmen stayed together this time. As they passed the Royal Flush, they saw that the window through which Chesterfield Pike had tossed the luckless gambler was already boarded up. Dodge Emerson would have to get another pane of glass freighted up here from Santa Fe, which might be an expensive proposition. Bo recalled that Jonas McHale owned the local freight line. He was willing to bet that despite McHale's dislike for Emerson, the mayor would take the saloon keeper's money when it came to hauling freight.

They didn't run into any more trouble this time, and they had returned to the bridge and were walking over the creek when Bo suddenly paused.

"Hold on a minute," he told Scratch. As he came to a stop as well, Bo tilted his head a little and listened intently.

"What is it?" Scratch asked before he heard the sounds of hoofbeats . . . and they were headed toward the two deputies in a hurry.

The swift rataplan of a horse's hooves carried through the night air, growing louder as the rider approached Whiskey Flats from the south. The two men turned to look in that direction.

"Sounds like whoever it is, is in a mite of a hurry."

"A mighty big hurry," Bo agreed.

Scratch said, "A fella who's ridin' that fast is usually either runnin' away from trouble or headin' straight into it."

"Town's quiet now, so the trouble must be behind him."

"Sounds like one horse," Bo said before the rider had reached the southern end of Main Street. Bo and Scratch could see him now as a fast-moving shadow in the darkness, although there wasn't enough light to make out any details yet.

"Let's get off the bridge," Bo said. "Maybe we can stop him and find out what's going on."

They hurried off the planks and took up positions at the southern end of the bridge. The horse and rider thundered closer. Bo waved his arms over his head and shouted, "Hold it! Hold it there, mister! Rein in!"

"Stop in the name of the law!" Scratch added.

None of it did any good. The horse continued to bolt. Bo could see now that the rider was slumped forward over the animal's neck, apparently either unconscious or dead. There was no telling how long the horse had been running. It looked to be out of its head.

The horse pounded on across the bridge. The way it was going, it might have kept running all the way to Colorado, if not for the fact that the slight jolt of going onto and then off of the bridge had unbalanced the rider. He swayed to the side and then toppled off, landing in the street and rolling over and over. He was lucky that neither of his feet had caught in a stirrup, Bo thought as he and Scratch ran across the bridge. If that had happened, the rider likely would have been dragged to his death.

Assuming, of course, that he hadn't already crossed the divide . . .

Relieved of the burden it had been carrying, the panic-stricken horse finally slowed and then stopped. Even from this distance, Bo could hear the heaving of its labored breath. As they came closer, he saw that the horse wasn't wearing a saddle; that was why the rider hadn't gotten a foot caught in a stirrup. The animal had only a rope hackamore strapped on its head.

Bo was more interested in the rider, who lay motionless in the street. He and Scratch hurried toward the man. When they came closer, they could tell that the rider wasn't a man at all, but rather a boy in his early teens. He lay on his side, gasping for breath and moaning in pain. Bo felt a cold chill go through him at the side of the dark blotches on the boy's shirt. Those were bloodstains, he knew, which meant that the youngster was hurt.

"We need to be careful with him," Bo warned as he knelt beside the boy. "Scratch, strike a match."

Scratch took a lucifer from his pocket and snapped it into life with his thumbnail. The harsh glare from the sulfur match revealed the youngster's pale, haggard face. He was a towhead, thirteen or fourteen years old.

"I never saw him before," Scratch said. "But that ain't surprisin', seein' as how we ain't been around these parts for very long. You know him, Bo?"

Bo was carefully pulling aside the youngster's shirt to check the wounds. "No, I don't recognize him," he said. Relief was evident in his voice as he went on. "Looks like the bullet just knocked a chunk out of his side. Probably hurts like blazes and he's lost quite a bit of blood, but if we get him to the doc right away, I think he'll be all right."

"Are you sure he was shot?" Scratch asked.

"The best I can tell in this light," Bo said. "Give me a hand with him, and then see if you can catch his horse. Might give us a clue as to who he is, although I'm betting somebody around here will know him."

With Scratch's help, Bo lifted the limp form and cradled it in his arms. He started toward the doctor's office, which he had visited a couple of times before to make the acquaintance of Dr. Edwin Summers and to check on the wounded prisoners who were still at the doc's place. Scratch followed behind leading the boy's horse. The mount had been too exhausted to even shy away as Scratch caught hold of the trailing reins.

"Boy must'a been bound and determined to make it to town," Scratch said. "He managed to hang on to the reins even after he passed out, so the horse'd keep on runnin'."

"Yeah. I hope the doc can bring him around so he can tell us what he was running from."

As far as Bo could tell, there had been no immediate pursuit behind the boy. The night remained quiet, now that the pounding hoofbeats were stilled.

Of course, that didn't really mean anything. Deadly danger was often quiet, like a water moccasin sunning itself on a creek bank, or a scorpion crawling in a man's boot, or a bushwhacker clutching a rifle in his sweaty hands while he waited for a target to appear in his sights.

Dr. Edwin Summers was waiting on the porch of his house when Bo and Scratch arrived with the wounded youngster. Rawhide was with him. Bo recalled that Rawhide had come up here to check on the injured gambler.

Summers stepped forward and said in a mild, intelligent voice, "Bring him on inside, Mr. Creel."

"It looks like the boy has been shot," Bo said. "The slug left a pretty deep graze on his right side."

Summers nodded and stepped aside. He was a slender man of medium height, with thinning dark hair and a neat goatee. His thin face usually had a solemn cast to it, probably the result of all the pain and suffering he had seen in his medical career. Bo recalled Summers saying during a previous conversation that he had been a field surgeon for the Union Army during the Late Unpleasantness. Bo and Scratch had stayed out of that war, except for a few times they had given a hand to some Confederate intelligence agents on missions that brought them West. Being Texans, they had supported the South, but they didn't hold any man's being a Yankee against him.

Bo carried the youngster on into the house, the front several rooms of which contained Summers's medical practice. The doctor ushered them into a small room furnished with an examination table and several cabinets full of medicine and medical instruments. A couple of lamps hung from the ceiling so that the table was particularly well lit. Following Summers's orders, Bo placed the boy on the table and stepped back. He had blood on his hands. Summers handed him a clean towel to wipe them, then bent to examine the wound in the boy's side.

"My God," Rawhide said as she crowded into the room along with Scratch. "I know that kid. He's the Thompson boy. Lester Thompson, I think his name is. His family has a little spread south of here, what some folks call a greasy-sack outfit. They raise horses mostly."

Summers looked up from the table. "I concur with your diagnosis, Mr. Creel," he said. "The bullet didn't penetrate, simply plowed a furrow through the upper layers of flesh, causing blood loss and tissue damage. There was a time when such a wound might have proven fatal due to blood poisoning, but now, as long as it's cleaned properly and kept clean, I see no reason why the boy shouldn't recover." He unbuttoned his shirtsleeves and started rolling them up. "I'll get started right away."

Summers cut the rest of the bloodstained shirt away. As he did so, Bo asked, "When do you think he'll wake up so he can tell us what happened, Doc?"

"There's no way of knowing," Summers said with a shake of his head. "He's passed out from loss of blood. He might come around at any time, or he may not wake up until tomorrow morning."

He began using a wet cloth to swab away the dried blood around the wound. When he had done that, he soaked another cloth with carbolic acid and started cleaning the wound itself.

That must have hurt, because Lester Thompson groaned and shifted slightly on the table. Summers looked around and said, "You men hold him so he doesn't move around."

Bo and Scratch stepped forward to do so. As they gripped Lester's shoulders, Summers resumed wiping carefully at the wound, which slowly welled blood.

Suddenly, the boy's eyes popped open, his head jerked up, and he screamed.

A second later, however, it became obvious that he wasn't screaming in pain, even though what Summers was doing must have hurt. Instead, Lester Thompson cried out, "Injuns! Oh, God, Pa, watch out! Apaches!"

Then his head fell back to the table as unconsciousness claimed him again.

CHAPTER 18

A stunned silence filled the room, broken only by Lester's strained breathing. Finally, Dr. Summers spoke up.

"Did he say . . . Apaches?"

Scratch nodded and replied in a bleak voice, "That's what he said, all right."

"But I thought . . . Indians used bows and arrows."

"They did in the old days," Bo said, his tone as grim as his fellow Texan's had been. "Some still do. But the white man taught 'em how to use guns, too . . . along with a lot of other things they learned from us, like scalping and breaking treaties."

Scratch added, "Most 'Paches are as good or better with a rifle than most white men. Some of 'em even carry revolvers and can handle them pretty well, although I never saw one who claimed to be a fast draw. They don't go in for such boastfulness. They take their killin' seriouslike."

Rawhide had gone pale under her golden tan.

"There hasn't been any Indian trouble around here for a long time. Close to ten years probably."

"What about what happened to Harry Winston's wife?" Bo asked.

Rawhide grimaced at the memory. "That was just one lone renegade, off on a loco killin' spree. It's not anywhere near the same as a war party attacking a ranch."

"We don't know for sure that's what happened here," Scratch pointed out. "All we've got to go on is what one kid said, and he's probably out of his head from the pain of his wound."

"Lester Thompson's a pretty level-headed boy," Dr. Summers put in, and Rawhide nodded in agreement with that opinion. "I don't think he would have imagined such a thing as an Indian attack."

"There's only one way to find out for sure," Bo said. "We'll have to ride out to the Thompson spread and have a look. Let's head back to the office and inform the marshal."

"Tonight?" Reilly practically yelped after Bo finished telling him the facts. Bo wished he'd get his nerves under control. Rawhide might start to wonder why the famous fighting marshal was getting so antsy all of a sudden.

Bo didn't answer Reilly's question directly. Instead, he asked Rawhide, "How far from town is the Thompson place?"

"Eight or ten miles," the young woman replied. "It's

pretty much due south of Whiskey Flats, so you can't miss it."

"I hate to say it," Scratch drawled, "but in the time it took that younker to ride from there into town, whatever was happenin' at his folks' place got over and done with. We'll ride out there in the mornin' and see just how bad it is. Be enough light then to pick up the trail o' the war party, too."

Bo nodded. "Scratch is right." He left unsaid the fact that Lester's escape was a miracle. The Apaches wouldn't have left anybody alive out there.

But he wouldn't say that in front of Reilly, who already looked shaken enough.

Instead, he went on. "For now, it would probably be a good idea if we kept what we've heard here tonight to ourselves."

"You mean we shouldn't warn the townspeople that the Apaches are raiding again?" Rawhide shook her head. "I don't like the sound of that. Folks have a right to know if they're in danger."

"I don't think there's much danger of the town being attacked. Apache war parties are usually small. They target isolated ranches, like the Thompson spread."

"They ain't like the Comanch'," Scratch added. "I recollect a time, back when Bo and me were young, when a giant war party rode down out of Comancheria and raided all the way to the Gulf Coast, layin' waste to the towns they come to on the way. 'Paches don't hardly ever do anything like that."

Reilly said, "But they could."

Scratch shrugged. "Fella could go plumb loco

tryin' to predict what an Indian will do. You can't never tell."

Bo said, "But I can guarantee that if you start running up and down the street yelling about Apaches, you'll have a panic on your hands, and probably for no good reason. Let us check it out in the morning, and then we'll figure out what we need to do next."

Reilly must have realized that he hadn't been acting like the lawman he was supposed to be, because he squared his shoulders, gave a decisive nod, and said, "That's exactly right, Deputy. The last thing we need right now is for the citizens of Whiskey Flats to panic. We'll stand guard all night, though, so that just in case there's an attack, the town will have some advance warning."

"Good thinking, Marshal," Bo said. He had been about to suggest the same thing, but Reilly had beaten him to it for once. Maybe the young man was finally starting to think like the lawman he was supposed to be.

"I suspect that the kid will be awake in the morning, if you want to talk to him before we ride out to his parents' ranch," Bo told Reilly. "Dr. Summers couldn't guarantee it, though, and he won't allow the kid to be disturbed if he's still resting."

"I reckon we've already got an idea what we're gonna find out there," Scratch added. "And it ain't gonna be anything good . . ."

The four of them switched off standing guard during the night, two at a time, one at each end of town. Just because the Apaches had attacked a ranch south of Whiskey Flats didn't necessarily mean that any attack on the settlement would come from that direction.

Since Scratch and Rawhide had worked together before, Bo suggested that the two of them take the first turn before Reilly could suggest that he and the young woman stand guard together. Bo figured that Reilly was too nervous about the Indians to get any romantic notions, and anyway, they would have been at opposite ends of the town, but in the long run it was better not to put temptation in Jake Reilly's path. He didn't have a good history of resisting it.

Reilly went to his room in the hotel to get a little sleep. Bo stayed in the marshal's office and jail, where Chesterfield Pike was still snoring peacefully, if loudly. Like most frontiersmen, Bo had picked up the knack of being able to doze off wherever and whenever he got the chance, so Pike's stentorian rumbling didn't disturb him at all. He took off his hat and coat—but not his gunbelt and boots—stretched out on one of the cots, and was asleep in less than a minute.

He slept dreamlessly until Scratch woke him with a hand on the shoulder and a low-voiced word. Bo came awake instantly, fully alert, another trait that most men in the West developed if they wanted to live very long.

"Everything's quiet," Scratch reported. "I ain't seen hide nor hair of any hostiles, and neither has the gal."

Bo swung his legs off the cot and stood up, stretching muscles that grew stiff every time he slept, no matter how comfortable the bed. That was just one of the prices a man had to pay for growing old.

"Doesn't surprise me," he said. "I figure it was a fairly small group of bucks. They wouldn't want anything to do with taking on a town this size."

"Want me to go wake up the kid?" Bo knew that Scratch meant Reilly.

"No, I'll do it," he said with a shake of his head.

Scratch grunted agreement. "I'll turn in then. I ain't so young as I used to be. These night watches get to be a mite long and tedious."

Bo knew the feeling. He put on his hat, shrugged into his coat, and left the marshal's office. By the time he went out the door, Scratch's snores were playing harmony with Chesterfield Pike's.

At this hour of the morning, the street on this end of town was quiet and dark, although a few lamps turned low still burned in a few of the buildings, and the lobby of the hotel was lit up. As Bo passed the alley that ran next to the Morning Glory Café, he glanced along it and saw a light burning in the kitchen window. Velma Dearborn and Ole Borglund were probably in there already, preparing for breakfast. Running a café in a frontier town meant long, hard hours.

At least, the window of the room where Harry Winston was staying was dark. Bo hoped that meant the former lawyer—and future judge, if everything went as planned—was sleeping. Winston ought to be getting over the worst of his sickness soon. Bo hoped that he wouldn't hear about the Apache raid on the Thompson ranch. Such a reminder of what happened to his wife might set him back and cause him to lose all the progress he had made so far. That was another reason for keeping the news quiet for now.

He went into the hotel lobby, which was deserted at this time of night. Keeping his steps light, Bo ascended the stairs and paused in front of the door to Reilly's room. He rapped softly on it.

Reilly didn't answer. Bo knocked again and called, "Marshal? It's Bo Creel."

Still no reply. Bo tried the door and found it unlocked. He opened it and stepped into the dark room, feeling his skin crawling as he did so. He had never liked setups like this. His hand dropped to the butt of his gun and his fingers closed around the walnut grips.

A raspy snore came from the bed.

Bo relaxed and grinned to himself. Everybody in Whiskey Flats was sawing logs tonight. The lamps in the hallway were out, but enough light came from downstairs for him to be able to make out Reilly's sleeping form in the bed. Bo stepped over to him and gave his shoulder a shake.

"Rise and shine, Marshal," he said.

Reilly let out a howl like Comaches had staked him out on an anthill, and went straight up in the air. "Indians!" he yelled.

Even though Bo was startled, he reacted quickly. He grabbed Reilly, pushed him back down in the bed, and clamped a hand over his mouth.

"Hush!" Bo hissed as he leaned over Reilly, who had started to struggle frantically, clearly confused about what was going on. "Marshal, it's me, Bo! Settle down now!"

Reilly's eyes were so wide that a ring of white showed all the way around them. He must have been having a humdinger of a nightmare, Bo thought, probably about being chased by savages.

But as the seconds passed, he stopped fighting. Bo put his mouth close to Reilly's ear and asked, "Are you all right now, Marshal? You know who I am?"

He felt Reilly's head bob up and down, and took his hand away from the young man's mouth. Reilly didn't say anything, just panted for breath.

Bo hoped the outcry hadn't waked up half the guests in the hotel. Reilly's voice had been strangled as he yelled, and even though Bo had understood what Reilly said, maybe anybody who happened to hear it would have taken it for the incoherent yelp some people let out upon waking up from a bad dream. Bo listened intently for any reaction. The rest of the hotel remained quiet and peaceful.

With a sigh of relief, Bo went on. "Time to wake up and stand our turn on guard, Marshal. Scratch and Rawhide didn't have any trouble during their turn."

Reilly sat up and scrubbed a hand over his face. "I was dreaming," he muttered. "This big Indian . . . as big as Chesterfield Pike . . . was trying to scalp me." He looked up at Bo. "Indians don't grow that big, do they?"

"Some do," Bo answered honestly, "but it's rare, just like it's rare to see a white man as big as Pike. Anyway, you don't have to worry about an Indian like that scalping you."

"Why not?"

Scratch was usually the jokester of the pair, but this time Bo couldn't resist. "Because any Indian that big would probably just pull your arms right off and beat you to death with them."

Reilly shuddered and didn't look amused at all.

Reilly's outburst was the most excitement either of them had the rest of the night. Whiskey Flats continued its tranquil slumber until the sky turned gray with the approach of dawn and folks started moving around. Bo, Scratch, Reilly, and Rawhide met at the marshal's office, Rawhide knuckling sleep out of her eyes as she came in.

"I stopped by Doc Summers' place, and Lester isn't awake yet. Doc says we can't wake him up either because he needs all the rest he can get. So do we get mounted up and ride out to the Thompson spread to find out what happened?" she asked.

"You don't," Reilly said. "We do."

Bo had discussed the plan with him before they returned to the marshal's office. Reilly didn't like it, since it involved him possibly putting himself in danger, but Bo had convinced him there was no way the townspeople would continue to accept him as John Henry Braddock if he shirked his duty.

"I'm not sure this even *is* my duty," Reilly had argued. "I'm the town marshal, remember. According to Rawhide, that ranch is eight or ten miles out of town."

Bo had shaken his head and said, "Doesn't matter.

You're the law in these parts now. You handle any trouble that might affect the town, even if technically it's not in your jurisdiction. That's why we need to get to the bottom of that rustling business, and we sure can't let an Apache war party go gallivanting around the countryside without even at least seeing what they've done."

"Yeah, yeah, I guess," Reilly had muttered, but he wasn't happy about it.

Just like Rawhide wasn't happy now about being left behind. "I told you that I wasn't gonna let you stick me here at the jail all the time," she said. "And now what do you do first thing?" She threw her hands in the air in exasperation.

"This is different, Rawhide," Bo told her calmly. "We may run into a whole band of Apache out there. I'm sorry, but no man is going to let a woman deliberately risk that."

"Especially not a Texan," Scratch added.

"Besides," Reilly said, "we have a prisoner here, remember? Somebody has to keep an eye on Pike. I want to keep him locked up here for another day, if we can, so when you talk to Jonas McHale about a hearing, see if he can't come up with some reason to postpone it for a day or two."

"Chesterfield won't like it, and neither will Dodge Emerson. He'll have that tame lawyer of his, Carrothers, up here spouting all sorts of habeas corpus malarkey and things like that."

"You'll just have to fend him off," Reilly said. "Tell him that you can't take the responsibility for making any decisions. Tell him I told you to keep Pike locked up, and that's it."

Rawhide continued to fume, but after a few minutes she agreed disgustedly to stay in Whiskey Flats. "But it's not fair, the three of you ridin' off to have all the fun!"

As the men headed for the livery stable, Scratch said, "I don't know what that gal expects us to find out there, but I'm sure as hell willin' to bet that it won't be fun!"

CHAPTER 19

They took their Winchesters and plenty of ammunition as they rode out of Whiskey Flats, heading south. McHale wasn't at the livery stable to ask where they were going, and Bo was grateful for that. He supposed that it was too early for the mayor to be stirring. Old Ike the hostler was there, though, and was clearly curious, but he didn't ask any questions.

Bo had a feeling that he would soon be scurrying around the settlement telling everyone he ran into that the new marshal and his deputies had ridden out of town armed and loaded for bear.

Or Apache, as the case might be.

"I'm still not sure about this," Reilly said as they rode along, generally following the course of the meandering stream that looped through Whiskey Flats and divided the town into two distinct sections. "I mean, Indian fighting doesn't fall under a marshal's normal duties, does it? Shouldn't we be getting the army to chase those Apaches or something?"

"We'll be a lot more likely to get some action out

of the army if we have something specific to report to them," Bo said.

"In other words," Scratch said, "those soldier boys don't like to jump until they know what they're jump-in' into."

"Well, what if the Indians are still there?" Reilly in-sisted.

"Don't worry, we won't just ride in blind," Bo assured him. "We'll do a little scouting first."

When Bo and Scratch thought that they had covered enough ground to be getting close to the Thompson ranch, they slowed their pace and began dismounting and checking before they topped each hill or rounded each sharp bend in the trail. It was still only mid-morning when Scratch came back down the slope of a wooded ridge on foot and said, "The spread's on the other side, about five hundred yards away." His voice held a tone of disgust as he added, "I didn't see nothin' movin' around except some buzzards."

Bo nodded grimly. "About what we expected." He pulled his rifle from its saddle sheath. "We'll go in slow and easy, ready for trouble."

Reilly nodded. He looked a little pale but deter-mined as he drew his own Winchester. "If you fellas are sure about this," he muttered. "After all these chances we've wound up taking since we came to Whiskey Flats, though, there had better be a damned good payoff when we get to the end of this."

"There will be," Bo promised.

Scratch mounted up again and they edged their horses forward, riding to the top of the ridge. Now all three men could see the layout. Rawhide had described the Thompson ranch as a greasy-sack outfit . . . a small ranch usually operated by a family, where the men would carry their lunch in a sack when they set out on the day's work, rather than returning to headquarters for the midday meal.

The Thompson place certainly qualified. The main house, from the looks of it once a sturdy log structure, was now a burned-out shell. The same was true of the barn and the other outbuildings. The raiders had set them on fire before leaving. The lack of a bunkhouse told Bo and Scratch that all the hands had lived in the main house and were probably related. They had seen dozens, maybe hundreds, of small spreads like this, both in Texas and in their wanderings elsewhere on the frontier.

"You were right," Bo said quietly to Scratch. "Nothing moving. They've been here and gone, just like we thought."

Scratch motioned to Reilly. "Spread out some. We want distance between us while we ride down there. No reason to clump up and give anybody who might be lurkin' around a bunch o' easy targets."

"I thought you said they were gone," Reilly said.

"Sometimes the next day, an Indian will come back to a place he's raided, just on the chance that he might be able to jump anybody who comes to check on it," Bo explained. "That doesn't mean they're here. Might not be an Apache within twenty miles."

"But that don't mean they *ain't* here either," Scratch added. "That's why we're bein' careful."

The riders spaced themselves out about twenty yards apart as they started down the slope toward the ranch. Their eyes moved constantly, always on the alert for any sign of danger. An eerie quiet hung over the place, broken only by the angry cries and flapping wings of the buzzards who rose into the air when the humans came too close.

Bo pointed to a couple of bloody, furry shapes and called, "There are the dogs. Looks like they've been shot to pieces."

"Man just inside the door of the barn," Scratch said as he pointed with his rifle. "He was probably runnin' out to see what was goin' on when they shot him. The slugs knocked him over backward."

"Where are the rest of the people?" Reilly asked. "I only see the one man Scratch pointed out."

"There's a fella by the corral," Bo said.

"I don't see . . . you mean that pile of rags?"

"Those ain't rags," Scratch said. "The 'Paches skinned him, bit by bit. That's what's left."

Reilly looked like he was going to be sick.

"That's a bad way to die," Bo said.

"One of the worst," Scratch agreed. He was even with the front door of the house now, so he reined to a halt and swung down from the saddle. Still holding his Winchester ready for instant use, he stepped to the doorway and peered inside for a long moment.

"Anything?" Bo called.

Scratch grunted. "Hard to tell because of the fire. Looks like a couple o' women . . . three . . . no, make that four little'uns . . . and a couple o' half-growed boys. From the looks of it, I expect they put up a hell of a fight."

Bo walked his horse over and stopped to look

around the place for another minute or so. Then he pointed toward the barn.

"Lester and his pa were in there tending to their evening chores. Somebody in the house spotted the Indians sneaking in and yelled. Thompson ran out and ran right into a bullet, like you said, Scratch. Before he died, he told Lester to grab a horse and ride for help. I reckon Lester didn't want to go, but he's a good boy and did what his pa told him. One of the Apaches winged him when he made his dash, but that didn't stop him. Then they laid siege to the house, and finally either got inside or just set it on fire and let that do the job for them. We'll know more when we get the bodies out to bury them."

Reilly listened to Bo's recreation of the attack and then asked, "How in the hell do you know all that?"

"Some of it's an educated guess," Bo admitted, "but the tracks tell the rest of the story. There were nine of the Apaches—"

"I make it ten," Scratch said.

"Nine or ten Apaches," Bo said. "Most of them, maybe all of them, were armed with Winchesters."

Reilly shook his head. "You can't possibly know that."

"Look at all the brass layin' around," Scratch said. "An Injun's got no way o' reloadin' cartridges, so he leaves his empty shells where they fall when the rifle kicks 'em out. There are enough of them around so that there had to be quite a few guns bein' used. Open your eyes, Marshal."

Reilly flushed angrily. "You can't expect me to know all this. I'm not a damned marshal! I'm a gambler."

"And a crook," Scratch drawled. "Don't forget that."

Frustrated, Reilly turned to Bo. "What was that about finding out whether the Indians got inside the house before they burned it down?"

"That's a good question. That's how you learn things, Jake, by asking questions."

"And by watchin' hombres who already know what they're doin', like me and Bo," Scratch said.

"If it's such a good question, what's the damn answer?"

Bo sighed. "If the children each have a single bullet hole in the head, it means the women finished them off before they could die in the fire and before the Apaches could get them. If that's the case, the women probably died of gunshot wounds to the head, too."

Scratch said, "But I'll bet those older boys went down fightin'. I just got a feelin' about 'em. That Lester's plenty tough, ridin' all the way into town with that bullet wound in his side, and odds are those other hombres were his brothers."

Reilly stared at the Texans. "My God. You sound almost proud of them."

"We are proud of them," Bo said. "How a man dies is sometimes just as important as how he lived. In a case like this, where those boys didn't get to live out their full span, the way they died is even more important."

"They stood up and fought," Scratch said. "Empty shells all around both of 'em. They didn't ask for what came at 'em, but they didn't run from it either." The silver-haired Texan spat on the ground. "Man who turns and runs from trouble ain't worthy o' being called a man. Lowest thing on the face o' the earth as far as I'm concerned. But I can tell you one thing right now . . . those two boys were *men*."

Bo nodded solemnly.

Reilly just shook his head. "I don't understand. Dead's dead, no matter how you got that way."

"You live long enough, you'll figure it out," Bo told him. He clapped a hand on Reilly's shoulder and went on. "We've got some burying to do."

"We're not going back to town to get the undertaker?"

"This was their home," Scratch said. "They died fightin' for it. Reckon this is where they'd want to be."

By the middle of the day, the ashes had cooled enough for Bo and Scratch to retrieve the bodies from the house. They had spent the time before that burying the man they had found just inside the barn and the one who had fallen beside the corral. They had buried the dogs as well, knowing that the animals had died fighting against the invaders and deserved to be laid to rest properly.

Reilly helped with that work, although he looked sickened during most of it. He refused to go into the house to help bring out the women and children, though.

"I can't do it," he declared. "Sorry, but I just can't."

"You'll learn one o' these days that there are a heap of hard, unpleasant chores in this life," Scratch told him. "Best to just face 'em head-on and get through 'em the best you can as quick as you can."

Reilly shook his head. "Maybe you're right," he admitted grudgingly, "but this is one chore I can't do yet."

Faced with that refusal to help, Bo and Scratch just carried on, since there was nothing else they could do.

As they had suspected, the younger children inside the house had each died of a gunshot to the head, one or both of the women choosing to spare them the agonies of dying in the fire. The women had given themselves the same mercy, one falling with a bullet in the back of the head, the other—the last one—snuffing out her own life with a shot to the temple. Probably the two teenage boys at the windows were dead by then, killed by Apache bullets. Bo couldn't imagine the horror that lone woman must have felt, surrounded by flames and by the bodies of her loved ones, in that moment before she pulled the trigger and ended it all. That final shot had been mercy indeed.

They couldn't dig graves for everybody, so they buried the little ones together, the boys in one grave, the women in another, the men in yet another. It wasn't a very satisfactory arrangement, but it was the best they could do. When they were finished and all the dirt had been heaped over the fresh graves, Bo and Scratch took off their hats, prompting Reilly to do so as well. The young man even bowed his head this time as Bo said a prayer for the souls of those who had died here. That was progress, Bo thought after he'd said "Amen." Reilly wasn't thinking only of himself all the time anymore.

Reilly turned away from the graves and lifted his hat to put it on, when a rifle suddenly cracked and a bullet tore the black Stetson from his hand. He let out a startled yelp and dived for the ground, even as Bo and Scratch slapped leather and spun toward the sound of the shot. Another rifle spat leaden death behind them, though, and only a swift, instinctive move by Scratch kept the bullet from hitting him. One of the pieces of fringe on his jacket jumped a little as the slug tugged at it.

"Spread out!" Bo called as he snapped a shot toward a flicker of movement at the corner of the barn. "Move, Jake! Don't let 'em pin you down!"

From the corner of his eye Bo saw Reilly scramble to his feet and dash for cover, triggering his six-gun as he ran. Reilly flung himself behind the horse trough near the barn, which had survived the fire and had been left alone by the Apaches except for defecating in the water to foul it.

Scratch, meanwhile, rolled under the bottom rail of the empty corral and came up in a crouch behind one of the corner posts. The post didn't provide much cover, but the silver-haired Texan didn't need much. As a bullet struck the post and sent splinters flying in the air, Scratch drew a bead and fired. He was rewarded by the sight of an Indian jerking back into cover behind some brush, his bullet-busted arm flopping limply as he did so.

That Apache wasn't dead, though, just wounded, so he couldn't be counted out of the fight. Scratch knew that, and took advantage of the brief respite to rattle his hocks and head for the far side of the corral.

Bo had cut away from the graves at an angle, putting some distance between himself and Scratch and Reilly. With bullets kicking up dirt and pebbles around his feet, he made it to some pines and ducked behind the shelter of the thick trunks.

The way the shots had been ringing out, it was impossible to tell for sure just how many attackers there were. Bo guessed three or four, which meant that he and his companions were pretty evenly matched. At the moment, though, he, Scratch, and Reilly were armed only with handguns. They had put their Winchesters back in the saddle sheaths while they worked on the graves. Since they were facing enemies with rifles, that put them at a disadvantage.

Nothing they could do except try to make the best of it, though. Bo began working his way through the trees, moving carefully and using every bit of cover he could find. Bullets hummed through the branches, but the riflemen were firing blindly, hoping to score with a lucky shot.

Over by the barn, Reilly lay on his belly behind the water trough, Colt clutched tightly in his hand. A few bullets had struck the heavy wooden trough, but they didn't penetrate.

A sudden cracking sound came from behind Reilly, causing him to roll over onto his back. It was the right reaction, because a rifle spouted flame in the ruins of the barn and the bullet smacked into the ground where Reilly had been lying. He jerked up his gun as he saw the Apache trying to lever the Winchester he had just fired. In the back of Reilly's mind, he knew the Indian must have stepped on a partially burned timber that had cracked the rest of the way under his weight, producing that warning sound.

He didn't take the time right then to ponder on that,

though, because he was too busy squeezing the Colt's trigger. It roared and bucked twice in his hand, and the Apache, clad in blue tunic, breechcloth, and buckskin leggings, was driven backward by the bullets plowing into his chest.

Scratch was making for the corner of the barn when he heard the shots and glanced over to see Reilly firing into the ruins. He didn't have a chance to see how that turned out because he reached the corner of the barn and ducked down behind the partially collapsed wall. The last time he'd seen the 'Pache he'd winged, the varmint had been coming this way. He heard a rustling in the brush now and turned in that direction.

Instinct warned him at the last second, or maybe it was a slight sound. Scratch ducked, and the Indian who had tried to lunge over the top of the ruined wall and grab him from behind got air instead. Scratch reached up, clamped his free hand around the Apache's arm, and hauled him forward over the wall.

The Indian sprawled on the ground as Scratch twisted hard on the arm he held, pressing it beyond the endurance of flesh and muscle and bone. The Indian screamed as his elbow dislocated.

Scratch stepped back and covered him. He saw that this was the Apache he had wounded before, as he had thought it would be. Now the hombre had two bum arms and wouldn't be a threat anymore.

That was what Scratch thought anyway. Even in agonizing pain from the bullet wound in one arm and the dislocated elbow on the other, the Indian came up off the ground and charged at Scratch, lowering his head as if he intended to butt the Texan in the chest.

"Damn it, don't make me shoot you!" Scratch yelled as he grabbed the Apache's tunic, used the man's own momentum against him, and flung him over the top of the wall.

There was a sickening sound as the Indian landed, and when Scratch looked over the top of the collapsed wall, he exclaimed in disgust, "Dadgum it!"

The Apache had fallen on a jagged piece of timber sticking up from the ruins, and his weight had been enough to drive the sharp wood right through his body. He was still alive, jerking and twitching as he stared at the bloody piece of wreckage protruding a good four inches from his chest. Scratch had time now to note that he was young, probably not out of his teens.

As Scratch watched, the Apache gave a bubbling sigh and then his head fell back in death. Scratch shook his head and started to turn away. He wouldn't have killed a helpless man intentionally, even one who'd taken part in the atrocity that had happened here at the Thompson ranch. Sometimes fate had other things in mind, though.

Like one of the bastards sneaking up on him and drawing a bead on him. Scratch knew as soon as he saw the Indian peering at him over the barrel of a rifle that he was done for. He didn't have time to raise the Remington and fire before the Apache could drill him.

The shot that blasted out didn't come from the Indian, though. Scratch saw the man's head jerk sideways as blood spurted out. The Apache folded up, dropping the rifle before he could pull the trigger.

Bo stepped out from behind a tree, lowering his

Colt, and Scratch said, "You took your damn time about it."

"If you want to overwhelm somebody with gratitude, better look the other way," Bo said with a nod toward the water trough. "I would've gotten here too late."

Scratch looked over and saw Reilly peering over the top of the trough. Smoke curled from the gun in the young man's fist. Scratch realized now that Bo was on the wrong side of the Apache to have fired the fatal shot.

"You mean *he* saved my life?" Scratch asked.

Bo grinned. "I reckon so."

Reilly looked and sounded amazed as he said, "I hit him! I aimed and all, but I didn't think I'd actually hit him. I just wanted to distract him."

"You distracted him pretty much to death," Scratch said. "And I'm obliged, Reilly. I really am."

Reilly looked around, suddenly worried again. "Are there any more of them?"

"If there were, they'd be shooting at us by now," Bo said as he walked toward the Indian Reilly had shot. He toed the man over onto his back. "Just a kid. Not more than sixteen, I reckon."

Scratch nodded. "Same with the one I killed in the barn. Might've been a little older than that, but not much. They must've been with the war party last night and couldn't resist comin' back today to see the results o' their handiwork." The Texan spat. "The older bucks had sense enough to stay away. Comin' back cost these young ones their lives."

Reilly got to his feet. "You killed one in the barn?

I killed one in the barn." His eyes widened. "Hey, I just realized . . . I got two out of the three of them. How about that?"

"Who gets how many ain't important," Scratch said. "What matters is that they're dead and we ain't."

Bo frowned. "Wish we could've taken one of them alive." He bent to pick up the rifle the Apache had dropped. "I'd like to know where they got these nice new Winchesters."

"Don't you reckon they stole 'em somewhere?" Scratch asked.

Bo shook his head. "Not rifles this new. I'd be willing to bet not more than fifty rounds have been fired from this gun. Let's check the others."

They found the Winchesters that had been used by the other two Indians, and the weapons were just as new and shiny as the first one Bo had looked at. A lot newer and shinier than the ones carried by Reilly and the Texans, in fact.

"Well, son of a bitch," Scratch said as the three of them gathered around to examine the weapons. "You know what this means, Bo."

Sounding irritated and impatient, Reilly said, "He may know, but I sure as hell don't. What are you two looking so grim about?"

"I haven't heard anything about any shipments of rifles being stolen in these parts lately," Bo said. "That means there's probably only one way these Apaches got their hands on these guns . . . somebody sold them to them."

CHAPTER 20

Reilly looked confused as usual. "What do you mean, sold them to them?" he asked. "Who'd sell guns to the Apaches? Surely you don't mean a white man would do something like that!"

"A white man who didn't give a damn about anything 'cept the money he could make from the deal," Scratch said. He added bitingly, "Fella like you ought to be able to understand that."

"What are you—" Reilly's eyes widened as he figured out what Scratch meant. "Why, of all the—Damn it, I never did anything as bad as selling guns to the Indians! None of my cons cost anybody their lives. These poor people might've died because those Apaches had new rifles. If they hadn't been so well armed, the Thompsons might have been able to fight them off!"

"You've swindled money from people who couldn't afford to lose it," Bo pointed out. "You don't know what effect that had on them. You had your loot, so you took off for the tall and uncut and never looked back."

Reilly glared at him. "So what? I'm not responsible for the well-being of every fool in the world! Anyway, you're a fine one to talk, Creel. You're the one who came up with the idea of me pretending to be John Henry Braddock so that we could make a killing from the people of Whiskey Flats!"

Bo shrugged and said, "Maybe so. We all have lapses."

"Not to hear you talk," Reilly shot back as he flung out a hand. "To hear you and Scratch tell it, you're both perfect! You know all there is to know about the frontier and how real men act! Well, blast it, I'm getting tired of it! I can be just as much of a man as either of you two!"

Scratch grunted. "I'll believe *that* when I see it."

Reilly's jaw jutted out belligerently. "Maybe you *will* see it. I say we find out who sold those guns to the Apaches and bring the son of a bitch to justice!"

"That's what you want to do?" Bo asked.

"Damn straight."

Bo rubbed his chin, apparently deep in thought. "It might mean postponing our original plans . . ."

"I don't care about that right now," Reilly snapped. "I'm tired of that superior attitude you and Scratch have all the time. I say we find those gunrunning skunks, no matter how long it takes!"

"Might help Rawhide run those rustlers to ground, too," Scratch suggested.

"Fine by me!" Reilly said.

Bo nodded. "All right then. We'll do it. For the time

being, we'll do more than act like real lawmen. We'll *be* real lawmen, as much as if you were really John Henry Braddock, Jake."

Reilly gave an emphatic nod of his own and said, "Now you're talking." He reached out to take the new Winchester Bo was holding. "We'd better play our cards pretty close to the vest, though. Whiskey Flats is the only settlement in these parts, so it's possible that somebody in town might be mixed up in selling these guns to the Indians."

"Somebody like that Emerson fella," Scratch said. "He seemed pretty slick, like the sort o' gent who might do something like that."

"We'll find out," Bo vowed. "But for now, Jake's right. We'll keep our suspicions to ourselves. We can tell folks in town about what happened here without mentioning the new Winchesters." He gestured toward the nearest of the dead Apaches. "We need to do something about these hombres, too. Nobody in town has to know about our fracas with them yet."

Scratch jerked a thumb over his shoulder. "We passed a nice deep ravine back that way. Drop 'em in there and nobody'd find 'em for a while . . . if ever."

Bo grimaced in distaste, but he nodded. "It's the practical solution," he said. "Let's take care of that, then head back to the settlement."

"Did they have any horses?" Reilly asked.

"Unlikely," Bo replied. "Apaches have a taste for horse meat, but not much use for them as mounts. An Apache warrior in his prime can trot all day and cover as much or more ground than a good saddle horse."

"We'll have to haul the bodies to that ravine on our horses," Scratch said. "I don't much cotton to that idea, but we don't have any choice."

They loaded the bodies on their horses. The animals were made skittish by the smell of blood, but Bo, Scratch, and Reilly were able to control them. As they started off toward the ravine, Reilly said, "I've noticed something about you two."

"What's that?" Scratch asked, sounding as if he didn't really want to know.

"Everywhere you go, sooner or later there are dead bodies to take care of."

Scratch sighed. "I know, and it's a plumb vexation, because we're peaceable men. Ain't that right, Bo?"

"Peaceable men," Bo agreed. "You can ask anybody."

"Not anybody," Reilly said with a shake of his head. He pointed toward the corpses. "You can't ask *them*, now can you?"

It was mid-afternoon when the three men rode back into Whiskey Flats, and one look at the townspeople calmly going about their business was enough to tell Bo that Rawhide and Doc Summers had succeeded in keeping the news of the Apache raid on the Thompson ranch a secret.

It couldn't stay under wraps forever, though. The folks who lived here had a right to know that they might be in danger, and besides, as Bo and Scratch and Reilly had discussed on the ride back into town, if someone in Whiskey Flats really *was* involved with selling rifles to the Apaches, it might be easier to flush him out if they revealed what had happened to the Thompson family.

Accordingly, they planned to talk to Mayor Jonas McHale and have him call a town meeting, at which Reilly could announce what had happened. Before that, though, they wanted to check in with Rawhide Abbott and find out if anything new had happened while they were gone.

Naturally enough, folks noticed their return, and as Bo had suspected, Ike had done his gossipy work well. Everyone was curious about why the three lawmen had ridden out early that morning, before most people were up. Reilly turned aside the questions that were called out to them from the boardwalk and asked by people in the street. His strength was responding to anything that called for a glib response. They reined in at the marshal's office and dismounted, leaving their horses at the hitch rail as they went inside.

Bo stopped short as he saw that the office was empty. The door to the cell block was open, though, and Chesterfield Pike's rumbling voice called from back there, "Hey, did somebody just come in?"

"Where's Rawhide?" Reilly asked as he stepped into the office. "I thought we told her to stay here."

"Might've been some trouble elsewhere in town," Bo said. "She might have felt that as a deputy she had to go see about it."

"Some commotion south o' the bridge, I'll bet," Scratch suggested.

Pike said, "If you fellas'll just come on back here, I'll tell you where Miss Rawhide went."

Bo and Scratch looked at each other and shrugged. Along with Reilly, they went into the cell block.

Pike stood there seeming to fill up the cell with his massive body. Both hands gripped the bars of the door, and he looked like he could simply tear it off its hinges without much effort. He said, "It's gettin' on past dinnertime. Is Miz Velma gonna bring me my food again? I surely do like her and her cookin'. She brought my breakfast this mornin'."

"Forget about eating for a minute," Reilly snapped. "You said you'd tell us where Rawhide is."

Pike scratched his head. "Oh, yeah. A fella came in and told her there'd been some more rustlin' somewhere . . . lemme see if I can recollect where . . . oh, yeah, someplace called the Star Ranch. The fella must'a been the owner, 'cause he sure was mad about his cows gettin' stole. Said him and his men was gonna ride over to the Rocking B and burn it down 'cause he was tired o' those no-good rustlin' skunks o' Bascomb's gettin' away with it." A big grin stretched across Pike's ugly face. "Say, I remembered that pretty good, didn't I?"

Bo, Scratch, and Reilly looked at each other in alarm. "How long ago did this happen?" Bo asked.

Pike's grin disappeared. "Hell, how would I know? I ain't got a watch, and I've dozed off a mite since then. Nothin' else to do in here. Say, I thought there was supposed to be a trial or somethin'. That tinhorn gambler needs to get what's comin' to him."

"Never mind that," Reilly said. "There'll be a trial soon enough." He turned to the Texans. "It's the middle of the afternoon now. North had to have come in sometime after we left." He looked at the prisoner again. "What did Rawhide say to the man who came in?"

"Well, she told him not to fly off the handle. Said she'd take care o' things 'cause she was a deputy now. The fella just laughed at that, though, and said he'd never heard of no gal deputy before. He left out right after that, and so did Miss Rawhide." A worried look began to form on Pike's face. "Say, Miss Rawhide's all right, ain't she? She's always been nice to me ever' time I come into town, one o' the few folks who treat me decent."

Reilly ignored him and said to Bo and Scratch, "What do you think she'd do in a situation like that?"

"You know damned well what that redheaded firebrand would do," Scratch said. "She lit a shuck for Bascomb's place, figurin' that she'd beat North and his crew there and try to head off the range war."

"I agree," Bo said, a look of concern on his face to rival Pike's. "We'd better get out there as fast as we can."

Reilly nodded, but said, "Yeah, there's one problem with that. I don't know where Bascomb's ranch is. Do either of you?"

Bo and Scratch looked at each other. Their silence was all the answer that was needed.

"Well," Bo said, "we'll have to ask somebody . . ."

"I can take you," Pike said.

They turned to look at him again. "You know where Chet Bascomb's ranch is?" Bo asked.

Pike nodded. "Sure. I know ever'body in these

parts. I just don't care to have much to do with 'em mostly. And sometimes I have trouble recollectin' names, mind you, but now that I think about it, I know where to find the Rocking B, and the Star Ranch, too. Lemme out and I'll show you."

Bo wasn't sure whether to believe the giant or not. It might be that Pike was just looking for a way to get out of the cell without having to bust out. But under the circumstances, they didn't have much choice. He glanced at Scratch, knowing from long experience that the same thoughts would be going through his trail partner's head. The silver-haired Texan nodded, signifying that he had reached the same conclusions.

"I'll get the keys," Bo said.

Chesterfield Pike's big mule had been taken to the livery stable the night before. Scratch went to fetch it, along with fresh horses for Bo, Reilly, and himself. Their regular mounts had already made the ride to the Thompson ranch today, and they weren't up to another hard run just yet.

Mayor McHale was in his office at the stable, but came out when he heard Scratch's voice. "Deputy Morton," he said briskly, without any greeting, "I heard that you and Marshal Braddock and Deputy Creel rode out early this morning as if there were some sort of trouble. What's going on?"

"Sorry, Mayor," Scratch said. "Ain't got time to talk about it right now. Me and Bo and the marshal got things under control, though, you can count on that."

McHale frowned. "That doesn't reassure me much,

Deputy. As mayor, I want to know what *things* you have under control."

"You'll have to take that up with the marshal." The horses and Pike's mule were saddled by now, and Scratch took all the reins from Ike. "We got to skedaddle."

"Deputy Morton!"

Scratch ignored McHale as he turned and led the animals away from the livery barn. The mayor could get red-faced and huffy all he wanted to, as far as Scratch was concerned. They had a range war to head off, not to mention keeping Rawhide Abbott from getting her pretty little hide shot full of holes.

By the time he got back to the marshal's office with the mounts, Pike had been let out of the cell and stood in the office stretching his back and swinging his tree-trunklike arms around. "Them cells is a mite crowded for a fella o' my size," Pike complained. "You need to make 'em bigger."

"You need to stop doing things to get arrested for," Bo told him. "That would solve the problem."

"I leave folks alone if they leave me alone. I never would'a thrown that gambler through the window if he hadn't tried to cheat me."

Bo shrugged. "I reckon you've got a point there. But as big and strong as you are, Chesterfield, you've got to realize that you can't just go around throwing people through windows and things like that. You might kill somebody one of these days, and I don't think you really want that. You might like to brawl a little now and then, but you're not a murderer."

Pike's shaggy eyebrows drew down. "I never murdered nobody!"

"And I'm sure you'd like to keep it that way. So think next time before you let your temper get the best of you."

"What are you, a preacher?" Pike looked Bo up and down. "You look a mite like a preacher with that black suit on."

Bo smiled. "Nope, just a deputy who just as soon not have to lock you up again any time soon."

Reilly was starting to look impatient. "Come on," he said. "We need to get moving. Rawhide's out there somewhere, maybe in the middle of a gun battle."

That put a look of concern on Pike's face, too. "The marshal's right," he declared. "We're wastin' time with all this jawin'."

The four men went outside and swung up into their saddles. They drew plenty of attention as they rode out of town, heading north. For the second time today, Whiskey Flats' lawmen were leaving with grim faces and determined attitudes, but they were headed in a different direction this time. Not to mention that the notorious Chesterfield Pike was accompanying them. They weren't just armed for bear this time . . . they had the next best thing to a grizzly riding with them.

Bo and Scratch had a general idea where Chet Bascomb's Rocking B Ranch was located, since they had run into Bascomb's foreman, Bill Cavalier, and some of the other hands chasing Rawhide on the first day they came to Whiskey Flats. As they followed Chesterfield Pike's directions, they could tell that the giant was taking them the way they should go. Evidently, Pike had been sincere in his offer to lead them to the Rocking B.

They kept the horses moving at a fast clip, so there wasn't really any opportunity for conversation. None of the men were interested in talking at the moment anyway. Bo and Scratch were worried about Rawhide, and Reilly and Pike shared that concern. And if the mutual suspicion and dislike between the Star and the Rocking B spreads flared up into a shooting war, the hostilities were almost certain to spill over into the settlement, since Whiskey Flats was the only place in the area where either side could get supplies.

When they had ridden for several miles, Pike pulled his mule back to a walk. The others followed suit. Now that the hooves weren't pounding so loudly, it was possible to talk, and Pike did so, saying, "We're about a mile from Bascomb's ranch house. I been doin' some thinkin', and since I'm helpin' you fellas out, it seems to me like I ought to be a deputy, too."

"A deputy?" Reilly repeated. "Hell, you're our prisoner!"

"Not now. You done let me out."

Bo said, "I'm afraid that until there's a hearing, you're still considered to be in our custody, Chesterfield."

"But you made Miss Rawhide a deputy after she helped you. I'm helpin' you, ain't I?"

"That doesn't mean you can be a deputy," Reilly said. "Good Lord, you throw people through windows! A deputy can't behave like that."

Bo and Scratch exchanged a quick grin at the idea of a former rascal like Jake Reilly lecturing somebody else on how a lawman should behave. Reilly had come a long way in a relatively short time.

"Well, I'm gonna try not to lose my temper so easy from now on, like Deputy Creel said," Pike declared. "To tell y' the truth, I'm a mite tired o' folks lookin' at me like I'm some sort o' monster ever' time I come to town. I can't even walk down the street without women grabbin' their kids and almost runnin' to get 'em away from me. Fellas on the boardwalk head for the other side o' the street when they see me comin'. I may not look like it, but I got feelin's, too, you know."

For a second Bo thought Reilly was going to laugh at Pike's plaintive statement, and he hoped that the young man wouldn't do that. He was glad when Reilly managed to keep a straight face and said, "You keep it up, Pike, and maybe someday you could be a deputy. Right now, though, you just think about getting us to the Rocking B as fast as you can."

"We're pert' near there," Pike said, lifting a hamlike hand to point. "Bascomb's spread is right over that rise in front of us."

They were close, all right . . . close enough to hear the sudden burst of gunshots that rang out in the afternoon air.

CHAPTER 21

Reilly managed to look angry and nervous at the same time as the guns continued blasting. "Some idiot had to start shooting!" he exclaimed. "Let's get over there!"

"We're with you, Marshal!" Bo told him as he heeled the borrowed horse into a run again. Scratch was right beside him, and Chesterfield Pike brought up the rear—but not by much—as he banged his big feet against the mule's flanks.

The four men charged up the hill, topped it, and thundered down the far slope. A valley spread out before them. A few hundred yards away lay the headquarters of Chet Bascomb's Rocking B spread: the ranch house, a long, slab-sided bunkhouse, a cookshack, smokehouse, blacksmith shop, a couple of big barns, and numerous corrals. The place gave every appearance of being a fine, prosperous outfit, a far cry from the unfortunate Thompson family's hardscrabble layout on the other side of Whiskey Flats.

At the moment, though, the Rocking B was a battlefield. A gray haze of powder smoke hung over the large open space between the main house and the barns. More smoke spurted from the windows of the house and the bunkhouse, as well as from the barns and around the corners of the other outbuildings.

As veterans of countless such battles, Bo and Scratch needed only a glance to know what was going on. Bascomb and his men were holed up in the main house and the bunkhouse, defending the Rocking B from the gun-hung crew of Steve North's Star Ranch. Bascomb and North might have had a parley before the shooting started, with North accusing Bascomb of being behind the rustling. Almost certainly, Bascomb would have fired back with the same accusation, laying all the blame for the widelooping at North's feet.

After that, it would have been only a matter of moments until the shooting started.

There was no sign of Rawhide Abbott, which was good news as far as it went. At least the redhead wasn't lying dead on the ground between the house and the barns. She might still be in danger, though, if she'd been here when the fracas started, as seemed highly likely given what Chesterfield Pike had told Bo, Scratch, and Reilly.

Bo held up a hand to signal a halt. As the others reined in, he said, "If we go charging in down there, we won't accomplish anything except to get ourselves shot full of holes."

"What should we do?" Reilly asked, forgetting for the moment that *he* was supposed to be in charge here. Pike didn't seem to notice, though.

"This is the same sort o' thing we ran into on our

first day in Whiskey Flats," Scratch reminded him. "Remember, Marshal?"

Bo added, "This fight is just on a lot larger scale."

"Yeah, of course," Reilly said. "We'll split up, find Bascomb and North, and force them to call off their men. Then we can figure out where to go from there."

The boy really *was* catching on, Bo thought. It was a solid plan, except for one problem.

"We've never met Bascomb or North. The only one of us who knows them by sight is Chesterfield here."

Pike grinned and crossed his arms over his massive chest. "Bet you wish now you'd made me a deputy."

"All right, damn it!" Reilly burst out. "Consider yourself a temporary deputy! All right?"

Still grinning, Pike nodded his shaggy head. "Sure. I'll be glad to give you a hand, Marshal."

"That doesn't solve all the problems," Bo said. "There's only one of Chesterfield."

"Damn right," Pike said. "When they made me, they busted the dang mold."

"How about me and Pike find Steve North?" Scratch suggested. "If you and the marshal can get in the house, Bo, you ought to be able to find Bascomb without much trouble."

Bo nodded. "That's true. I've got a hunch that Rawhide is in there, too, and she'll know Bascomb." He tightened his grip on the reins and lifted his other hand in farewell. "Good luck, boys."

The group parted, Bo and Reilly riding to the left so they could circle behind the ranch house, Scratch and Chesterfield Pike heading right so they could close in on the barns from the rear. Down below, the shots continued to roar.

Scratch and Pike followed a line of trees, staying behind the cover of the trunks for the most part. With the battle going on, Scratch didn't figure anybody around the Rocking B headquarters would be paying too much attention to what was going on elsewhere, but it wouldn't hurt anything to be careful about their approach. When he judged that they had gone far enough, he waved for Pike to follow him and turned his horse down the slope.

This really was like the shoot-out between the hardcases at the Top-Notch and Lariat saloons, Scratch mused, only instead of a feisty redheaded gal siding him, he had the man-monster called Chesterfield Pike. Scratch realized that Pike wasn't armed, so before they reached the barns, he asked, "You want to borrow my Winchester or one of my Remingtons?" He didn't like the idea of handing over one of the fancy ivory-handled revolvers, but he wouldn't send a man into battle without any way to protect himself.

But Pike shook his head and said, "Naw, I ain't much of a hand with guns. A revolver like that is plumb puny, and I'm too clumsy to handle it. A rifle's almost as bad."

"Well, I don't have a damn cannon to offer you," Scratch snapped. "That might be the only thing big enough for you."

"A cannon, eh?" Pike sounded intrigued by the idea. "Too bad we don't have one. I bet it'd make them fellas stop shootin' if I opened up on 'em with a cannon."

"Well, what *are* you gonna use if you have to fight?" Scratch asked.

Pike held up a huge fist. "Same thing I gen'rally use."

Scratch sighed. It was too late to do anything about the situation now. Pike would just have to take his chances. Scratch said, "Stay behind me anyway. I'll do my best to cover you."

"Much obliged, but I won't need your help, Deputy. I can take care o' myself."

Scratch didn't doubt that. Pike was big enough to handle most anything.

They reined in and dismounted at the edge of the trees, about fifty yards behind the barns. Scratch spotted several men in range clothes crouched behind some wagons parked next to one of the barns. They had rifles and handguns and were firing toward the house.

Scratch nodded toward the men and told Pike, "Let's see if we can cut down the odds a mite first." He didn't bother lowering his voice when he spoke. Nobody but Pike could hear him over the nearly continual gunfire.

Pike nodded his agreement, grinned, doubled his fists, and tapped them together in anticipation.

Scratch drew his guns, crouched slightly, and headed toward the wagons at a run. Pike loped along beside him, barely doing more than walking since his long legs covered so much ground with each stride. The Star cowboys didn't notice them coming until it was too late. Then one of the men must have caught a glimpse of them from the corner of his eye, because he suddenly twisted around and yelled, "Look out, boys!"

Before any of the rest of them could even react, Pike was on them. His fists lashed out with surprising speed, and two men went flying through the air as the blows connected with bone-crunching power. That left three men, and Pike grabbed two of them, lifting them off their feet and driving their heads together. The resounding thud that resulted as the men's skulls met would have made Scratch wince if there had been time. Instead, he was busy walloping the fifth and final man with one of his Remingtons. The hombre folded up, out cold.

In a matter of a couple of heartbeats, Scratch and Pike had laid out five men, all of whom sprawled around in a senseless state. Of course, Pike had done most of the work, Scratch reflected. The big fella was a fightin' fool.

"All right," Scratch told him. "Let's head for the back o' the barn. If you see Steve North, let me know. If we can get our hands on him, chances are we can get the rest o' his crew to hold their fire."

Pike nodded. He followed as Scratch made his way along the side of the barn to the back corner. They turned it and headed for the rear doors, which were closed.

When they got there, Scratch tried to swing the doors open and bit back a curse as they refused to budge. "They must be barred inside," he said.

"That ain't a problem," Pike said. He wedged his fingers between the doors and heaved. They didn't give at first, and Pike let out a grunt of effort as he threw more strength into it. The doors began to inch outward, creating a bigger gap between them and allowing Pike to get an even better grip on them. He growled, as if angered that the doors would dare to resist him.

They didn't resist for long. With a sharp crack, the bar that held the doors closed inside broke in two. The doors flew outward with such speed that Scratch was glad he had decided to step back; otherwise he would have gotten hit by one of them. He wished there had been a quieter way in. The breaking bar had to have alerted some of the men inside the barn that they faced a new threat.

As Scratch and Pike charged inside, the dimness made it hard for them to see at first. Scratch saw muzzle fire spurt toward them and snapped a shot in return. He didn't want to kill any of Steve North's men, or the rancher himself, but he wasn't the sort of gent who could get shot at without shooting back.

"Dadgum it!" Pike howled. "I'm hit! Feels like a damn bee sting."

Scratch looked over at the giant and saw Pike pawing at his upper left arm. There was a small blood-stain on the sleeve of his homespun shirt, but it didn't seem to be spreading very fast. He'd probably just been nicked by one of the bullets flying around.

"Those bastards must be some o' Bascomb's wad-dies!" a harsh voice yelled. "Get 'em, but don't kill 'em! We'll use 'em as hostages to make Bascomb give up, the rustlin' son of a bitch!"

The guns fell silent and booted feet pounded on the ground as several men rushed at Scratch and Pike.

North didn't know it, but he had just played right into their hands. Scratch didn't care what the odds were. Based on what he had seen so far, in a rough-and-tumble brawl, his money was on Chesterfield Pike.

Six men charged out of the shadows. A couple of them looked surprised and started to slow down as they caught sight of Pike and realized who they were facing. They might have turned to run, in spite of North's orders, but by then it was too late. Pike was among them, flailing right and left with his tree-trunk arms and keglike fists.

One man turned a backflip, Pike hit him so hard. Another doubled over, stumbled backward, and collapsed. A third man clutched his chest and gasped for air after one of Pike's fists landed on his sternum. Yet another flew through the air, crashed into one of the thick posts that held up the hayloft, and bounced off it to land on his face.

Scratch holstered his guns as the remaining two men leaped on Pike. One of them landed on Pike's back and looped both arms around the giant's thick neck in an attempt to strangle him. The other grabbed him around the knees and heaved, trying to upset him. Neither man got very far with those efforts. Pike reached up, got hold of the man on his back, and heaved him up and over his head. The man had time for a yell before he crashed down to the ground.

The last man gave up on trying to yank Pike's legs out from under him. He might as well have been struggling with a pair of redwoods. He let go and turned to run before Pike could swing around.

Unfortunately for that hombre, he ran right into the

hard right fist that Scratch had launched in a perfectly timed uppercut. The blow landed solidly on the man's jaw, lifted him off his feet, and deposited him on the hard-packed dirt floor of the barn, just as senseless as the others in the bunch.

"Son of a *bitch*!"

The exclamation came from the man who had ordered that Scratch and Pike be captured, not killed. He found himself alone in the barn now, with all his men either stunned and moaning or knocked out cold. He stood about ten feet away, staring at the carnage, a sharp-faced man in range clothes that didn't look like he actually worked in them and a Stetson with a tightly curled brim. A white mustache bristled under his hawklike nose.

"By God!" he suddenly yelled. "Nobody treats my men like that!"

His hand clawed at the revolver holstered on his hip.

Before the gun could clear leather, the man found himself staring down the barrels of both of Scratch's Remingtons, which the silver-haired Texan had drawn in a swift, smooth motion. "Let it slide back into the holster, amigo," Scratch ordered, "and then unbuckle that gunbelt and drop it."

The man hesitated, fury darkening his face. Clearly, he wasn't used to anybody telling him what to do. That attitude was confirmed by the words he choked out.

"Do you know who I am?"

"Don't really give a damn," Scratch said, "but I've got a hunch you're Steve North."

"He's North, all right," Pike rumbled before the

man could say anything. "I seen him around town a time or two."

North squinted at him. "You're that fella Pike everybody is so scared of. Well, I'm not scared of you, mister." He glared at Scratch. "Nor of you, whoever the hell you are."

"Deputy Marshal Scratch Morton, that's who the hell I am."

North snorted in contempt and said, "That don't mean nothin' to me. I heard there were some new lawmen in Whiskey Flats, but your jurisdiction ends at the edge of town, Mr. Deputy."

Scratch hefted the left-hand Remington while keeping the one in his right hand trained squarely on North. "I got all the jurisdiction I need right here." He used the left-hand gun to motion toward the front of the barn. "Now, you're gonna go out there and call a cease-fire. Tell your boys to stop shootin', and be quick about it."

"What if I don't?" North asked with a sneer. "You plan to shoot me?"

Scratch shook his head. "Nope. I'll just let Pike here reason with you."

North tried to maintain his arrogant attitude, but he couldn't do it in the face of that threat, especially when Pike gave him a toothy grin of anticipation. Scratch didn't know if the big galoot was just playing along with him, or if he really thought Scratch might let him rip the rancher limb from limb. It didn't really matter, because North turned pale under his permanent tan and started backing away. He held up his hands and said, "Hold on, now. Just hold on,

Deputy. I've always been a law-abidin' man. I'll do what I can to help you, whether you got any real jurisdiction out here or not."

Scratch nodded and gestured with the Remington again. "That's more like it. Now move."

As North turned and started toward the barn's entrance, he said over his shoulder, "If you really want to do somethin' to bring law and order to these parts, you'll arrest that thievin' bastard Chet Bascomb. Son of a gun's been rustlin' my stock for months now."

"We'll talk about that once the shootin' stops. Keep movin'."

Shots still blasted from the house and from the Star Ranch cowboys who were scattered around the place, defenders and attackers each trying to take a toll on the other. The damage that Scratch and Pike had done to North's men had decreased the amount of gunfire from that side, but the battle still raged.

Maybe not for much longer, though, Scratch thought . . . depending on how much luck Bo and Reilly were having.

CHAPTER 22

A narrow creek ran close to the Rocking B ranch house, and Bo and Reilly used the cover of the trees that grew along its banks to shield their approach to Chet Bascomb's headquarters. The attackers from the Star Ranch were concentrated on the far side of the big house, so Bo didn't figure there would be too many defenders watching in this direction.

If Bascomb was smart, though, he would have posted at least few men on this side of the house, knowing that it was always possible North's men might try some sort of circling maneuver. Bo knew that he and Reilly couldn't just waltz in.

They dismounted while still in the cover of the trees and started toward the house on foot. The cookshack and smokehouse were on this side of the spread's headquarters, so those buildings furnished some cover, too. Bo stopped at one of the rear corners of the cookshack and edged an eye past it to study the ground between there and the house.

The Rocking B ranch house was a two-story,

whitewashed frame structure with a sprawling look to it that told Bo it had probably been built in stages, with new additions being tacked on around a much smaller, central part of the house that was likely Bascomb's original dwelling.

"Couple of riflemen in second-story windows," Bo said to Reilly. "If we make a run for the house, they'll spot us and probably gun us down, thinking that we're some of North's men. That means we have to distract them somehow."

"How do we do that?" Reilly asked.

Bo leaned back so he could look up at the shack's roof, where a tin pipe stuck up from the stove below. "Smoke screen," he said with a grin.

The shack had a window in the back wall. Bo slipped over to it and risked a look inside. He didn't see anybody. Chances were that the cook was inside the main house. He had probably fled there when the shooting started. Bo shoved the window up and said, "Come on."

He climbed inside the shack first, followed by Reilly. The cook probably slept out here, which meant there would be some bedding in the cubbyhole where he spent his nights. Bo intended to use some of that bedding to kindle a fire in the stove that would produce a lot of smoke. While he was doing that, Reilly would have to climb onto the roof and use another blanket to direct the smoke toward the house, like an Indian sending up smoke signals. The stovepipe was on the back side of the roof, so it might not be too visible to those sentries on the second floor of the ranch house.

On second thought, Bo decided, maybe *he* ought to be the one to climb up onto the roof. Reilly was younger and sprier, but he might not be able to handle a blanket well enough to make the smoke do what it needed to do.

Bo was taking a second to ponder that question when a Chinaman jumped out from behind a stack of crates and swung a hatchet at his head.

Instinct was all that saved Bo from having that keen blade buried in his skull. His Colt was in his hand, so when he jerked it up in self-defense, the hatchet hit the revolver's barrel with a clang. That was enough to deflect it so that the hatchet swept harmlessly past Bo's shoulder.

Reilly swung his gun toward the furious Chinese man, but Bo didn't want a shot to give them away. He moved quickly, jabbing a hard left-hand punch into the cook's face. The man's head rocked back under the impact of the blow. The next second, Bo rapped him on the head with the Colt's barrel, stunning him. The hatchet fell from nerveless fingers as the man crumpled.

"Good Lord!" Reilly said. "Where'd that Chinaman come from?"

"He'd be Bascomb's cook," Bo explained. "This is his shack. I figured that he'd holed up in the house with the rest of them, but I reckon I was wrong." He holstered his gun and pulled loose the sashlike belt that went around the cook's waist. "Give me a hand and we'll get him tied up so he can't bother us while we're working."

"Better gag him, too," Reilly suggested. "I remember

running into a Chinaman out in San Francisco who could scream like the very devil."

That was a good idea, Bo decided. It took them only a couple of minutes to truss up the cook where he couldn't move and tie a gag in his mouth to keep him quiet. Then they were ready to put Bo's plan into action.

He explained to Reilly what they were going to do, and pulled the sheets and a couple of wadded up blankets from the cook's bed in a tiny alcove. There was kindling in a box beside the stove, which was cold at the moment, as well as a small stack of firewood in the corner. Bo got a fire going without much trouble, opened the flue all the way, and crammed one of the blankets into the stove.

As he closed the door, he said, "Be ready to make a run for the house as soon as the smoke is thick enough."

"Won't the guards realize that something's wrong and start shooting into the smoke?" Reilly asked.

"Maybe, but we're going to be moving fast. It'd just be blind luck if they hit us."

"Blind luck can get you just as dead as good aim," Reilly muttered.

Bo chuckled as he draped the other blanket over his shoulder. "That's true. You're learning, Jake."

"Yeah, you keep saying that, but I haven't learned how to keep you and Scratch from getting me into these messes, have I? I swear, you get shot at by Apaches in the morning and land smack-dab in the middle of a range war in the afternoon!"

There was nothing Bo could say to that. Reilly was right.

"Give me a hand," Bo told the young man as he began clambering out through the window. He got his feet on the sill and stood up in the window, reaching up for the roof. When he got hold of it, Reilly laced his hands together and gave him a boost onto the tar-papered slope. Staying low so that his head didn't stick up over the roofline, Bo climbed up to the stovepipe, where thick gray smoke was beginning to well out.

Bo whipped the blanket off his shoulder and opened it enough to spread it around the pipe. The blanket trapped the smoke, and when Bo judged that there was enough built up, he snapped the blanket open and waved it, sending the smoke toward the house. He did that again, although he couldn't hold the smoke as long the second time. The wind helped, spreading the gray cloud across the open space between the cookshack and the house. Bo pulled the stunt for a third time, then judged that his and Reilly's approach would be about as obscured as it was going to get.

"Go, Jake!" he called as he dropped the blanket and swung down from the roof. "Head for the house!"

The sentries had noticed the smoke, of course. Bo heard their yells of alarm; then seconds later rifles began to bark. None of the bullets came close enough for him to hear them whining past his head. Most of the smoke was higher than his head, so it didn't sting his nose and eyes too much, and he could see Reilly running toward the house just ahead of him.

They made the back porch almost at the same

time, bounding up the stairs with guns drawn. Reilly seemed to be getting caught up in the heat of battle again. Barely slowing down, he lifted a booted foot and kicked the door open. It slammed back against the wall inside the house.

And shots slammed out, coming from the defenders who had run to the back of the house in response to the sentries' outcry. Reilly might have been riddled by the flying lead if Bo hadn't grabbed his coat and jerked him off his feet. Both men sprawled on the floor just inside the door.

"Hold your fire!" Bo shouted. "We're friends! Hold your fire!"

"Don't shoot!" a high-pitched voice cried. "That's Bo Creel!"

"Rawhide?" Bo called back to her as the guns fell silent. "Rawhide, is that you?"

"Everybody hold your fire, damn it! That's an order!"

That was Rawhide, all right, Bo thought . . . although in this case he was mighty glad she was quick to give orders. He climbed to his feet along with Reilly as the redheaded deputy came up to them.

"What the Sam Hill are you two doing here?" Rawhide demanded. "I've got this situation under control!"

"Yeah, it looked like it when we rode up and saw all these fellas trying to kill each other," Reilly said with a disgusted snort. "You had no business riding out here and trying to stop a range war all by yourself, Deputy."

"Well, somebody had to do it," she shot back at

him. "Nobody else was in the marshal's office, and when Steve North came in and said he was gonna ride out to the Rocking B and settle the score with Bascomb, what was I supposed to do?"

"Wait for orders maybe?" Reilly suggested. "Instead of rushing off like some damn reckless hothead."

Rawhide looked like she wanted to torch him with some equally fiery reply, but she stopped herself. "You're the marshal," she said grudgingly.

"And don't you forget it," Reilly said. He looked around. "Where's Bascomb?"

A stocky man with thinning hair and a white goatee stepped forward holding a Winchester. "I'm Chet Bascomb," he rasped in an unfriendly voice. "You'd be the new marshal."

Reilly nodded. "That's right. And I'm ordering you to have your men cease fire."

The shooting still continued from elsewhere in the house and from outside as well as the battle raged on, although at a less intense level now. Bascomb cursed in response to Reilly's order and said, "If you really want to do your job, Marshal, you'll arrest Steve North for bein' the wideloopin' coyote that he is."

"North has lost stock, too," Rawhide said. "I told you that over and over while I was trying to get you to listen to reason, Mr. Bascomb. If you and Mr. North would just talk to each other without getting mad, you'd see that somebody's trying to stir up trouble between you, as well as line their pockets with the profits from those stolen cows."

Bascomb waved off her argument. "North's just

tryin' to throw everybody off his trail. He's guilty, I tell you. Guilty as sin."

"Why not let the law decide that?" Reilly asked.

"When the law keeps me from bein' robbed blind, then maybe I'll pay more attention to it," the rancher snapped.

"You'd better pay attention now," Bo advised him. "Call off your men, Bascomb, and let us get to the bottom of this."

Bascomb frowned and rubbed his jaw in thought. "You swear you won't let Steve North take you in with his lies?"

"We'll listen to both sides," Bo promised. "All we want is to get at the truth . . . which I suspect is a lot different than either of you think."

"Well . . ." Bascomb was clearly wavering now. "I suppose it wouldn't hurt anything to let you fellas have a try at stopping this damned rustlin'."

Rawhide let out a wounded cry and threw her hands in the air. "That's all *I* asked you to do, Mr. Bascomb, and you wouldn't even hear of it! You and North both just bulled ahead, called each other names, and started shootin'. Why is lettin' the law handle things such a good idea *now*?"

"Well, shoot, Rawhide . . . you're a girl. And I've known you ever since you were a little bitty thing, runnin' around Whiskey Flats with your drawers droopin'."

Rawhide made a strangled, incoherent noise of rage and reached for her gun. Bo took hold of her wrist before she could draw the weapon, and said to the rancher, "We appreciate your cooperation, Mr.

Bascomb. Now, if we could put a stop to all the powder burning for a while . . ."

Bascomb nodded and headed for the front of the house.

"I swear," Rawhide said, "sometimes I think I'd like to shoot every stubborn, addlepated man on the face of the earth . . . and that includes practically the whole damned species!"

"Settle down, Rawhide," Reilly told her. "You couldn't expect Bascomb and North to listen to you. You weren't even a deputy until today."

"And those two old mossyhorns have been building up to this for a long time," Bo added. "Chances are, they were some of the first settlers in this part of the country. They're used to having things their own way and bulling right over anybody who tries to stop them. Fact of the matter is, they're not quite civilized yet . . . but give them time. They will be."

And in a way, it would be a shame when they were, Bo added silently to himself, because civilization never would have come to the West at all without the old curly wolves like Steve North and Chet Bascomb who came first.

Bascomb's shouts blended with the roar of gunfire, which gradually diminished as Bascomb's yelling got louder. As the guns fell silent, Bo realized that no more shots were coming from outside either. He grinned at Reilly and said, "Sounds like Scratch and Pike did their part, too."

"Pike!" Rawhide exclaimed. "You brought that loco galoot along with you?"

"Worse than that," Bo said. "The marshal made him a deputy, too."

Rawhide looked like she didn't know whether to sputter in disbelief or cuss in outrage, so she settled for rolling her eyes and shaking her head.

Bo said, "Come on. Let's see if we can get Bascomb and North to talking again, instead of trying to kill each other."

The tension in the air was so thick you could have whittled on it with a bowie knife, Bo thought as the two veteran cattlemen confronted each other on the front porch of the ranch house. Bascomb's men stood along the wall behind him, bristling with guns. Likewise, North's heavily armed crew was arrayed behind their boss, equally deadly. Between those two bunches wasn't a very safe place to be.

So of course, that was exactly where Bo, Scratch, Jake Reilly, Rawhide Abbott, and Chesterfield Pike found themselves. Pike was the only one of the five who didn't appear to be overly concerned. Maybe he thought that he was immune to bullets, Bo mused. He hoped that Pike wouldn't get the chance to find out that that assumption was wrong.

Bo saw nervousness lurking in Reilly's eyes, but the young man hid it well. Confidently, he said to Bascomb and North, "All right, you'll both get a chance to speak your pieces. North, you first. Why did you come into my office this morning and tell Deputy Abbott you were going to attack the Rocking B?"

"Because I'm tired o' my stock bein' stolen," North

snapped. "Not only that, but one o' my punchers was shot last night by Bascomb's varmints when they widelooped another jag o' cows."

"My men never shot anybody who didn't have it comin'," Bascomb put in. "And they sure didn't shoot anybody on your ranch, North, because they got standin' orders to steer clear of that hellhole." A frown creased Bascomb's forehead. "The puncher who got shot . . . is he gonna be all right?"

The question didn't surprise Bo. If he was right— if neither Bascomb nor North were behind the rustling—then Bascomb had a cattleman's natural regard for the men who worked at the demanding profession of cowboy. He might hate Steve North, but he would respect the men who rode for North's brand.

"Well . . . I think he'll pull through," North said. "You mean to say that none of your crew was on my range last night?"

Bascomb turned to look at stocky, bearded Bill Cavalier. "What about it, Bill? Any of the boys unaccounted for last night?"

The foreman shook his head. "Nope. Ever'body was right here 'cept for Burke and Holmes up at the line shack, and those two wouldn't rustle anybody's stock, not even North's. Hell, I've known 'em both for nigh on to twenty years."

Bascomb swung back toward North and glared at him defiantly as he asked, "Is that good enough for you? You've got my word and Bill's."

North rubbed at his bristly jaw. "I never heard anybody say that Bill Cavalier wasn't an honest man.

Anyway, there were half a dozen hombres in the bunch that stole the cows and plugged that waddie."

Bascomb crossed his arms over his chest and glared even more darkly. "That don't explain how come *I've* been losin' stock, too," he said. "I figure you're behind it."

"That's a damned lie!"

The tension grew even thicker as hands tightened on pistol butts and rifle stocks. Most men wouldn't stand for being called a liar. It was a matter of honor . . . a killing matter, most of the time. Chet Bascomb's face turned white around the mouth, and fires blazed in his eyes.

Knowing that he was taking a chance, Bo stepped between the two men and said, "Hold on a minute. North, you believe Bascomb when he says he didn't have anything to do with your cattle being stolen and your man being shot?"

"Well . . ." North said grudgingly, "I don't want to. I purely don't. But I've known the old bastard for so many years I don't think he'd lie to me. Steal from me, yeah, if he thought he could get away with it, but not lie to my face."

Bo turned to look at Bascomb. "Then you ought to be able to accept North's word for it if he says that he and his men haven't been rustling your stock either, Bascomb."

"I never said *he* wouldn't lie to *me*," Bascomb replied with a snort.

"Has he ever?" Bo asked bluntly. "Has Steve North ever lied to you?"

Bascomb frowned and didn't reply for a long moment, then admitted, "No, not that I recollect."

Bo didn't bother trying to keep the anger and frustration out of his voice as he said, "Then for God's sake, are you both just too stubborn to admit that somebody's been playing you both for fools and rustling your cattle while you waste time blaming each other?"

Bascomb and North looked at each other for a long moment as if considering what Bo had just said, and once again Rawhide couldn't suppress her irritation. "I told them the same blasted thing!" she exploded. "They wouldn't even listen to me! They were too eager to start shooting at each other!"

North said, "Well, that ain't all of it, Rawhide. This fella here looks like he's been around some and seen some things. And you're just—"

"Deputy . . ." Reilly said warningly as Rawhide started to take a step forward. "Don't make me take your badge away when you've been a deputy for less than a day."

"I don't *have* a badge!" Rawhide said. Fuming, she turned away. "Do what you want. I don't care anymore."

Bo doubted that, but there were more pressing matters to attend to. "How about it, gents?" he prodded Bascomb and North. "Are you willing to call a truce and let the law get to the bottom of this rustling?"

Bascomb shrugged. "I reckon I can hold off a few days."

"So can I," North said with a nod.

"But if I lose any more cows . . ." Bascomb began warningly.

"That goes double for me, damn it!" North shot back.

"All right then, it's settled," Bo said quickly before the two old ranchers could start arguing again. "Mr. North, why don't we start by you showing us where you lost those cattle last night? Maybe we can pick up the rustlers' trail."

North looked doubtful. "We tried to follow the tracks, but we lost 'em in the hills. What makes you think you can follow the trail when me and my boys couldn't?"

"Well, for one thing," Scratch said, "we're from Texas, and everybody knows Texans are natural-born trackers."

Under his breath, Bascomb said, "They're natural-born *something,* all right."

"You can say that again," North added, maybe the first time the cattlemen had agreed in quite a spell.

"Say . . ." Scratch began, his expression clouding up.

Bo headed off that argument. "Let's get our horses and ride." He looked at Reilly. "If that's all right with you, Marshal."

Reilly nodded. "Sure, sure. Let's go hunt down some rustlers. And when we get finished with that—"

He caught himself, and Bo was glad for the unaccustomed show of discretion. He knew what Reilly had been about to say.

After they tracked down those rustlers, then maybe they could find out who was running guns to the Indians . . .

CHAPTER 23

Rawhide wouldn't hear of going back to Whiskey Flats until Bo pointed out that the marshal's office was sitting there unattended. "I know we don't have any prisoners right now . . ." he began.

Rawhide gave an unladylike snort and jerked a thumb at Chesterfield Pike. "Only because you let this big varmint out, which I never would've done."

"I helped, Miss Rawhide," Pike said, tugging his hat off and holding it in front of his massive chest as he spoke to her. "I showed the marshal and Bo and Scratch how to find this place."

"And stove up half a dozen or more o' my men once you got here," Steve North said. "Those boys may not be able to do a full day's work for a week. By all rights, I ought to get you as a hand until they're all back on their feet."

Pike shook his head. "No, sir. I don't do no cowboyin'. My pa said that cowboys was often unwholesome individuals and that he didn't want me growin' up to be one of 'em."

Bo said, "Chesterfield, you ought to go back to town with Miss Rawhide. Technically, you're still under arrest, even though the marshal did appoint you as a temporary deputy."

"If you're goin' up in them hills to look for rustlers," Pike said with a frown, "you'd best take me along. Nobody around here knows that country better'n I do. I've been roamin' all over 'em since I was just a little sprout."

Bo found it hard to believe that Chesterfield Pike had ever been a little anything, but Chet Bascomb said, "He's right, Deputy. Pike hunts and traps for a living, and he knows those hills."

"See? I told you," Pike said with a triumphant grin.

Bo thought it over and nodded. "That's actually a pretty good idea. If you want to keep on helping us, Chesterfield . . ."

The giant nodded eagerly. "I do. Bein' a deputy's the most fun I had in a coon's age."

"Let's go, then," Reilly said. "Rawhide, we'll see you back in town. Hold down the fort while we're gone."

The redhead rode off grumbling, heading for Whiskey Flats. Bo, Scratch, Reilly, and Pike headed for the Star Ranch, accompanied by Steve North and the men who had come with him to attack the Rocking B. The ones who had tangled with Pike had regained consciousness and were able to ride, but they looked plenty the worse for wear.

North's spread was deeper in the foothills of the mountains than the Rocking B, and so the terrain was rougher. The grass wasn't as good either, and Bo wondered if jealousy on North's part had contributed to the ill feelings between the two men.

On the other hand, it was still good cattle country, and judging by the number and quality of the grazing stock they passed once they were on Star range, North had done all right for himself. His ranch was probably the second most successful one in these parts.

It was a two-hour ride from the Rocking B to the high pasture where a hundred head of North's cattle had been grazing until the night before. Along the way, most of North's men veered off and headed for the ranch headquarters at North's orders, the rancher saying that after they had been bounced around by Pike like that, they wouldn't be worth anything in a fight anyway. Three of the Star hands accompanied them, making the party number eight.

When they reached the pasture, North pointed out the line shack where the puncher who had been shot, Teddy Arrington, normally stayed.

"He was out checking on the cows because he heard a commotion," North explained as they rode on past the shack. "We get wolves around here from time to time, and that's what he thought it was, some old lobo after a calf or something. But when he got out there, he saw riders pushing the herd toward that canyon over yonder. He knew he couldn't stand up to six-to-one odds and tried to get turned around and go for help, but one o' the bastards spotted him and opened fire. Teddy caught a slug, but got away and made it back to the ranch house." Emotion roughened

North's already gravelly voice. "Kid ain't but eighteen years old."

By the time Bo and Scratch were eighteen years old, they had helped free Texas from the Mexican dictator Santa Anna and had had other adventures, too, some of them pretty harrowing. But the Texans didn't point that out to North, figuring that he wouldn't appreciate it at the moment.

They rode toward the canyon where the rustlers had taken the stolen stock. "Where does that go?" Scratch asked. "Can't be a box canyon since them cows had to go somewhere."

"It cuts through that ridge to some malpais breaks on the other side," North explained. "The ridge is the boundary line for my property. Nobody claims the breaks, since they ain't really good for anything. Hell, it's such a maze over there that nobody could find his way through it."

Pike spoke up. "I know my way through the breaks. Tramped over every foot of 'em, many's the time."

"Then maybe you can follow the trail," North said. "That's where we lost it, a mile or two into those badlands. To tell you the truth, I was just glad we were able to find our way back out without strayin' into that damn lava. Stuff'll cut a horse's hooves to ribbons and leave a man afoot."

Bo and Scratch had seen the black malpais before—hardened lava left over from volcanic eruptions many, many years earlier, possibly before the dawn of recorded history. They knew that it was indeed treacherous and that the razor-sharp edges of

· the lava deposits were dangerous to man and horse alike and had to be avoided.

The men rode into the canyon, which was about a hundred yards wide in most places, with sheer walls that rose between twenty-five and thirty feet to the rimrock. They could plainly see the tracks of the stolen cattle on the dusty floor of the canyon.

"Easy enough trail to follow," Scratch commented.

"Yeah, a Texan'd think so," North said.

Pike said, "It'll get harder later once we get into the malpais. But I reckon I can find them cows."

North snorted. "I hope you're right, big boy."

It was late afternoon by the time the men reached the far end of the canyon. The breaks that lay beyond looked dark and forbidding in the shadows cast by the mountains. As they reined in, Pike said, "It'd be easier to follow the trail in the mornin'."

"That would mean leaving Rawhide on her own back in Whiskey Flats overnight," Reilly pointed out. "I don't know if that's a good idea."

Bo said, "That girl's got a good head on her shoulders. She'll be all right."

"I don't know. Maybe I'd better go back, too. I couldn't get there by dark, but it wouldn't be too late."

Bo frowned. He didn't like the idea of Reilly and Rawhide being alone together in town. Reilly still had romantic notions about the girl, more than likely, but Bo wasn't worried too much about that. From what he had seen of Rawhide's handiness with both fist and gun, she could take care of herself. But she was smart, too, and Reilly might do or say something to give away the fact that he wasn't really John Henry Braddock.

On the other hand, he and Scratch wouldn't be around forever to look after Reilly and help him maintain the masquerade. The day would come when they had to ride on and resume their wandering ways. And Reilly would have to decide if he wanted to reveal to the townspeople who he really was . . . or continue being John Henry Braddock from now on.

So maybe it would be a good thing for Reilly to go back to the settlement. Let him get started now seeing what it would be like to the marshal of Whiskey Flats without his two "deputies" around.

"Sounds like a good idea, Marshal," Bo said, well aware that Scratch gave him a quick glance that asked if he had gone plumb loco. "We can track these rustlers, can't we, Scratch?"

"Uh, sure," the silver-haired Texan replied. "We'll handle this little chore, Marshal. Don't you worry none about us."

Reilly nodded. "It's settled then. Mr. North, since I'm new in these parts, how about sending one of your men with me to make sure I find the trail to Whiskey Flats all right?"

The rancher nodded. "I reckon I can do that." He gestured to one of his punchers. "Max, you go with the marshal as far as he needs you to."

"Sure, Boss," the cowboy responded. "To tell you the truth, I wasn't much lookin' forward to ridin' into that hellhole tomorrow anyway."

"I don't reckon none of us are," North said. "But it'll be worth it if we can find them damn wideloopers."

And not get shot to pieces in the process, Bo added to himself.

* * *

During the night, the wind blew through the pinnacles and spires of the breaks with an eerie howling sound that made a shiver go through a man if he listened to it for too long. Because of that, the members of the group camped on the edge of the badlands didn't sleep too well as they waited for morning. They didn't build a fire, and their supper had been a skimpy one because they didn't have many supplies with them. Pairs of men stood guard in turn, just in case the rustlers who used this route came along again.

Bo and Scratch took the same shift on watch, and as they hunkered beside a boulder that blocked the chilly night wind, Scratch said in a low voice that only his trail partner could hear, "I hope it wasn't a mistake sendin' that boy back to Whiskey Flats by himself."

"He'll do all right," Bo predicted. "He's got to start standing on his own two feet sometime."

"You really think he'll do that?" Scratch shook his head. "I figure he'll cut and run if any real trouble comes at him."

"He hasn't so far. He handled himself all right during that shoot-out in town and at the Thompson ranch."

Scratch snorted. "Pure luck."

"I don't think so," Bo said. "I think there's a good man in there. I've felt like that all along. It's just a matter of bringing the good man out."

"We'll see," Scratch said, but he didn't sound convinced. He changed the subject. "North should've known better than to accuse Bascomb o' bein' behind the rustlin'. This trail is a long way from the Rockin' B."

"Maybe so, but Bascomb could still be involved. I don't think he is, mind you, but just because the rustlers came through the canyon doesn't clear Bascomb."

"Hide and watch. You'll see that there's some bunch o' scruffy owlhoots up in the hills who've been doin' the wideloopin' all along."

Bo nodded. "Chances are that you're right. But if Pike can really follow the trail through the breaks like he says, maybe we can prove it."

Both Texans were quiet for a while. Then Scratch chuckled and said, "We get mixed up in some o' the damnedest messes, don't we?"

Bo smiled in the moonlight. "We do for a fact."

When morning came, the men ate a quick, cold breakfast and then hit the saddle. Pike led the way into the breaks on his mule with the rest of the group strung out behind him.

The temperature climbed quickly as the sun rose, and by mid-morning it was sweltering in the haunted badlands. The riders followed a twisting, turning course that never ran straight for more than fifty yards or so. That was because there was always some obstacle to avoid: a lava flow, a spiny ridge, a huge boulder. It must have been hard work taking those stolen cattle through here. In most places, the trail was so narrow that no more than two or three of the animals could have walked abreast. On the other hand, there was no place for them to spread out and scatter. Once they started through the breaks, they sort of had to keep going. All the rustlers had to do was prevent them from trying to turn back.

"We've already come a lot farther in here than we got yesterday," Steve North told Bo and Scratch. "I was gettin' so turned around I was afraid we'd never find our way out, and then we'd die o' thirst or starvation in here. Anyway, we couldn't see the tracks of those stolen cows anymore, so we didn't know if we were on the right trail or not." North nodded toward Pike. "That big hombre must have eyes like a hawk."

Several times during the morning, Pike had paused, dismounted, and hunkered down to study the rocky ground before straightening and pointing to the sign he'd been looking for that told him which way the cattle had gone. Once Pike pointed out the tiny indications, Bo and Scratch could see them, too, but even though they were both good trackers, they knew they would have lost the trail without having Pike's almost supernatural abilities at their service.

"What's on the other side of these breaks?" Bo asked.

North shrugged. "Hell if I know. We're well off my range now, and I never rode over there. Never had any reason to until now. From the looks of it, though, they may run right up to the foot of the mountains."

That looked possible to Bo, too, but he supposed they would find out when they got there.

That happened around midday, when Pike led them around another flow of the black malpais and up a long slope. When they reached the crest, instead of the gray and brown and tan of the rocky badlands through which they had been riding, the verdant green of a grassy hillside fell away before them. It dropped down into a pocket valley, thickly grassed, dotted with trees, and watered by a small stream that twisted through it. The pastures at one end of the valley were packed with grazing cattle. There had to be more than a thousand head, Bo estimated.

"Son of a bitch!" North burst out. "So this is where they've been goin'!"

Bo said, "And I'll lay you odds that if you check the brands on those cattle, you'll find just as many Rocking B animals as you do Star. Like I said, they've been looting both ranches and counting on the fact that you and Bascomb would blame each other rather than looking for the real thieves."

"Well, I feel like a damn-blasted fool." North rested his hand on the butt of this gun. "But I'll feel better once we've rode down there and cleaned out that rat's nest!"

"It won't be that easy," Bo warned. "They've probably got sentries out watching this approach."

As if to confirm his words, at that moment a shot blasted out, and Chesterfield Pike's battered old hat leaped from his head as if slapped off by a giant hand.

CHAPTER 24

Pike let out a yelp of surprise and anger as he made a futile grab for his hat, which was already well out of reach. More shots continued to roar, shattering the midday stillness, and as a slug whipped past Bo's head, he realized where some of them were coming from.

"They're behind us, too!" he shouted. Probably those sentries he had mentioned to North.

A dozen riders burst out of some trees down the slope and charged toward the group, guns blazing. Bo, Scratch, and the others were caught in a deadly cross fire. If they stayed where they were, they would be shot to pieces in a matter of minutes.

"Fall back!" Bo called. "Back into the breaks!"

North had already unleathered his gun and begun firing at the men charging toward them. He paused and said, "I don't like runnin' from trouble!"

"Neither do I, but this ain't runnin'," Scratch said. "It's what you call a strategic retreat! Ain't that right, Bo?"

Bo didn't answer directly. He just wheeled his horse around and called, "Come on!"

Twisting in their saddles to fire behind them at the group giving chase, the men turned their horses and galloped back into the breaks. Pike, who had been in the lead, now brought up the rear. Since he was un-armed, he couldn't fight back. All he could do was lean forward over the neck of his mule to make himself a smaller target, but he was so big to start with that that didn't help much.

Bo spotted a puff of powder smoke from the corner of his eye and realized that one of the gunmen in the breaks was hidden behind a boulder on a ledge about twenty feet up a rock wall. He swung his Colt in that direction and squeezed off three fast shots, aiming not at the boulder or the narrow slice of bushwhacker he could see, but rather at the wall near the concealed rifleman. Those slugs bounced off, ricocheting wildly from the almost sheer rock, and Bo was rewarded by the sight of the man reeling out from behind the boulder, clutching his belly where a flying chunk of lead had struck him. That deformed ricochet had probably done even more damage than a regular bullet would have. The man pitched off the ledge and plummeted to the ground as Bo and the others flashed by.

Even though Pike had had to lead them through the breaks, once Bo and Scratch had been over a trail once, they had no trouble backtracking along it. The Texans led the way now, keeping their horses moving at a near gallop as they weaved around the lava flows and the towering spires. One good thing about the twisting trail was that the pursuers had trouble getting a clear shot at them. Rocks were always in the way.

Scratch pulled alongside Bo and shouted over the

pounding hoofbeats, "Those hombres will keep chasin' us! They can't afford to let us get away now that we know where this place is!"

"I know!" Bo replied. "I'm hoping we can turn the tables on them!"

Since he and his companions were outnumbered, they couldn't make a straight-up, head-on fight of it. Instead, they had to find someplace where they could fort up and hold off the rustlers. Bo pulled his horse to the side and waved North and his men on past. Scratch did likewise.

Chesterfield Pike was still bringing up the rear on his mule. Bo and Scratch fell in with him, one on either side of the giant. "Chesterfield!" Bo said. "Do you know of any place around here where we could make a stand?"

"Hornpipe Rock!" Pike replied. "It ain't far!"

"Lead the way!" Bo told him.

Pike urged his mule to a harder run. Bo and Scratch yelled for North's men to move over and let them past. In a moment, Pike was in the lead again, veering off from the trail they had followed through the breaks onto an even more narrow, twisting trace with black lava flows on either side. If a man fell off his horse and landed in the malpais, the razor-sharp stuff might cut him up badly.

Pike headed up a slope. Gravel rattled and flew under the mule's hoofs. They came to a jutting shoulder underneath a giant, oblong rock with dozens of holes bored through it by water, wind, and time. It bore a slight resemblance to a hornpipe, and Bo imagined that when the wind blew through those holes, it produced a musical note.

At the base of the rock was a cavelike overhang partially shielded by a cluster of boulders. As soon as Bo saw them, he knew that was where Pike intended for them to make their stand against the rustlers.

"Head for the rocks!" he called to the others as he reined in. He holstered his Colt and pulled the Winchester from its saddle sheath.

"Oh, no, you don't," Scratch said as he brought his mount to a halt and drew his own rifle. "You ain't gonna stay here by yourself to slow down those varmints."

"I don't have time to argue with you," Bo said while North and the cowboys from the Star Ranch rode past him. He had spotted movement at the bottom of the slope, and brought the Winchester to his shoulder and squeezed off a shot in one smooth motion. The bullet sent the sombrero flying from the head of the Mexican hardcase who had been the first to start up the hill after them. The man jerked his horse around so quickly that its legs almost went out from under it.

Bo and Scratch sent several more shots whistling down the slope to discourage anybody else from trying it right away, then whirled their horses and galloped toward the boulders at the base of Hornpipe Rock. Pike, North, and the others had reached them by now and were dismounting and pulling their rifles. They covered Bo and Scratch as the Texans galloped toward the shelter of the boulders, but since none of them fired, Bo figured the rustlers were hanging back now, trying to decide what to do next.

They hauled back on the reins as they reached the boulders and dropped from the saddles almost before the horses had stopped moving. Carrying their rifles, the Texans ran back to kneel behind a couple of rocks and peer toward the spot where the trail reached the top of the slope.

"I found us a good place, didn't I?" Pike called over from his position behind one of the other boulders. "You can pick 'em off when they get to the top o' the trail. They can't get to us without goin' through a bunch o' lead, and they can't go around because o' the malpais on both sides o' the trail. We're safe here."

"Yeah, safe as can be," Scratch said, and the bitter edge to his voice told Bo that his trail partner had realized the same thing he had.

The rustlers couldn't get to them . . . but they couldn't get out either.

They were trapped here just as surely as if iron bars stood in their way.

It was amazing how much hotter the sun was when you knew you couldn't get out of the place you were in, Bo thought as he knelt behind the boulder and peered over the barrel of his Winchester at the top of the trail.

He and Scratch and the others had been holed up at the base of Hornpipe Rock for about an hour, and during that time the gang of rustlers had tried twice to rush them, only to be turned back both times by heavy fire from the defenders. Bo didn't think any of the rustlers had been killed, but a couple of them had been wounded before they withdrew.

In the long run, that didn't matter. If the rustlers settled in for a siege, only one outcome was possible. The defenders didn't have much food or water, and their supply of ammunition wasn't unlimited. Eventually, hunger and thirst would force them to make a break for it, and then the rustlers would be waiting to gun them down.

Scratch had removed his buckskin jacket and rolled up the sleeves of his shirt over his forearms. He grinned over at Bo from behind another boulder and said, "Gettin' a mite warm, ain't it?"

"You can say that again." Bo laid down his rifle and shucked his long black coat. He left his vest and his string tie on, though. Some habits were hard to break.

North spoke up. "I say we charge the sons o' bitches. They can't get all of us."

"I think you might be wrong there, Mr. North," Bo said. "They outnumber us quite a bit, and I'm sure that by now they've found some pretty good cover, too. I think there's a good chance they'd kill us all before we got to the bottom of the trail."

"Well, hell, we can't just squat here and fry!"

Bo turned his head to look over his shoulder at the massive rock looming above them. "The sun will get around behind Hornpipe Rock eventually," he said. "That'll give us some shade . . ." His voice trailed off as he frowned in thought.

"I know that look," Scratch said. "You got some idea percolatin' in that brain o' yours, don't you, Bo?"

"Maybe," Bo said slowly. "Those holes go all the way through the rock, don't they, Chesterfield?"

Pike squinted up at the rock and nodded. "Most of 'em do, I reckon. You can tell that by the way the sun's shinin' through 'em, see?"

"So if a man could get up there, he might be able to crawl through one of the holes and get out the other side."

"If a fella could sprout wings and fly up there, you mean!" Steve North put in. "He sure as hell couldn't climb up that rock."

Bo pointed. "No, but see that little knob of rock. A man could dab a loop on that, and I think it would hold his weight while he climbed up."

"Hell, nobody could rope that," North said with a frown. "Anyway, I reckon a lariat would slip right off once a fella put his weight on it."

"Only one way to find out," Bo said.

Scratch stood up. "One o' you punchers loan me your lasso," he said. "This is a job for a Texan."

"The hell you say!" North exclaimed. "Jack Brodie there is the best roper in the whole blamed New Mexico Territory! Ain't that right, Jack?"

"I swing a lasso pretty good," the cowboy said with the modesty typical of his breed.

"Think you could catch that rock?" Bo asked, turning his head so that he could wink at Scratch without any of the others seeing him. Scratch's comment about it being a job for a Texan had had the desired effect.

"I reckon I could sure give it a try," Brodie said. He went to his horse and got his rope from the saddle. He paid it out and formed a loop, then moved over so that he stood under the little knob that Bo had pointed out. Brodie backed up a couple of steps to give himself a better angle, then lazily twirled the loop a couple of times before he cast it upward with a flick of his wrist.

The rope landed on the knob, but slid off without catching. Brodie brought in the slack, grinned, and said, "Could be a mite challengin'." Then he twirled it and cast again.

It took four throws before the loop landed exactly right. Brodie pulled it tight around the rock and hauled hard on it. "Looks like it's gonna hold," he said.

North shook his head, not in disagreement but in amazement. "I didn't think it could be done. A fella would still have to climb up there, though, and there ain't no place to brace his feet until he's a good fifteen feet in the air. That part of it'd have to be hand over hand, and that won't be easy."

"I can do it," Pike said.

They all turned to look at him. "Chesterfield, no offense," Bo said, "but you're a mighty big hombre. I don't know if that rope will hold you."

"It'll hold a steer, won't it?"

Jack Brodie said, "Dang right it will. It's a good rope."

"Then it'll hold me," Pike declared confidently.

"What about them holes?" Scratch asked. "I ain't sure your shoulders'll go through any of 'em."

"I reckon they will," Pike said. "Might have to scrape a little skin off, but I can make it. And once I'm through, that rope's plenty long enough for me to haul you fellas up one by one."

Bo hadn't gotten that far in his thinking, but he saw that Pike's suggestion might work. It was a way out for all of them. They would have to leave their horses behind, and they would still be stuck here in these badlands with a gang of vicious rustlers on their trail, but they would be able to move around again and put up a fight.

"Let's give it a try," Bo said. "If we can get out of here, maybe we can circle around and get the drop on those fellas."

Pike took hold of the rope. If any of them was strong enough to pull himself up with only his arms, it was Chesterfield Pike.

"Let's give him a hand, boys," Scratch said as he stepped forward and made a stirrup with his hands. "Somebody pitch in here."

The men crowded around and lifted Pike as he hauled himself up hand over hand. Pretty soon he was too high for them to help anymore, though, so all the burden was on him. The muscles in his arms and shoulders bulged dramatically as he strained to lift his own great weight. A groan of effort came from him.

Then he was high enough so that one of his flailing feet found the overhanging rock face. That eased the load on his arms somewhat. He got his other foot braced against the rock, and from there on it would be much easier. He could just walk up the face of Horn-pipe Rock until he reached the lowest of the holes, which was only a couple of feet above the knob where the lasso was caught.

It should have been simple enough. It would have been . . .

If guns hadn't begun to crack at that moment and bullets hadn't started slamming into the rock around him, stinging him with rock splinters and startling him so that his feet slipped. He began to fall, roaring in pain as the rope burned through his clutching hands.

CHAPTER 25

Bo whirled around to see where the shots were coming from, and spotted powder smoke spurting from a flat-topped rock spire that thrust up out of the malpais about a hundred and fifty yards away. Some of the rustlers must have climbed up there, he realized, so that they could take potshots at the men forted up at the base of Hornpipe Rock. They had spotted Pike climbing the rope and targeted their shots at him.

Pike didn't fall all the way to the ground. He stopped himself after he had dropped about five feet. Bullets still pelted the rock around him, but so far none of them had hit him.

"Give him some cover!" Bo shouted as he lifted his Winchester. "We've got to keep those varmints off Chesterfield's back!"

He drew a bead on the pinnacle the rustlers were shooting from and squeezed off a round, then cranked the rifle's lever and fired again. Scratch, Steve North, Jack Brodie, and the other Star cowboys joined in, pouring lead at the distant upthrust. Their shots must have come close enough to make the rustlers duck, because slugs stopped smacking into the rock face.

"Climb, Chesterfield, climb!" Bo called.

Pike started hauling himself up the rope again as the men below continued their covering fire. He quickly regained the five feet he had lost and got his feet braced on the rock again. From there, he practically lunged upward and reached the knob where the lasso was caught. One of his arms swung higher, and his huge hand gripped the edge of the nearest natural tunnel in the rock.

Scratch glanced up and said worriedly, "It ain't gonna be big enough for him to get through."

"It's got to be," Bo said as he squeezed off another round.

Pike lowered his head and began to wriggle into the hole. As Scratch had predicted, his shoulders were a little too wide for it. But he twisted and pushed his arms out in front of him and narrowed the span of his shoulders as much as he could. His fingers dug against the rock and pulled . . .

When Bo and Scratch glanced up again, the upper half of Pike's body had disappeared into the hole. "Son of a gun!" Scratch said. "He might just make it after all!"

The rustlers had started shooting again. Ricochets whined wickedly around the rocks. The Texans kept up their own deadly accurate fire, along with North and his punchers.

Suddenly, a man plummeted off the spire the

rustlers had climbed, and North let out a triumphant yell. "Got one of the bastards!"

"What do you mean, you got him?" Scratch demanded. "That was my shot knocked him off there!"

"The hell it was!"

"Keep shooting," Bo reminded them. "Chesterfield's still a sitting duck up there."

A moment later, though, he glanced up to see that Pike had vanished completely into the narrow tunnel, pulling up the rope after him. Several more minutes of fierce firing went by. Then suddenly the rope slithered back down, this time from the top of Hornpipe Rock.

"Somebody grab hold!" Pike bellowed. "I'll pull you up!"

Bo didn't doubt that Pike had the sheer strength to lift the other men right up the rock. Unfortunately, they would be prime targets while he was doing so.

North gestured toward the dangling rope and called to Bo, "Go ahead! Get outta here while the gettin's good!"

Bo wasn't sure how good the getting would be, but once he was on top of Hornpipe Rock, he would have an even better vantage point to shoot at the rustlers. If Pike could lift him up there, he could help cover the ascent of the others . . .

He looked at Scratch, who gave him a curt nod. "Go on," the silver-haired Texan said. "I'll see you up top."

"All right," Bo said. "You come next, though."

"Right behind you, pard."

Bo ran over to the rope and grabbed it. He wound

it around his waist once and then got a good grip on it with his right hand. His left still held the Winchester, which he figured he would need once he was on top of the rock. He gave the rope a tug and shouted over the gunfire, "Haul away, Chesterfield!"

The sensation was a little disorienting and not very pleasant as Bo rose into the air and the ground fell away under his feet. Pike's enormous strength allowed him to lift Bo fairly quickly. A bullet whipped past the Texan's head. He almost banged into the overhang because he reached it faster than he thought he would. He got a foot up and fended it off, then used both feet to practically run up the rock face as Pike continued to lift him.

Rustler lead came close enough for him to hear another couple of times, but then he was at the top and Pike reached out to haul him to safety. Bo fell forward and rolled a short distance down the sloping formation before he caught himself. Then he scrambled back up, stretched out on his belly, and thrust the Winchester's barrel over the crest. Just as he had hoped, from there he had a good vantage point from which to fire down at the distant rustlers.

Judging wind and elevation with an expert sense developed over the long years of danger and adventure, Bo opened up, cranking off four fast shots. He saw the rustlers diving for cover behind the boulders that dotted the flat top of the spire.

"Toss that rope back down there, Chesterfield!" he told Pike. "I'll cover you while you're hauling Scratch up here!"

Pike nodded and threw the end of the rope down to

the waiting men. "Grab hold, Deputy Morton!" he shouted. A moment later, he began to haul away.

Bo edged forward so he could see down the rock face as he continued to fire. He glanced along the rope and saw Scratch rising toward him as Pike pulled it in hand over hand, grunting and straining.

Scratch was about halfway up the rock face when pure bad luck took a hand in the game. One of the bullets fired from the distant spire found the taut rope, slicing it cleanly about a foot above Scratch's head. Shocked, Bo yelled his friend's name as Scratch started to fall.

Despite his age, Scratch had the reflexes of a much younger man. Pike had lifted him high enough so that some of the tunnels that gave the rock its name were within reach. Scratch dropped his Winchester and lunged for the nearest one, catching the edge with both hands and stopping his fall. He yelled in pain as his weight hit his arms and shoulders, but he hung on for dear life. The rope that was around his waist slithered loose and fell the rest of the way to the ground.

"Hang on!" Pike shouted. "I'll lower this part of the rope to you, Deputy!"

That was Scratch's only chance, Bo knew. He thumbed fresh cartridges into the Winchester and opened fire again, covering Pike as the big man slid as far forward on the rock as he could without sliding right off it. He found a handhold with his left hand, and clung to it tightly as he extended his right arm and dangled the part of the lariat he still held toward Scratch.

"Grab on!" Pike called.

Down below, Scratch gritted his teeth as he tried to pull himself up far enough to grasp the end of the rope. Then he hesitated and shouted, "Damn it, Chesterfield, if I do I'm liable to pull you off! No use in both of us gettin' killed!"

"No, I can do it!" Pike insisted. "Grab the rope!"

"Go ahead, Scratch!" Bo urged. "If Chesterfield starts to slip, I'll grab hold of him!"

The idea that Bo could hold up both Scratch's weight and Pike's massive bulk was so ridiculous that Scratch had to laugh. But he gathered his strength, pulled himself up as much as he could, and let go with his right hand to make a grab for the rope.

He got it, twisting it around his wrist a couple of times. Then he let go of the rock with his other hand and used it to grab the rope, too, as quickly as he could so that his entire weight wouldn't be on his wrist any longer than it had to be.

Up above, Bo watched anxiously as the fingers on Pike's hand that was clinging to the rock slipped a little. Then Pike's hold strengthened, and he groaned as he heaved upward. He shifted, braced his feet, and was able to use both arms to lift Scratch. Bo wanted desperately to go to his aid, but he knew that the best way he could help right now was to continue peppering the rustlers with lead so they couldn't concentrate their fire on the drama playing out on the rock face.

Somehow, Scratch's cream-colored Stetson had stayed on his head despite all the banging around. It rose into view, then his head and shoulders, and then Pike reached out, got hold of Scratch's arm, and pulled the Texan to safety. Both of them rolled down the slope where the rustlers' bullets couldn't reach them.

Bo slid down to join them. "You all right?" he asked Scratch.

"Yeah." Scratch rotated his right wrist, testing it. "Still works good enough to shoot a gun anyway. I banged against the rock pretty hard, but I ain't worried about a few bruises."

"How about you, Chesterfield?"

Pike's great chest rose and fell like the ground heaving in an earthquake. "Yeah," he said. "Just lemme . . . catch my breath."

Bo picked up the rope and looked at the end of it where the bullet had sliced through it. "That was a mighty lucky shot," he said. "Or unlucky, depending on how you look at it. Neither piece of rope is long enough now to reach from up here to down there."

"Yeah," Scratch agreed grimly. "North and his boys are stuck."

Bo climbed back up to the top of the rock. The shooting had fallen off once Scratch reached safety. "North!" Bo called down. "Can you hear me?"

"I hear you, Creel!" the rancher replied. Bo couldn't see him from here, but North sounded as strong as ever. "You hombres all right up there?"

"Fine," Bo said, "but we've got a problem."

"You mean *we've* got a problem. We're still stuck here."

"I'm afraid so, unless you've got another rope long enough to reach up here."

"Let me check," North said. A couple of minutes later, he called up with the bad news. "Nope! Jack's lariat was the longest one we had. You fellas go on and get the hell out of here! We'll keep those damned rustlers occupied!"

"We're not going to abandon you, North," Bo insisted. "We'll find some way of pulling you out of there."

"Forget it! Just get back to Whiskey Flats and tell the marshal about finding those rustlers' hideout. Clean up that rat's nest, boys. That'll square accounts for us."

Scratch had climbed up beside Bo while North was talking. He shook his head and said to Bo, "If we leave those fellas here for those bastards to kill, it'll stick in my craw from now on."

"Mine, too," Bo agreed. "That's why we're not going to do it." He called down again to the men below. "North! Don't give up. Save your ammunition as much as you can, and make your food and water last! We'll turn the tables on those varmints somehow!"

"Damn it, Creel—"

"So long," Bo called, cutting into North's protest. "We'll see you later."

Then he slid down the rock and motioned for Scratch and Pike to follow him.

They were up pretty high here, high enough to look down and see the lava flows snaking through the breaks. "Can you get us down from up here, Chesterfield?" Bo asked.

"I reckon," Pike said with a nod. "You got to understand, though, I never been up here in this particular place before. I only seen Hornpipe Rock from down below. But I reckon I can find a trail for us."

"A trail fit for a damn mountain goat more'n likely," Scratch put in.

Pike grinned. "I been accused o' smellin' like a goat a time or two in my life. Reckon now it's time to see whether or not I can climb like one."

CHAPTER 26

For the next hour, the three men made their way down from the heights, carefully testing each foothold and handhold before they trusted their weight to it. As they descended through the rugged landscape, they could hear the shots coming from the vicinity of Hornpipe Rock as Steve North and his men continued to swap lead with the rustlers. That was a good sign, because it meant that North and the Star Ranch punchers were still alive.

Pike led Bo and Scratch around a large boulder, and then stopped so short that the Texans almost ran into his broad back. "That don't look good," he said as he leaned to one side so they could see past him.

A ledge little more than a foot wide ran for nearly a hundred yards along a cliff face above a fifty-foot drop. Just as dangerous as the distance, though, was the fact that at the bottom lay one of the lava flows. Those razor-sharp black rocks could slice a man into ribbons if he fell into them, especially from such a height. No one would survive a tumble like that.

"Any way around it?" Scratch asked.

Pike shook his head. "Not that I can see."

"Well, then, we'll just have to be careful," Bo said. "Let's rest a minute and catch our breath before we start across."

But even as they paused, the distant sounds of gunfire seemed to be trying to prod them into motion again. None of them could bear to stand there for very long doing nothing while North and his men were still under siege.

"All right," Bo said when little more than a minute had passed. "Let's give it a try. I'll go first."

"Nope," Pike said, "better let me. I weigh the most, so if that ledge is gonna crumble, it'll do it under me. If it holds me up, you know it'll hold you fellas, too."

That made sense, so Bo motioned for Pike to go ahead. The giant shuffled out onto the ledge, facing the cliff and pressing his big hands against the rock. He moved sideways, sliding each foot in turn, and soon had covered twenty or thirty feet without mishap.

Pike paused and started to turn his head, but Bo called to him, "Don't look down, Chesterfield. You're really not that high, but it might be enough to throw you off balance anyway."

"Yeah, that's smart," Pike said with a nod. He started moving again, sliding his feet along the ledge.

After a moment, Bo said, "He's gone far enough. I'm starting out there, too."

"Be careful," Scratch told him. "I'll bring up the rear, I reckon."

Bo followed Pike's example, facing the cliff and shuttling along the ledge. The ledge itself seemed sturdy and was fairly level, so if a fella could make his mind forget the big drop that was at his back, then making his way along here wasn't really that difficult. Seeing movement from the corner of his eye, Bo turned his head and saw Scratch starting out onto the ledge as well.

It took a good ten minutes for all three of them to reach the other end of the ledge, but they all made it safely. After that going became a little easier, and Bo noticed after a while that the shots were louder now.

"You're leading us around behind the rustlers, aren't you, Chesterfield?" he asked.

"That's what you wanted, ain't it?"

Bo nodded. "That's exactly what I wanted. If we can take them by surprise, maybe we can get North and the others out of that trap."

A few minutes later, they emerged from a long, narrow ravine and found themselves at the base of the flat-topped spire from which the rustlers had been firing at the defenders of Hornpipe Rock. Bo, Scratch, and Pike all went belly-down as they spotted a couple of men holding some horses.

"Looks like the whole gang is up there trying to root out North," Bo said quietly, "except for those two they left with the horses."

Pike pointed. "You can see the trail windin' back and forth up the rock. That's how they got to the top."

Scratch said, "If we can get past those hombres without them givin' the alarm, the rest o' the bunch won't have any idea we're behind 'em until it's too late."

"Yes, but first we've got to get past those two," Bo said. He thought about it and then asked,

"Chesterfield, how do you feel about being a Trojan horse?"

"I dunno. Is that anything like bein' mule-headed?"

Bo chuckled. "Not exactly. Here's what we're going to do . . ."

A couple of minutes later, the two men holding the gang's horses and standing guard at the base of the rock reached for their guns in surprise as they saw a giant form striding toward them. They drew the weapons, but held their fire as they noted that Pike was carrying two limp, apparently either lifeless or unconscious forms, one under each arm. One of the rustlers called out, "Hold it right there, mister!"

Pike kept coming. He rumbled, "These are two o' the fellas you're lookin' for. I'll trade 'em to you."

The second rustler laughed harshly. "Who the hell says we're interested in a trade?"

"They don't mean nothin' to me," Pike insisted. "Hell, they locked me up. They're deputies from Whiskey Flats. They made me come along and help 'em find the trail through the breaks, but as far as I'm concerned you can have 'em."

The two rustlers frowned and looked at each other. "You reckon he's tellin' the truth?" one of them asked the other. "I know this fella. He's always been a troublemaker, not the sort to help the law unless he had to."

"Then maybe he really did turn on 'em." The second rustler motioned to Pike, who hadn't slowed down but had strode steadily closer. "Let's see those deputies, Pike. Are they dead?"

"Not hardly," Pike said. Suddenly, he let go of Bo

and Scratch, who dropped to the ground and caught themselves on their hands and feet as they landed. Pike sprang ahead, moving with speed surprising in such a big man, sort of like the deceptive speed of a charging grizzly bear. He grabbed both rustlers and slammed them together. The collision jolted the guns out of their hands but didn't knock them out. They writhed in Pike's grip and swung frantic fists at his head.

Bo brought the butt of his Colt down on the head of one rustler, who went limp and slid out of Pike's hand. At the same time, Scratch slammed the barrel of a Remington against the other man's head, knocking him out cold. Pike dropped him as well.

Then he looked down at the two unconscious rustlers with a somewhat sorrowful expression and said, "That one fella was right. I always been a troublemaker. I always lost my temper and raised hell ever' time I came into the settlement, like tossin' that tinhorn gambler through Dodge Emerson's window."

"That's in the past, Chesterfield," Bo told him. "You've been a lot of help to us."

"Hell, without you we wouldn't even be here," Scratch added.

"As far as I'm concerned, you've more than justified being made a temporary deputy." An idea occurred to Bo. "Maybe if you talked to Marshal Braddock about it, you might convince him to make it permanent."

Pike's eyes widened. "Really? I never had no real, respectable job like that. Folks might look at me different if I was a real deputy. They wouldn't think I was such a monster."

"You're no monster, Chesterfield," Bo assured him. "Let's tie these hombres up and then see about getting the drop on their friends."

When the two rustlers had their hands and feet lashed together, Pike started toward the trail that led up to the top of the spire. Bo stopped him, saying, "Better let me and Scratch go first this time."

"Yeah," Scratch said, "this is liable to be gun work."

Pike nodded reluctantly. "I'll be right behind you, though."

The firing was intermittent now. Bo said, "North and his boys must be running short on ammunition by now."

"Not to mention gettin' hungry and thirsty," Scratch said.

They slowed as they neared the top of the trail. Bo took off his hat and risked a look. No trees grew on top of the spire, but it was dotted with boulders and brush. The rustlers were crouched behind rocks as they fired toward North and his men. Confident that no danger lurked behind them, they didn't even glance in Bo's direction.

Scratch edged up alongside Bo and joined him in studying the layout. After a moment, the silver-haired Texan said, "I make it an even dozen of the varmints. We gonna give 'em a chance to surrender?"

"I've never been one to shoot a man without giving him a fair break," Bo said with a solemn expression on his face.

"But you'll consider it now, won't you?"

Bo frowned. "I don't reckon we've got much choice in the matter. There are just too blasted many of them."

"That's sorta the way I look at it, too." Scratch's hands tightened on the ivory grips of the Remingtons as he lifted them. "Make every shot count, old hoss."

"Yeah," Bo said as he nodded. "Every shot."

Crouching, the Texans moved up from the trail onto the flat top of the spire itself. They walked forward, getting as close to the rustlers as they could before opening fire. No shots at all were coming now from the men holed up under Hornpipe Rock. Either North and his cowboys had run out of cartridges, or they had spotted Bo and Scratch closing in on the rustlers and were holding their fire so the Texans wouldn't be threatened by any stray slugs.

Scratch and Bo were within thirty feet of the nearest rustler when the man's instincts must have warned him. He twisted around, got a good look at them, and opened his mouth to shout a warning. Scratch fired his right-hand Remington before the man could make a sound, and the shot was lost in the other gun blasts coming from the rustlers. The man who had tried to warn his companions was driven backward by Scratch's bullet slamming into his chest. He flopped under some brush.

Bo drew a bead on another man and fired. His slug broke the hombre's gun arm between the shoulder and elbow and sent him spinning to the ground, howling in pain. That got the attention of the others, right enough, and yelling in anger and alarm, they whirled around to confront this new threat.

Bo seemed to hear the strains of "Come to the Bower" playing in his head as he and Scratch strode forward steadily, the guns in their hands roaring. A couple of pipers had been playing that song on the spring afternoon in 1836 when a few hundred men of the Texas Army had advanced across a grassy field toward the camp where thousands of Mexicans, the soldiers of Santa Anna, were enjoying their daily siesta. That restful interlude had ended a few moments later in blood and death and confusion as the chaos of battle ensued . . . and before the day was over, Texas had won its freedom.

The stakes weren't that high here . . . just the lives of Bo, Scratch, Chesterfield Pike, Steve North, and the rest of the Star Ranch crew. But the pounding of the heart was the same, and the smell of gun smoke in a man's nose, and the way the roar of the shots slammed against his ears.

Bo squeezed off a shot, saw a man fall, shifted his aim, fired again. A bullet tugged at his shirt, and he heard another whistle past his head. He pivoted and saw smoke spurt from the barrel of a gun just as he drew a bead on the man holding that gun and triggered his own shot. He waited that awful split second for the sledgehammer blow of the bullet striking his body, and when it didn't come he knew his time hadn't come. He would go on living . . . for another few heartbeats anyway.

Beside him, Scratch had both of the long-barreled smokepoles working. He was almost as good with his left hand as he was with his right. Suddenly, there was a hitch in his stride, and his left leg threatened to fold up underneath him. He stiffened it and kept going, ignoring the fiery pain from the bullet burn on his thigh.

Eight of the twelve rustlers were down, either lying motionless in death or writhing in pain. But that still left four of them, so Bo and Scratch were still outnumbered. And the hammers of their guns were about to fall on empty chambers.

That was when Chesterfield Pike rushed past them, roaring like the grizzly bear he resembled as his long legs carried him right into the midst of the rustlers. They were too startled by the brazen attack to get out of his way, and he grabbed up two of them like sacks of flour and ran toward the edge of the spire, which was less than twenty feet away.

It looked like Pike was going to run right off the brink with the two men still in his grip, but he threw on the brakes just before he ran out of room and slung the luckless rustlers ahead of him. Screaming, they sailed over the edge and dropped out of sight as they plummeted toward the ground far below. Those cries ended abruptly in a pair of soggy thuds.

Pike's assault was so shocking that the other two rustlers had forgotten about Bo and Scratch. When they realized their mistake and tried to swing their guns up again, the Texans' weapons blasted a split second faster. The final pair of wideloopers crumpled as lead ripped through them.

"It's a good thing that's the last of 'em," Scratch said as he lowered his Remingtons. "I'm plumb empty."

"Me, too," Bo said, checking the cylinder of his Colt. He took a handful of fresh cartridges from his shell belt and began thumbing them into the revolver. "Better reload. Some of those other hombres could still have some fight in them."

That proved not to be the case. In fact, all twelve of the rustlers were dead. The ones who hadn't been killed immediately had bled to death.

Bo shook his head when he saw that and said, "At least we've got the two we took prisoner down below. I want to question them and find out who they're working for. Chesterfield, do you recognize any of these men?"

Pike studied the hard-bitten faces of the corpses, then shook his head. "I don't recollect ever seein' any of 'em before."

"Not in any of the saloons in Whiskey Flats?" Scratch asked. "Especially Emerson's place?"

"Nope, I'm sure of that," Pike declared emphatically. "I never saw any of 'em in Mr. Emerson's saloon."

Scratch rasped a thumb along his jaw. "Well, now, that don't hardly make sense. I had Emerson figured as the fella who was behind the rustlin'."

Bo said, "So did I, but it's starting to look like we were wrong." He turned to Pike again. "Chesterfield, I hate to ask it of you, but do you reckon you can carry these fellas down to their horses? We ought to take them back to town."

Pike nodded. "Sure. I reckon I've carried worse things in my life." He bent and picked up two of the corpses, carrying them like he had carried Bo and

Scratch earlier when they had fooled the rustlers holding the horses.

When they got to the bottom of the trail, they stopped short and Scratch let out a curse. "Gone!" he said. "Dadgum it, we tied those fellas up good! They shouldn't'a been able to get loose."

"One of them must have had a knife and was able to get his hands on it," Bo said, feeling the sharp sting of disappointment. "We didn't really take the time to search them. Reckon we should have."

"How are we gonna find out who they were workin' for?"

"Maybe somebody in town will recognize one of them," Bo said. "We might get a lead that way."

Even as he said it, though, he wasn't very hopeful that would turn out to be the case. He had a feeling that the ringleader of this gang had a knack for covering his trail.

But they would close in on him sooner or later. Bo was convinced of that.

CHAPTER 27

Steve North and his men rode up while Bo, Scratch, and Pike were loading the dead men on their horses. The two rustlers who had fled had been in such a hurry to get away that they had taken only their own mounts.

"We saw you wipin' out those varmints and figured it was safe to go round up our horses," North explained. "Never saw anything like that before in all my borned days. Don't mind tellin' you, it sent chills down my back, the way you fellas just marched right ahead like that, shootin' down those wideloopers one after the other."

Scratch grunted and gestured toward his left leg, where a bloodstained rag was tied around his thigh. "It ain't like we got off without even bein' nicked," he said. "Reckon I'll live, though."

"Anything me and my boys can do to help you?"

Bo shook his head. "No, we can take these bodies back to Whiskey Flats."

"We'll start roundin' up those cows that're stashed

in that valley then. It'll be a big job, gettin' 'em back out and sortin' out Chet Bascomb's stock from mine."

"I reckon the feud between the two of you is over now?"

North grinned sheepishly. "I reckon so. Chet and me got more in common than differences. We're both stubborn damn fools, fallin' for a stunt like this and blamin' each other."

"Don't feel bad," Bo told the rancher. "That was exactly what you were supposed to do, according to the fellow who laid out this plan."

"You got any idea who that might be?"

"Not yet," Bo admitted with a shake of his head. "One thing you and your men can do before you go . . . take a look at these bodies and see if you recognize any of them."

That effort proved to be just as futile as Pike's study of the corpses. North and his punchers didn't know any of them. "I can tell you this much," North said. "They must've been mighty careful to steer clear of Whiskey Flats. Otherwise, we would've seen at least a few of them around the saloons on the south end of town."

"Yeah," Bo said, frowning in thought, "that's the way it looks to me, too."

North lifted a hand in farewell as he turned his horse away. His men followed him as he rode toward the valley where the stolen cattle were hidden. He had brought Bo and Scratch's horses with him, as well as Pike's mule, so they were able to mount up as well and head for Whiskey Flats, leading the rustlers' horses carrying their grisly burden.

The ride out of the breaks and back to the settlement took the rest of the day. It was after dark when the group reached Whiskey Flats. Bo, Scratch, and Pike had decided to keep moving when night fell. None of them wanted to camp out with a dozen corpses for company.

As they approached the town from the north, Bo was surprised to see that not very many lights were burning in the buildings. It wasn't *that* late. Some of the businesses should have still been open. He reined in and called softly to Scratch and Pike to stop as well. Instinct told him that something was wrong, and as he listened intently, he realized what it was.

"There's no music coming from the saloons," he told the other two.

"The saloons *never* close down," Pike said.

"It's mostly dark south of the bridge, too," Bo pointed out. He rested his hand on the butt of his Colt. "Let's take it slow and easy until we know what we're riding into."

They started forward again, but they hadn't gone fifty yards before a challenge rang out from a clump of trees close to the trail. "Hold it, whoever you are!" a man's voice called. "Don't come any closer or we'll shoot!"

Bo reined in. Scratch and Pike followed suit. "Hold your fire," Bo snapped. "What in blazes is going on here?"

He didn't receive a direct answer, but a voice muttered from the shadows under the trees, obviously talking to another sentry, "Well, at least they're not Apaches."

Bo sighed. In the time he and Scratch had been gone from Whiskey Flats, word had leaked out about the raid on the Thompson ranch. Well, that came as no surprise. The news probably would have been announced by Mayor Jonas McHale at a town meeting by now, if the brewing range war between the Rocking B and the Star hadn't cropped up.

"No, we're not Apaches," he said to the unseen sentries. "I'm Deputy Creel, and Deputy Morton and Deputy Pike are with me."

"Deputy Pike!" one of the men exclaimed. "You don't mean that big galoot Chesterfield Pike?"

Pike started to growl a reply, but Bo held up a hand to stop him. "Where's Marshal Braddock?"

"In his office, I reckon. Him and that redheaded Rawhide Abbott are gettin' the town ready to defend itself from those bloodthirsty redskins who wiped out the poor Thompson family."

Scratch leaned over in the saddle and said quietly to Bo, "There were less'n a dozen 'Paches in that war party. They ain't about to attack a whole blamed town, even with new rifles."

"I know," Bo said. "Folks don't think too straight, though, when they see something like what happened at the Thompson spread." He raised his voice. "We're riding on in. Keep your fingers off the triggers, boys."

"Go ahead, Deputy," one of the guards called out. "Best be careful, though. Folks are a mite nervous right now."

Bo was well aware of that. And a town full of nervous settlers with guns in their hands could be mighty dangerous.

As they rode past the trees, one of the sentries let out a low whistle of surprise at the sight of the horses being led. "What the hell you got there, Deputy?" he asked. "Those look mighty like dead men."

"There's a good reason for that," Bo said. "That's what they are. These are the men responsible for the rustling that's been going on around here recently. They'll be at the undertaker's. When you get a chance, go by there and see if you recognize any of them."

"Sure thing, Deputy." The sentry stepped out of the shadows and lifted a hand in farewell as the party rode on.

They stopped at Ed Chamberlain's. The place was dark, but Chamberlain was obviously still awake, because he stepped out onto the porch with a shotgun in his hands.

"It's a pure relief to see you boys," the jovial little undertaker said. He didn't seem so jovial at the moment, though. He sounded downright scared as he went on. "When I heard horses comin', I was afraid they were Indian ponies."

The settlement was on the verge of panic, Bo sensed. He had been afraid that would happen once the townspeople found out about the Apache raid.

"Got some business for you, Mr. Chamberlain," Bo said.

Chamberlain pointed the Greener at the porch and stepped forward as his instincts took over. "I see that!" he said. "Who do you have there, Deputy?"

"The gang of rustlers that've been causing so much trouble hereabouts. Take a good look at them and see if you know any of them, Mr. Chamberlain."

"I sure will. Just leave 'em right there. Me and my helpers will tote 'em in."

Bo, Scratch, and Pike turned the corpses over to Chamberlain and then headed for the marshal's office. A small light burned inside the building. The door opened as the three men rode up. Jake Reilly and Rawhide Abbott hurried out.

"Bo! Scratch! God, it's good to see you again! I didn't know when you would get back, and folks are going crazy over this Apache business—"

"You can't blame them for being worried," Rawhide interrupted Reilly. "Not after what happened to the Thompsons." She turned to Bo, Scratch, and Pike as they swung down from their saddles. "What happened? Did you find the rustlers?"

Scratch grinned and jerked a thumb over his shoulder. "They're down at the undertakin' parlor right now."

Rawhide's eyes widened. "You killed them? All of them?"

"Except for a couple that got away," Bo said. "And we found most of the cattle they stole, hidden away in a little valley on the other side of those malpais breaks beyond North's range. There won't be any range war between the Star and the Rocking B."

Rawhide looked like she didn't know whether to be relieved or angry. "I poke into that mess for weeks and don't get anywhere, and you ride out for two days and come back with it all cleared up!"

"I reckon we were just lucky," Scratch said. He slapped his wounded leg and winced. "If you call nearly gettin' killed half a dozen times bein' lucky."

Reilly asked, "Did Pike behave himself?"

"He did more than that," Bo said. "He found the rustlers' hideout and saved our bacon several times." He reached up and clapped a hand on the big man's shoulder. "You might think about making that deputy's job permanent, Marshal."

"Yeah, I guess I could—" Reilly stopped short, and Bo knew what he was thinking. Reilly had never intended for his pose as Marshal John Henry Braddock to be permanent. He had no business hiring full-time deputies.

But he didn't say that, of course. Instead, he went on. "We'll see, Pike. You've got to answer for those charges against you first."

Pike nodded. "I know that, Marshal. But I'd be right pleased if you'd consider keepin' me on after that."

Bo nodded toward the open door. "Let's go inside and see if we can figure out what to do about this Apache business."

The five of them went into the marshal's office. The cell block door was open, and Bo could see that the cells were all empty. Everybody was too worried about being attacked by Indians to cause any trouble, he supposed.

"First of all," Bo said as he took off his hat, "I don't think the settlement is in any danger from the Apaches. The war party that attacked the Thompson ranch was too small to threaten the town, even with new rifles. They'll steer clear of Whiskey Flats."

"But just because the bunch that wiped out the Thompsons was small doesn't mean there isn't a bigger war party out there," Rawhide argued.

"Other than the fact that most of the Apaches are over in Arizona Territory or below the border in Mexico. This was just an isolated band of renegades, out for blood."

Reilly said, "You can't be sure of that. Anyway, since they were able to get their hands on those rifles, that might draw even more of them over here. Whoever sold them the guns needs more customers."

Bo frowned. What Reilly said actually made sense. If word reached the larger bands of Apaches holed up in the mountains of Arizona and Mexico that new Winchesters could be had in this part of New Mexico, more of them could flock to these parts.

"That's a good reason to get to the bottom of that gun smuggling *now*," Bo said.

"How do you suggest we go about doing that?" Reilly asked.

An idea was lurking in the back of Bo's head. He didn't answer Reilly's question right away. Instead, he went over to the stove and poured himself a cup of coffee from the pot that sat there keeping warm. He took a couple of sips of the Arbuckle's and then turned to face the others, who were watching him curiously.

"We've got somebody bringing in guns to sell to the Indians," he said slowly, "and we've got somebody who set up that rustling scheme so that Chet Bascomb and Steve North would blame each other for the stock they were losing. What I'm wondering is if the same *somebody* is behind both plans."

"We got no reason to think that," Scratch pointed out. "One don't have to have anything to do with the other."

"But how likely is it that two varmints capable of coming up with such schemes would be here in Whiskey Flats?" Bo argued.

Rawhide said, "Bo may be on to something. It'd take a smart man, and there aren't that many around here. Well, not outlaw smart anyway." Her eyes narrowed. "But Dodge Emerson could do it. By God, I wouldn't put either one of those schemes past him!"

Scratch said, "What we need is some way to tie those rustlers in with Emerson. If we had that leverage, we might be able to find out if he's got anything to do with runnin' guns to the 'Paches, too."

Reilly went over to the desk and opened the middle drawer. "I've got a whole bunch of new reward dodgers in here. Came in from Santa Fe with yesterday's mail. That's how the folks here in town found out about what happened to the Thompsons. The stagecoach that makes that run had a horse throw a shoe, and the driver detoured over to their ranch to see if anybody there could take care of it. He found the burned-out ruins and the fresh graves and unhitched one of the team to gallop on into town to warn everybody."

"He didn't have any passengers on this run, so he just brought the mail pouch with him," Rawhide added.

Reilly shrugged. "Once the news was out, I didn't see any point in keeping any of it secret. I explained what we found to Mayor McHale and had him break the news to the citizens, just like we talked about, Bo. He was sure unhappy when I showed him those brand-new Winchesters we brought back from out there. Folks didn't like it much when they found out we knew about the Apaches and didn't tell anybody."

"Let's see those wanted posters," Bo said. "Scratch and I studied the faces of those dead rustlers. Maybe one of them will turn up."

Reilly took the thick stack of papers from the desk drawer and handed them to Bo. With Scratch looking over his shoulder, Bo began to go through them, taking a good look at the pictures drawn on each of them. It was a hard-bitten, desperate-looking bunch of owlhoots.

Bo's fingers suddenly tightened on one of the posters, and he sensed Scratch tensing beside him. Scratch said, "Ain't that—"

"Yeah," Bo said. "It sure is."

"One of the rustlers?" Rawhide asked.

Bo shook his head. "No, just a fella we ran into once. You don't have to worry about him being mixed up in the rustling or the gun-running, though. He's dead."

"No doubt about it," Scratch added.

"And no need for this poster to be cluttering up the place," Bo said as he folded the paper and thrust it inside his coat. He went back to studying the others, but after a few minutes he shook his head and tossed the stack back onto the desk.

"You didn't recognize any of them?" Reilly asked.

"Only that one, and it doesn't have anything to do with this," Bo said. "Whoever brought those hardcases in to handle the rustling must have sent for them in some other territory and told them to lie low once they got here. He's a smart son of a gun, whoever he is."

"What do we do now?" Reilly wasn't even trying to sound decisive now. He needed help and advice and didn't bother trying to hide it.

"Try to convince people there's no reason to panic, I suppose," Bo said. "That can wait until morning. The town looks like most folks have already hunkered down for the night, so we won't disturb them."

"To tell you the truth, I wouldn't mind gettin' some shut-eye," Scratch said. "I thought I wanted a big steak from Miz Dearborn's place first thing when we got back, but I reckon I'm tireder than I am hungry. Anyway, it was dark over there. I wouldn't want to wake her."

Bo put his hat on again. "Scratch and Chesterfield and I will take our horses over to the livery stable and tend to them," he said. "Then we'll come back here and trade off getting some rest while one of us stands guard the rest of the night. You can go back to the hotel, Marshal, and I reckon you can go on home, Rawhide."

"All right," the redhead said with a nod. "We'll figure out everything in the morning, I guess."

"All we can do," Bo said.

He and Scratch and Pike left the office, untied their mounts' reins from the hitch rail out front, and led the horses and the mule up the street toward the stable. The town was quiet and dark, although the feeling of tension in the air dispelled the idea that everyone was sleeping peacefully. The settlers were too on edge because of their fear of the Apaches.

The doors of the stable were locked, and no light showed in the office window. "Let's go around back,"

Bo suggested. "Maybe that door will be unlocked, and if it's not, Ike's quarters are back there. We can knock and wake him up."

They led the horses and the mule around the big barn and into the shadows at the rear of the structure. Surprisingly, a light was visible back here, although it was only a narrow line that came through an inch-wide gap where the rear door was ajar.

"Somebody's up," Scratch said. "Must be—"

He stumbled before he could finish whatever he was about to say. Bo reached out to grasp his old friend's arm and steady him. "Trip over something?" he asked.

"Yeah. Hold on a minute." Scratch dropped to one knee and felt around in the darkness, finding an old blanket that he pulled aside. "I didn't like the feel of it either. I think . . . yeah, take a look at this, Bo."

Bo took a match from his pocket and used his thumbnail to snap the lucifer to life. He bent over so that the glow from the flame washed over the figure of a man lying on his back. He recognized the man's face.

"It's Ike," Scratch said. "And he ain't ever gonna spread any more gossip. Somebody stoved his head plumb in."

CHAPTER 28

Bo checked for a pulse, just to make sure. It took only a moment to confirm that the hostler was dead, all right.

"Maybe a horse kicked him in the head," Scratch suggested, his voice little more than a whisper.

"If that had happened, McHale would have sent for the doctor, or for Ed Chamberlain if he knew it was too late to help Ike," Bo said. "Somebody hauled him out here and then covered him up so he wouldn't be found right away. It was just pure luck you tripped over him. To me, that adds up to murder."

"Mur—" Chesterfield Pike started to rumble in surprise, but Bo clamped his free hand on Pike's arm to silence him. Even when Pike was trying to keep his voice down, he sounded sort of like an avalanche. If Ike's murderer was still inside the barn, Bo didn't want to warn him that they were out here.

He shook the match out and dropped it, then slipped his Colt from its holster. "Let's have a look," he whispered. "Chesterfield, stay behind Scratch and me."

They catfooted toward the door. Bo put his hand on it and eased it open more. The low sound of voices came to his ears. One of them was familiar, but he couldn't make out the words.

Then they became clearer as the man moved closer to the rear of the barn, and Bo suddenly knew who the voice belonged to. That realization came as no real surprise, considering that the man who was speaking owned this place.

"—careful," Mayor Jonas McHale was saying to someone. "Once things have quieted down, we can dig up those crates. My plans have been postponed, that's all. We'll still make a fortune off those rifles."

Scratch heard it, too, and looked over at Bo, mouthing *McHale?* Bo nodded. Jonas McHale owned the freight line that ran between Whiskey Flats and Santa Fe. He could have bought the rifles in Santa Fe and smuggled them into Whiskey Flats along with the regular freight his wagons carried. Then they could be slipped out of town a few at a time and sold to the Apaches. It made sense.

Bo pushed the door back a little farther. He saw McHale now. The mayor stood holding a lantern while two men struggled to move a heavy crate into a hole that had been dug in an empty stall. Bo recognized both men. The last time he had seen them had been earlier today, out in the breaks. They were the rustlers who had been holding the horses, the pair of varmints who had gotten away.

Their presence here in the livery stable, following McHale's orders, was proof that the mayor was behind both the rustling and the gunrunning. Just as Bo had begun to wonder about in the marshal's office, one man had come up with both plans. Obviously, having a successful business and being the mayor of Whiskey Flats wasn't enough for Jonas McHale. Greed and ambition had prompted him to cross the line into law-breaking.

"Too bad about Ike," McHale commented as the two rustlers wrestled the crate of rifles into the hiding place. "Usually, he sleeps like a log. Once he saw what we were doing there, though, I knew we couldn't trust him to keep his mouth shut."

One of the rustlers grunted. "I'm a mite surprised you took care of him yourself, Boss. Fella like you usually don't want to get his own hands dirty."

"Just get those guns covered up now," McHale snapped.

Scratch had filled his hands with his Remingtons, and by the look on his face, Bo knew that his partner was ready to crash in there and settle the score for everything McHale had done. Since the two rustlers had their hands full and McHale didn't appear to be armed, Bo figured he and Scratch could get the drop on the men fairly easily. He was about to nod when somebody pounded on the front doors of the barn.

"Mayor!" Jake Reilly called. "Mayor McHale, are you in there?"

"What the hell's *he* doin' here?" Scratch asked in a whisper.

Bo just shook his head. They had left Reilly and Rawhide at the marshal's office, and had figured that the young man would stay there until they got back.

McHale was just as surprised as the Texans. He

turned quickly toward the door and motioned for the two rustlers to keep quiet. Carrying the lantern, he went to the door and called through it, "Marshal? Is that you?"

"Yeah. Sorry to bother you, Mayor, but have you seen my deputies, Creel and Morton? They came over here to put up their horses, but I thought they'd be back by now." Reilly gave a clearly audible yawn. "They were supposed to come back to the office—"

"I haven't seen them, Marshal," McHale cut in. "Sorry."

"Damn it," Reilly said. "I wonder where they could be."

Bo nodded to Scratch and Pike and then stepped forward, leveling his Colt. "We're here, Marshal!" he called. "McHale, unlock that door!"

The two rustlers were half in and half out of the hole where they were burying the rifles. At the sound of Bo's voice, they dropped the crate with a resounding crash and clawed at the guns on their hips. "Kill them!" McHale shouted, and then he did the one thing Bo hadn't been expecting.

He slung the lighted lantern right into a big pile of straw.

The dry stuff went up almost like it was as combustible as coal oil. The rustlers opened fire as the flames leaped up. Bo called, "Pike, get down!" Then he went one way and Scratch went the other, outlaw lead whistling through the air between them where they had been a heartbeat earlier.

Bo dropped to a knee and squeezed off two shots, both of them hitting the rustler closest to him. The man cried out in pain as he slid all the way into the hole. He landed on top of the crate, and struggled to bring his revolver into line for another shot. Bo fired again, and this time the man's head jerked back as the slug bored a hole in his forehead and exploded out the back of his skull.

Meanwhile, both of Scratch's Remingtons roared as he limped hurriedly to the side. The bullets hammered into the other rustler, who folded up and collapsed on top of his dead comrade.

That left McHale to bring to justice, but the fire had already spread across the stable so that the flames blocked the Texans' view of the entrance. They heard shots, but couldn't see what was going on. Bo whirled to Chesterfield Pike, who was scrambling to his feet after having dived to the ground when Bo warned him.

"You all right, Chesterfield?" Bo asked.

"Yeah, fine," the giant rumbled.

"Go around the back of the barn and spread the word about the fire. We need to get a bucket brigade going before it spreads!"

Pike nodded in understanding and dashed out the rear door of the barn.

"You see McHale?" Scratch asked.

"No, he must have gone out the front. Maybe the marshal stopped him."

Even as Bo spoke the words, though, he felt doubt strike him. Jake Reilly had grown up a lot since coming to Whiskey Flats, but he still had a lot to learn and he wouldn't be expecting trouble from the town's mayor. McHale might have knocked the bar loose from the front door, rushed out, and gotten his hands on Reilly's gun before the young man knew what was going on.

Those shots Bo had heard could have been Jake Reilly dying.

"We can't get through that fire," he said. "Come on!"

They ran out the back as Pike had done and circled toward the street, hoping that they wouldn't be too late.

As they rounded the corner of the big building, smoke began to boil from the doors and the opening into the hayloft. The garish orange light of the flames spilled into the street. Its glare revealed Jonas McHale backing away, a desperate look on his face as he pressed a gun to the head of Rawhide Abbott. His other arm was looped around Rawhide's neck, pressing cruelly against her throat. Facing them about twelve feet away was Jake Reilly, gun in hand, an anxious expression on his face.

Bo and Scratch hadn't seen what had happened, but it was easy enough to figure out. That was Rawhide's pistol McHale gripped in his hand. She must have been with Reilly when he came over to the livery stable in search of the Texans, and the renegade mayor had grabbed her when he rushed out, jerking her gun from its holster and taking her hostage with her own weapon.

"I'll kill her!" McHale threatened. "I swear I will unless somebody brings me a horse!"

"But . . . but you're the *mayor*!" Reilly said.

"Not until this little bitch's father finally died! I

worked as hard for this town as Norman Abbott ever did, but never got any of the credit! I couldn't even get elected mayor until he was dead!"

Bo came up on one side of Reilly, Scratch on the other. "So you decided to make as much money as you could and get your revenge on the town at the same time," Bo said. "You tried to start a range war between Bascomb and North that would have spilled over into the settlement, and you got the idea of selling rifles to the Apaches, too. Maybe you thought you could prod them into attacking the town and wiping it out."

Reilly didn't take his eyes off McHale and Rawhide, but he yelped, "What? McHale did all that?"

"That's right," Scratch said. "He's plumb loco with hate and greed, and now maybe he's gonna be responsible for the whole town burnin' down."

McHale grinned over Rawhide's shoulder. "It's what the place deserves."

Behind Bo, Scratch, and Reilly, the street was filling up with people as the settlers rushed out of their houses in response to Chesterfield Pike's thunderous shouts of "Fire! Fire!" Men yelled and ran to get buckets to form a bucket brigade that would stretch from the public well to the stable. Flames were eating at the building's roof by now. With all the chaos ensuing from the blaze, nobody seemed to be paying any attention to the small drama being played out by the light of the flames.

"Get me a horse," McHale demanded again. "I'm riding away from here, and nobody's going to stop me!"

"Let go of my deputy," Reilly said, sounding for all the world like a real marshal.

"The hell I will! This redheaded bitch is coming with me, so you won't get any ideas about chasing me down. You'll give me a day's head start, or she dies!"

Reilly shook his head. "No. You're under arrest, Mayor."

Quietly, Bo asked, "Are you sure you know what you're doing, Marshal?"

"I know exactly what I'm doing," Reilly said. "I'm doing my job, Deputy." He raised his voice. "Are you going to surrender, McHale?"

McHale jabbed the pistol's barrel harder against Rawhide's head, so she cried out in pain. "Go to hell!"

Reilly lifted his gun and sighted carefully over the barrel. "Here's the thing," he said with a faint smile playing about his lips. "I figure I can put a bullet through your brain and kill you before you can pull the trigger, McHale. You know why I believe that?"

McHale didn't say anything, just bared his teeth in a grimace of rage and insane hatred.

"I figure I can do that," Reilly went on, "*because I'm John Henry Braddock!*"

"You son of a bitch!" McHale screamed. He jerked the gun away from Rawhide's head, whipped it toward Reilly, and fired. At the same time, Rawhide twisted in his grip, slammed an elbow back into his belly, and tore free. She lunged away from him, throwing herself to the street out of the line of fire.

Reilly rocked back as McHale's bullet crashed into his body. He held off on the trigger of his own gun, though, until Rawhide was clear, then he fired. Bo's

Colt and Scratch's twin Remingtons roared at the same time, the shots all coming so close together they sounded like one. McHale was lifted off the ground and thrown backward a good five feet by the impact of four slugs smashing into him at once. The gun flew out of his hand. He landed hard on his back. His arms and legs twitched a couple of times, and then he lay still, staring sightlessly at the night sky as it was lit up by the hellish glare of the flames.

As Rawhide scrambled to her feet and ran to Reilly's side, Scratch stalked forward, keeping both guns trained on McHale just in case the man had any fight left in him. Scratch toed his shoulder, making McHale's head loll loosely on his shoulders. "Dead," the silver-haired Texan announced.

"That's good, I reckon," Reilly said as he slid his gun back in its holster. "I never would've taken Mc-Hale for the man behind all this, but he made it pretty clear that he—"

His head tipped back and his knees folded up underneath him as he dropped to the ground. "John Henry!" Rawhide cried. She fell to her knees beside him and ripped his coat open. "Damn it, his shirt's all bloody! He's hurt! John Henry, blast your hide, don't you die!" She looked around wildly, her eyes wide with fear. "Somebody get him to the doc's house!"

Chesterfield Pike stepped up, bent over, and picked up Reilly, cradling his body gently in massive arms. "I been helpin' out with the bucket brigade," he said, "but it looks like they're gonna keep the fire from spreadin'. I'll take the marshal down to the doc's, Miss Rawhide."

"Be careful with him," Rawhide urged as she went with them, half running alongside Pike to keep up with the giant's long strides.

Scratch watched them go and asked, "Reckon he'll be all right?"

"I hope so," Bo said. "If he is, I've got a feeling that Whiskey Flats has found itself a marshal for real."

"Did you see the way Rawhide was fussin' over him?"

"I saw," Bo said, smiling now. He started reloading his Colt, and Scratch began thumbing fresh cartridges into each of his Remingtons in turn as the two Texans walked down the street toward Dr. Summers's office.

Behind them, the livery stable continued to burn, casting the light of its destruction over the body of Jonas McHale.

CHAPTER 29

"I swear, if you two stay in Whiskey Flats much longer, I'm not going to have room for any more patients," Dr. Edwin Summers said with a smile as he wiped blood from his hands with a clean rag.

"What about Marshal Braddock?" Bo asked, thinking that the news must be good; otherwise, the sawbones wouldn't be smiling.

"He'll be fine," Summers said. "The bullet missed anything important and went straight through him. He lost enough blood so that he'll be laid up for a while, regaining his strength, but in a month or so he ought to be fine . . . especially with Pamela Abbott helping me look after him."

"I heard that, Doc!" the pretty redhead called from the other room. "My name's Rawhide, dang it!"

Bo smiled and asked, "Can we see him?"

"Of course. Just don't tire him out too much."

Bo, Scratch, and Chesterfield Pike all crowded into the little room where a bandaged-up Jake Reilly lay in bed with Rawhide perching a hip on the mattress beside him.

"How's things in town?" Reilly asked, only a slight tremor in his voice betraying the weakness he had to be feeling.

"Pretty quiet now," Bo said.

"Livery stable's burned to the ground," Scratch added, "but the buildings around it got wet down enough so that they didn't catch on fire. Mighty lucky, if you ask me."

"Yeah," Reilly agreed. "And it was lucky that you and Bo discovered what McHale was doing."

"I don't know about that," Bo said as he held his hat in front of him. "He would have overstepped himself sooner or later. Fellas who let greed get the best of them always do, sooner or later. With McHale, it just happened to be tonight."

"Say what you want," Reilly replied, "but you and Scratch have a knack for running smack-dab into trouble."

Scratch chuckled. "I don't reckon we can argue with that, Marshal."

Reilly turned his head to look up at the young woman. "Rawhide, you don't mind if I talk to Bo and Scratch alone, do you?"

Rawhide frowned. "You heard what the doc said. You're not supposed to tire yourself out."

"It'll just take a minute." Reilly got a solemn look on his face. "Anyway, all the representatives of law and order in Whiskey Flats shouldn't be here together. What if there's some more trouble tonight? I want a couple of deputies out there keeping the town safe. You and Chesterfield there are elected."

"Well . . . all right." Rawhide reached out and smoothed back Reilly's blond hair with unaccustomed tenderness. "But I'll be back to check on you later."

She stood up and left the room, taking Pike with her. Reilly gestured toward the door and said to Bo, "Shut that, will you?"

Bo eased the door closed and turned back to the man in the bed. "Something on your mind, Marshal?"

"Yeah." Reilly motioned the Texans closer and lowered his voice even more. "I . . . I don't think I can go through with it."

"Through with what?" Bo asked, although he knew perfectly well what Reilly was talking about.

"You know . . . swindling the folks in town by pretending to be John Henry Braddock."

Scratch said, "Seems to me you meant it when you told McHale you were Braddock."

Bo nodded. "That's the way it sounded to me, too."

"Well . . ." Reilly looked back and forth between them. "Who's to say it couldn't really be that way?"

"You mean you'd just keep on pretending?" Bo asked.

"It's not exactly pretending," Reilly argued. "The real Braddock is dead. Nobody would ever know the difference, especially if . . . if I could be a good marshal for these folks. And I think I can. I'm learning how."

"You are, at that," Bo agreed.

"And I'd have Rawhide and Pike to help me, and a good judge in Harry Winston."

Scratch nodded. "Sounds like it just might work out."

"And you fellas, too, of course."

"Now, there's where you're wrong," Bo said.

"We got to be ridin' on," Scratch said.

"But why?" Reilly insisted. "If *I* can settle down here, there's no reason you can't, too."

"We've been on the drift a lot longer than you have, Ja—" Bo stopped himself. "I mean John Henry. Putting down roots is something that Scratch and I . . . well, we just can't do it."

"There might be a place out there we ain't seen yet," Scratch explained, adding with a grin, "and some trouble we ain't got into."

"But . . . but . . ." Reilly sighed. "I can't change your minds, can I?"

"Not hardly," Scratch said.

Reilly pushed himself a little higher in the bed and asked, "Is it because of that wanted poster?"

"Wanted poster?" Bo repeated.

"You can't fool me. I saw the way both of you reacted when you saw one of those reward dodgers, the one you put in your coat, Bo. It had your pictures on it, didn't it? You're wanted, and you don't want people here to find out about it."

Bo chuckled. "That's not quite it, John Henry. But I reckon you've got a right to know." He reached inside his coat, took out the paper he had put there earlier, unfolded it, and smoothed it out so that Reilly could see it.

Reilly's eyes widened in amazement as he recognized the man in the drawing on the poster. "But that's . . . that's . . ."

"John Henry Braddock," Bo said. "Or at least, the fella we *thought* was John Henry Braddock. The one who died in that avalanche."

Reilly pointed a shaky finger at the reward poster. "That says his name is Halliday. It says he's wanted for murder."

Bo nodded. "That's right. Bart Halliday's a hired killer and an outlaw."

"But he had the badge. He had that letter addressed to John Henry Braddock . . ."

"Only one thing makes any sense," Bo said.

"Halliday ambushed and killed the real John Henry Braddock and took his place," Scratch said.

"Why would he do that?"

"The same reason you pretended to be Braddock," Bo said. "He figured on taking the town for whatever he could. Of course, in your case things, worked out a mite different."

"Yeah," Reilly said, nodding slowly. "I reckon they did." He thought for a moment and then asked, "If McHale was responsible for the rustling and the gun-running, why did he hire a lawman like Braddock in the first place? Wouldn't he have been afraid that Braddock would find out what he was up to?"

"I'm sure he didn't want to. But the rest of the town leaders pretty much boxed him in so he didn't have any choice. He had to just hope that Braddock wouldn't interfere with his plans."

"Like we did," Scratch added with a grin.

Reilly sighed and shook his head. "I still have a little trouble believing that Dodge Emerson wasn't behind all the trouble."

"Oh, you'll have to keep an eye on Emerson," Bo cautioned. "I don't think he's crooked, but he's ambitious. One of these days *he's* liable to be the mayor of Whiskey Flats. You may be working for him."

Reilly closed his eyes and winced. "I guess I'll have to deal with that when and if it happens. It would sure be easier if you two were still around, though."

"Sorry, John Henry," Bo said as he put on his hat. "I think we're heading south."

"Been a while since we been to Mexico," Scratch said. "Tequila and plump, brown-skinned señoritas . . ."

"Chili so hot it'll make your eyes water," Bo said.

"Pretty little señoritas . . ."

Bo took hold of Scratch's buckskin jacket and tugged him out the door. The Texans might not leave Whiskey Flats right away, but in their minds they were already on the drift again, answering the call of the frontier, bound for new places and hoping that at the end of the trail there would be peace this time, instead of some new ruckus.

After all, they couldn't keep riding into trouble forever . . . could they?